HOUSE
OF
SECRETS

HOUSE

OF

SECRETS

TRACIE

PETERSON

BETHANY HOUSE PUBLISHERS
a division of Baker Publishing Group
Minneapolis, Minnesota

Published by Bethany House Publishers
11400 Hampshire Avenue South
Bloomington, Minnesota 55438
www.bethanyhouse.com

Bethany House Publishers is a division of
Baker Publishing Group, Grand Rapids, Michigan

Printed in the United States of America

Library of Congress Cataloging-in-Publication Data
Peterson, Tracie.
    House of secrets / Tracie Peterson.
      p.   cm.
    ISBN 978-0-7642-0922-2 (alk. paper)
    ISBN 978-0-7642-0618-4 (pbk. : alk. paper)
    ISBN 978-0-7642-0930-7 (large-print pbk. : alk. paper)
    1. Sisters—Fiction. 2. Family secrets—Fiction. I. Title.
PS3566.E7717H68 2011
813'.54—dc23   2011025210

Cover design by Andrea Gjeldum

Cover photography by Chris Strong Photography, Chicago

11 12 13 14 15 16 17   7 6 5 4 3 2 1

With thanks to Angie Breidenbach for her
help and willingness to share.
You are a wonderful author, teacher,
and friend,
and I love how God put us together
at just the right time.
http://www.AngelaBreidenbach.com

BOOKS BY TRACIE PETERSON

www.traciepeterson.com
House of Secrets • *A Slender Thread* • *Where My Heart Belongs*

BRIDAL VEIL ISLAND*
To Have and To Hold

SONG OF ALASKA
Dawn's Prelude • *Morning's Refrain* • *Twilight's Serenade*

STRIKING A MATCH
Embers of Love • *Hearts Aglow* • *Hope Rekindled*

ALASKAN QUEST
Summer of the Midnight Sun
Under the Northern Lights • *Whispers of Winter*

ALASKAN QUEST (3 IN 1)

BRIDES OF GALLATIN COUNTY
A Promise to Believe In • *A Love to Last Forever*
A Dream to Call My Own

THE BROADMOOR LEGACY*
A Daughter's Inheritance • *An Unexpected Love*
A Surrendered Heart

BELLS OF LOWELL*
Daughter of the Loom • *A Fragile Design* • *These Tangled Threads*

LIGHTS OF LOWELL*
A Tapestry of Hope • *A Love Woven True* • *The Pattern of Her Heart*

DESERT ROSES
Shadows of the Canyon • *Across the Years* • *Beneath a Harvest Sky*

HEIRS OF MONTANA
Land of My Heart • *The Coming Storm*
To Dream Anew • *The Hope Within*

LADIES OF LIBERTY
A Lady of High Regard • *A Lady of Hidden Intent*
A Lady of Secret Devotion

RIBBONS OF STEEL**
Distant Dreams • *A Hope Beyond* • *A Promise for Tomorrow*

RIBBONS WEST**
Westward the Dream • *Separate Roads*

WESTWARD CHRONICLES
A Shelter of Hope • *Hidden in a Whisper* • *A Veiled Reflection*

YUKON QUEST
Treasures of the North • *Ashes and Ice* • *Rivers of Gold*

*with Judith Miller   **with Judith Pella

TEAR DOWN THESE WALLS

by Becky Milesnick

Tear down these walls.
I need to see what's been hidden
By this pain, this hurt
This fear, this brokenness.

Only You can take this away,
Only Your presence
Can lead me to say

It's all in the past
I'm moving on
Forget what's behind me
I'll look to Your throne.
Remove all these stains
Wash me in love
Restore my innocence
Breathe life from above.

www.worshipprojectfoundation.com

CHAPTER 1

At twenty-seven, it feels silly to admit that my biggest fear in life is getting a certain phone call. You know the kind I mean—where someone announces they've arranged for your family to be on one of those hideous daytime television talk shows. Screaming, yelling, family secrets upchucked for all the viewers to see. What's worse, our family is a trash TV dream-come-true.

I would like to tell you I've exaggerated, but I can't. As the oldest of three girls, I've long been the headmistress in our strange house of secrets.

My sister Geena turned twenty-three last February. She's always been the genius in the family; she devoured college like a two-year-old with a bowl of sugar-laden cereal and moved right on to a main course of law school. She also is model thin and a bit taller than me, which irritated me to no end when I hit my teens and people thought she was the oldest. All three of us have brown hair, but Geena's is more a dark blond, almost a burnt gold, and long. Mine is a deeper brown, and I usually grab it back in a clip to keep it out of my face.

Our little sister, Piper, graduated college last month. At twenty-one she's all moodiness and distraction. Petite and delicate and pretty, Piper has always had hauntingly elfish features, with dark brown hair worn in a stylish bob. She also grew into the spitting image of our dead mother. I often wondered if it unnerved our father as much as it did me, but of course, I would never ask that question aloud.

In the Cooper family, we learned early to never ask questions. Those only stirred up conflict, and conflict was unacceptable.

Then there's me. Being the eldest, I fit the stereotype—conscientious, responsible, a workaholic . . . probably more than a tad dull. Which may be why I found myself sitting in a rather old-fashioned, stuffy conference room listening to a barrage of reasons for why I should immediately accept the job being offered.

The vice president of the company, Ron Delahunt, leaned forward on the polished oak table. "We have been pleased with the work you've done, Bailee. A full-time position with Masters and Delahunt Publishing is yours if you want it." I'd been working for just over three years in my current position as a freelance editor, so the fact that I was being offered a job heading up the freelance editorial team was quite an honor.

I gave a sidelong glance at Mark Delahunt—Ron's son and my immediate supervisor. Not to mention the heir apparent to the throne. Mark was yet another difficult part of my life. My brain kept telling me he was everything I could want in a man—if I would only allow myself to want one. Given my history, however, I was determined to go through life solo. It would have been something akin to cruelty to force anyone else to endure what the Cooper family had to offer. Don't get me wrong; I'd tried to have a boyfriend. When I was younger I convinced myself not once but twice that I could overcome the past and all the ugly issues that surround my family. But just as I started to give my heart—began to believe I could actually trust another person—something happened and I retreated to my fortress of solitude. Twice, as I mentioned.

The other day I figured I'd spent something like four hundred hours in therapy to learn that I've got trust and abandonment issues. I could have figured that out on my own, saving myself time and my father a great deal of money. Mark's grin drew me back into the present.

"I need to consider your offer," I said trying hard to sound nonchalant about the entire matter. It wasn't every day that an offer of this magnitude came along, and frankly it would be the answer to a lot of my problems. However, it would also cause problems. For instance, I would need to leave Boston and move to New York City. That would mean leaving my sisters.

"Take as much time as you need," Ron said, getting up from the table. His assistant, Madge, quickly gathered the papers he'd left and got to her feet. Madge had been working here nearly as long as the publishing house had been in operation. Rumor held that she would retire at the end of the year, but as we'd seen with numerous sports figures who retired only to reappear the following season, I didn't believe Madge was going anywhere.

"Mark can further explain the benefits," Ron said as he moved to the door. "I have a four o'clock across town and need to leave. Good to see you again, Bailee."

And just as quickly as he'd entered the room a half hour earlier, he was gone. I saw Mark's assistant, Sandy, peek into the room. "You two want any coffee? I'm making a run."

I smiled. "A skinny latte sounds great."

"Make mine a mocha latte," Mark declared.

Sandy nodded. "Be back in a jiff."

Once the door was closed, I turned to Mark. "Did you know he was going to do this today?"

He smiled and ran his hand through his wavy brown hair. "I did. I suppose I should have mentioned it, but I thought you might prefer to be surprised."

"You know I hate surprises." I leaned back and studied him for a moment. Mark and I had a history that went back several years. And in the course of that time, I'd never failed to appreciate his rugged good looks.

"Well, you know these opportunities are few and far between. You'd be in charge of all the freelance projects and represent those editors at the editorial meetings."

"I know, Mark. Believe me, I feel rather honored that your family would take a chance on someone as young as me."

"Well, we kind of like you around here."

Which in and of itself complicated matters. Mark liked me, and I liked Mark. Maybe too much. He had the heart of a poet, the mind of Einstein, and the face of . . . well, let me just say the man was definitely dealt a fair hand in the looks department. Several business magazine covers featured his impish grin and smiling blue eyes, and rumors buzzed that a top fashion magazine wanted to cast him as the spokesperson for the hottest new clothing line aimed at career-minded women.

"Look, why don't you stick around the city this weekend?" Mark leaned toward me. "You can stay at the apartment Dad mentioned— the one you'd be offered if you take the job. You can get a feel for it and see what you think. You and I could take in a show—maybe do some sightseeing or go to the art museum. Then on Sunday you could go to church with me."

And there was the other reason I needed to be careful where Mark Delahunt was concerned: He had all these nicely arranged beliefs in a God who cared and loved him enough to intercede when bad times threatened. That was a god I didn't know—didn't believe existed.

"I need to get home. I shouldn't even wait for the coffee." I got to my feet and gathered my things. Opening my case, I stuffed them inside without worrying about the order of things. "I have people counting on me, as you know."

"Your sisters?"

I met his raised-brow expression and doubting tone. "Yes. My sisters count on me. They always have."

"Don't you think it's time you focused on *your* life—what *you* need and want? You can't even consider this job without first weighing the consequences to them. That hardly seems fair—or healthy."

"Look, it's just the way it's always been. Our father has been . . . well . . . busy building his empire. We girls rely on each other. That's just the way it is."

"So how will that work when you start pairing off? Getting married?" he asked with a grin.

Shaking my head, I headed for the door. "This isn't open for discussion. I have too much on my plate right now to let you distract me."

He was at my side in four quick strides. Reaching out, he took hold of my arm. "Bailee, at least have dinner with me. You can catch the late train." His eyes all but danced, as if amused at my discomfort. Was it wrong of me to think he rather enjoyed making me feel aflutter in his presence? On the other hand, maybe he didn't realize the temptation he presented.

"Please. Just dinner."

"I can't, Mark. I need to get back." I hurried from the room, knowing that if I didn't I might well give in.

My weekend in Boston didn't turn out like I'd figured it would. Piper refused to go shopping on Saturday, telling us that she had a splitting headache and just wanted to sleep. Geena and I quickly grew bored with checking out sales and headed instead to my condo in the city. We both ended up taking a nap and before we realized it, the day was gone—a complete waste. I ended up going back to the family house in Newton to spend the night, unable to stop thinking about what my Saturday might have been like had I stayed in New York.

From the time we girls hit our teens, Sunday had represented nothing more than the day we were to head back to our boarding school—if we even came home on the weekend. This morning I slept late and then tried to interest my sisters in going out for brunch, but neither of them wanted to bother. I felt listless, roaming around my family home, so I soon found myself working on a manuscript and thinking I should just head back to my condo. Something was happening to the three of us, and I didn't know quite how to take it. All of my life—at least as far back as I could remember—I've felt responsible for Geena and Piper. Part of that came from my mother's encouragement. She always said that as the oldest sister, it was my job to set an example and keep watch. For most of our lives, we three girls have been close—either bound by our secrets or the uncertainty of our future— and so we stuck together. Now, however, that was all changing.

"I'm going to meet some friends," Geena announced after spending most of the day on the phone.

"I thought we were going to get some dinner together—maybe catch a movie." I looked at Piper for confirmation.

She shrugged and seemed to mold herself even more tightly in the confines of the leather chair where she'd curled up to read. "I don't feel like doing much of anything," she replied. "You two go ahead if you want."

"I didn't think we had firm plans," Geena said, looking rather annoyed.

Sighing, I gathered my things. "I'll walk to the T with you." And that was my weekend. The weekend that was so important that I turned down the chance to spend time with Mark in New York City. Maybe Mark was right. Maybe it was time to break away—start fresh.

So on a rainy Monday evening, I considered the pros and cons of just such a move. The logistics were on my side for once. In New York I would be able to sublet an apartment owned by the publishing house. I'd have a good job in place—people who cared about me. I would receive a substantial raise, acquire new benefits, and move ahead in my career. It seemed like the decision should be an easy one.

But there were nagging cons that kept me from taking the position. My life in Boston was fairly regimented. I had a routine that was long established. Our father was so often gone that I'd taken it upon myself to be both mother and father to my sisters. Not that he'd ever really asked me to, but after our mother died it seemed that in his absence it was my only choice. Of course, if this last weekend proved anything, it was clear that my sisters didn't feel the need to have a guardian any- more. And who could blame them? They were grown women. I had no right to direct their lives.

My stomach clenched at the thought that they no longer needed me.

"So why not take the job?" I asked aloud. Just be bold and forget about everything else and take the position in New York City. It was what I wanted. It was what I'd dreamed of. So why was I so afraid?

I knew the answer, but I didn't really want to voice it. It was impossible to move forward with the future when I couldn't seem to let go of the past. I carried the past around like a set of luggage that, though shredded and ugly in appearance, still managed to contain my things. I didn't really want to keep it. But I felt guilty about casting it aside.

Spying the clock on the wall, I pushed aside those facts and fears and settled into my work. I'd been given a rapid-turnaround project to edit—some governor who hoped to one day run for president had written a book timed to coincide with the next saga of campaign hoopla. Fortunately, I was nearing the end. Most of the book was written like a frat boy tasting his first spoonful of success. A braggart at best, and an out-and-out liar at worst. The project bored me to tears, but I'd taken it on as a favor to Mark. It would also be a nice piece of change in my pocket.

The standard ring of my cell drew me back to task. I'd assigned specific ringtones to my family and my therapist, so I knew this had to be either work or a total stranger. I hoped it was Sandy, Mark's assistant. She was supposed to get back to me and let me know about my next editorial project.

"Bailee Cooper," I answered in my professional voice.

"Hello, Bailee. It's Mark."

I looked at my phone again. It wasn't his usual number, and that kind of surprised me. Shrugging, I jumped right in. "I wasn't expecting to hear from you, but since you called, I'll let you know that this project is clearly one of the lamest I've ever worked on. This man is positively full of himself. To hear him tell it, he's single-handedly nearly put an end to hunger, disease, and war. A job for everyone and a chicken in every pot."

Mark laughed. "I felt the same way when I gave it a quick read, but Dad is good friends with the man and believes he'll one day be president of the United States."

"I hope the man loses his fondness for Speedos by then."

"I hope you edited that part," Mark said, sounding serious now. "Readers aren't going to want to read ten pages on the virtues of swimwear."

I nodded and made a note. I hadn't been entirely sure how much of a free hand I had on this project.

"But, Bailee, that's not really why I'm calling."

I steeled myself. I knew very well why he was calling. At least I had a pretty good idea. I said nothing.

"Bailee, you still there?"

"I am. Just waiting for you to tell me why you called. Something to do with my next project, I hope?"

"In a sense. I want to know if you've thought about the job."

I rubbed at my temples. "Of course I've thought about it. I just haven't made up my mind. I hardly think one weekend is time enough to make a decision that will affect the rest of my life." I knew this wouldn't be what he wanted to hear, but I couldn't help it.

"I thought you and I might discuss it in more detail tonight."

I frowned. What more could he tell me about the job than what we'd already been over several times?

"Bailee?"

"I'm sorry, Mark, my mind. . . . Well, I really need to go. I'll talk to you more about this later. I promise—"

"Bailee, wait."

"Bye for now," I said and quickly clicked off. It was a good thing too. Someone was pounding on my door as if the building were on fire. Probably Mrs. Nelson from the condo around the corner. She used a nightstick instead of the usual knock. She carried the stick for protection, although I had a hard time imagining the seventy-something woman successfully wielding it against some nineteen-year-old punk. Mrs. Nelson noted, though, that many of her friends were half deaf.

I opened the door a few inches, to the limit of the security chain, only to find Mark grinning like he was delivering a contest winner's million dollar check. "What are you doing here?" My heart skipped a beat. Okay, it actually skipped three, which frightened me more than I wanted to admit. I needed to get control of myself—and in a hurry.

"I'm here to see you."

"How did you get in the building?" We had very strict doormen and concierges who guarded the high-rise like it was home to royalty and celebrities. So far as I knew, however, neither lived here.

"I've gotten to know Gunther," Mark said. "He's interested in writing a book about his experiences in East Berlin before the wall came down." He flashed me that smile again. "Doesn't that sound like a winner?" When I didn't respond, he said, "So . . . might I come in? Please?"

My resolve quickly dwindled. I lifted the chain and opened the door wider. "I still don't understand why you're here. It's a long way—"

"I explained it on the telephone," he said, losing the smile. "I want to do my best to persuade you to join Masters and Delahunt on a full-time basis. In a world where most publishers are eliminating in-house jobs, this is an opportunity few will ever get."

I motioned him inside and closed the door. "Have a seat," I said, waving him to a chair in the living room, "and I'll try to clarify why I'm not ready to give you an answer just yet." I told myself that I wasn't furthering the relationship angle—only offering an explanation related to my professional career.

"Nice what you've done here," Mark said, looking around. "Minimalist in white."

I frowned and followed him into my modest apartment. The main living area was designed in a great room fashion. The kitchen flowed into the dining room which flowed into the living room. My office was tucked into the little alcove to the side. Okay, so I hadn't done much in the way of decorating. I'd only been in this condo for what . . . two years? With my schedule I could hardly be expected to paint walls, hang pictures, and worry about accessorizing to make color pop against my white sofa and overstuffed chair.

I shrugged. "I laid a blue towel over the white ottoman. Think it adds a nice touch of color?"

Mark laughed. "It's probably just as well. I mean, if you're going to be moving, this place will already be set—a clean slate for someone else to decorate."

"Yeah, if I were going to move."

He sank down on the edge of the chair, fingers steepled in front of him, and leaned forward. "Haven't I convinced you yet?"

"Even if I did take the job, it doesn't necessarily mean moving. I could commute."

"But that would waste a lot of hours in the day. Even by the fast train, it would be three and a half hours one way. You'd spend more time on the rails than at home."

"I could spend that time reviewing projects."

He gave me a patient smile. "A complete waste of your time—others can do that for you. Besides, like I told you—the company has an apartment ready for you to sublet."

All my life I'd battled with the need to confide in a friend, yet fearing that once I did, they would immediately terminate the friendship and run screaming in the opposite direction. That's why I found it so hard to make a commitment. Well, one of the reasons, according to my therapist. Dinah said I needed to face the past, and that in doing so it would somehow lift the burden of guilt or fear or humiliation or whatever else I was hiding.

"Bailee, this isn't just about the job." I could see his Adam's apple move up and down as he swallowed. "I care about you."

Okay, there it was. And something in me wanted to level with him. Mark was a good man, and he'd been great to work for. If I could ever bring myself to believe in love and romance—which for me meant commitment and marriage—I would want a man just like

Mark. I'd even told the psychologist that very thing last week. But telling a counselor sworn to secrecy and confessing my feelings to Mark himself were two entirely different things.

"Mark, I've told you my family needs me here. I have to consider them first."

"You also told me that one of your sisters is finishing law school in the fall, and your youngest just graduated with a degree in business management or some such thing."

I nodded. "But that doesn't mean I can just take off. Besides, it's less expensive to live here."

"Not with the sublet this job offers," he replied.

I turned away to stare at the open window. Fact of the matter, I was terrified of moving. New York represented a real change, and I didn't know if I was ready for that. It had been hard enough to leave our family home in the suburb of Newton and take this condo in the Back Bay area of Boston.

I closed my eyes for a moment. Truthfully, it hadn't been that hard. Dad purchased the elegant condo as an investment and then enticed me to live in it. He figured in time I'd move on and pass it along to Geena and Piper. Just like always, Dad thought he could show his affection and fatherhood by buying us something.

"Look, I know you're concerned about what it all will mean, but we can just take it one step at a time." Mark's voice reminded me of a warm cappuccino—smooth and rich. "We already know we get along well, and if it doesn't work out, I promise you it won't affect your job." His tone was heavy, weighted by the layers of meaning in his words.

"That's good. The last thing M&D Publishing needs is a sexual harassment suit," I said, attempting to balance my emotional seesaw with sarcasm and casual wit. I decided to give him just a hint of truth. "I have a lot of baggage . . . too much for a relationship, Mark. It's just that simple."

"Everybody's life has a lot of baggage."

He wasn't making this easy. "I need to eliminate some of the past before I even think about looking to the future."

"But maybe we could work on that together. I believe things happen for a reason, and our friendship and the connection we share didn't just happen by chance."

Now he'd done it. He was going to tell me that God had a hand in this. I turned away and shook my head. "I'm not religious, Mark. You know that."

"I'm not religious either."

"Yes you are. Don't give me that. Call it what you will, but you are totally into the Bible and God's love and walking hand-in-hand with Jesus and living happily ever after."

He grinned. "What's wrong with happily ever after?"

"It isn't real. That's what's wrong." I sighed and finally took a seat on the far end of the sofa. I folded my hands and tried to think of how best to explain. In the fewest number of words. "Mark, without getting into the details of my past—"

"I'd love to get into the details of your past," he interrupted, now leaning back in his own corner like he was going to stay awhile. He was so good-looking. I loved the way his brown hair held just a hint of curl. But it was his blue eyes that completely set my heart aflutter. He could give me a look that . . . well . . . let's just say I'd never felt that way when anyone else looked at me.

I frowned. I was losing track of my argument. "Be that as it may, I have to tell you that God and I haven't been on good terms for most of my life. At a time when I needed to count on a higher power—a heavenly Father, a gentle Savior, whatever—He wasn't there."

"Of course He was," Mark answered matter-of-factly. "Maybe He didn't look like you expected."

I thought of all the times I'd prayed as a child—the times I'd gone to church hoping for some sort of proof that God was real. After Mom died, I gave up all thoughts of God, trading them in for cynicism and anger. Now, all these years later, I found the edges of my grief had worn down and the pain had faded some. But in its place, fear had very nearly paralyzed me. I was like a child staring at a roller coaster, wanting to climb on, but backing out at the last minute because I just couldn't get up the nerve to take that ride.

I caught sight of Mark's caring expression and shrugged. "Well, despite whether God was in disguise or not, I don't feel about Him like you do. Now, correct me if I'm wrong, but I have to believe that such an attitude would be deadly to any relationship we might have."

He nodded. "I agree. If we were to get serious about each other, we would need to be on the same page."

I leaned further back and relaxed a bit. Perhaps honesty had been the best choice. "See, there you have it. I'm not on the same page with you. In fact, I'm not even reading the same book." I was kind of proud of my clever quip—you know, "book," Bible.

I figured this would end the matter and free me from further pressure for an entanglement I didn't want or need. But that wasn't honest either. I was drawn to Mark, but I'd barely allowed myself the luxury of indulging in thoughts of "us" and a future together.

"But you could be," he replied softly.

I was not at all sure I'd heard correctly. "I don't even *own* a Bible."

"That can be rectified."

I was growing more frustrated by the moment. "I don't *want* to own a Bible. God let me down. I don't need Him now. End of story."

For a few minutes Mark said nothing. I was beginning to get hopeful again that he had come to terms with our differences. Instead, he surprised me once more. "How about dinner together? I won't mention God, and you can talk about anything you like. A deal?"

My cell phone startled me, the ringtone was the one I had assigned to my father. "I need to take this," I told Mark. I crossed the room to my tiny office alcove, keeping my back turned. "Hello, Dad?"

"I'm glad I got ahold of you instead of your voicemail," my father said. "I have some great news. We're all going to the summer house."

I felt like I'd just been elbowed hard in the side. The wind went out of me and my stomach knotted. "In Washington?"

"Do we have another summer house that I'm unaware of?" he said good-naturedly.

"Of course the one in Washington. Look, I've already arranged the tickets for you and your sisters. You'll fly out tomorrow. I'll join you in a couple of days. Plan to stay several weeks. It'll be great fun, and I have a very important announcement to make." His in-charge mentality never gave him pause to consider the possibility that any one of us—or all of us—might not want to go.

"But, Dad . . . I mean. . . ." I went silent. How could I explain to him all I was feeling? We hadn't been back to the summer house since Mom died. Fifteen years ago. In fact, no one had even suggested such a trip. Why now? Why was Dad suddenly instigating a reunion there? "I thought you had the place rented out to summer visitors." Stalling tactic.

"No, I took it off the listing for this year. You could stay the entire summer if you'd like."

"What about your job? What about—?"

"Look, just be at Logan tomorrow evening for your flight on Alaska Airlines. You'll leave at six twenty and get in to Seattle around nine thirty. I'll email you the details. When you get to Seattle, rent a car and take the ferry over to Bremerton. You should be able to catch the last one. Oh, and be sure you get a GPS so you can find your way to the house. It's a little tricky, and I know you won't remember the way."

"But, Dad . . ."

"I have to finish up the plans. Geena and Piper will meet you at the airport. Love you, babe."

And he was gone. Just like that. No further explanation. No other comment. After fifteen years of avoiding anything that referenced our mother and the place where she'd died, our father was suddenly plunging us back into the nightmare. This wasn't at all like him. In fact, his entire demeanor was different. Could he be on drugs?

I must have been as pale as I felt, because when I turned to face Mark, he was up and across the room in a matter of seconds.

"What is it? What's wrong?" he asked.

I put the cell phone down on the desk and shook my head. "My father . . . he . . . well. It's hard to explain. He's called a family meeting of sorts. I'm supposed to fly to Seattle tomorrow."

"Seattle?"

For reasons beyond me, I found myself spilling out more information than I'd ever intended. "We . . . Dad has a summer house in Bremerton. We haven't been back there— well, since I was twelve. Dad said he had something important to tell us." I couldn't imagine what it might be, but the very thought of it left me trembling. Was he sick? Getting married?

"Are you all right?" Mark put his hand on my shoulder.

"I'm fine," I lied. "Just surprised, is all. My father isn't really the type to pull these secret get-togethers. It has me somewhat concerned."

"Did he sound like something was wrong?"

I shook my head. "No, in fact, he sounded . . . what can I say? Happy, excited?"

Mark smiled. "Then don't borrow trouble. Maybe it's something really good."

I looked at him oddly, eyebrows raised. Something good? In the Cooper family? "I'm sorry, Mark, but I think you'd better go. I'll need to pack, and I still have to finish this edit tonight. I'll send it in before I go. If you have another project ready for me, please just email it. I promise to keep up with the work no matter what happens in Washington or how long I'm gone."

"Really, Bailee, are you sure you wouldn't just like some time off?"

"No!"

He almost flinched at the sound of my harsh reply. His left brow lifted slightly, and he narrowed his gaze, question marks filling his expression.

"I'm sorry, Mark. I'm just trying to sort everything out in my mind. There's so much to do to get ready. I need to talk to my sisters too."

He seemed reluctant to let the topic drop, but I was grateful when he didn't ask anything further. "I guess I'll see myself out. You're sure you can't take an hour out for dinner? You have to eat—"

"I'm sure," I said, moving toward the door. "I'm sorry, Mark. I'll talk to you soon."

He paused and studied me intently. "If you want to talk about this . . . I'll be there for you."

"Thanks," I replied, opening the door and practically pushing him through it. But I paused and our eyes locked for a long moment. "I'll be in touch," I said softly.

I closed the door and rested my head against it, suddenly weary. I wanted to call Dad back and tell him that I wouldn't be joining them. I wanted to tell him I could never go back to that place—to those memories. My therapist had been urging me to make just such a trip, but I hadn't been able to convince myself. Now it seemed the decision had been taken out of my hands. Could I really refuse?

I leaned hard against the door and slid to the floor. At last I was being drawn back to that house of secrets—to those hidden memories of loss and sorrow. For so long I had fooled myself into believing the past would never catch up with me. But now the moment of truth had come . . . and if there was a hell, I just knew that demons were dancing in delight.

CHAPTER 2

Yesterday I was arguing with Mark in Boston, and now I was waiting in a rental car to pull onto the ferry for Bremerton. A misty rain fell, putting a chill in the air and sending me back to a time I'd hoped to forget.

"Momma, does it always rain here?" I'd asked my mother. In my mind's eye I was standing at the window in the ferry lounge. Water streaked the window and obscured my view.

"I don't know," she told me. "Seems like every time we come here it rains. Maybe God is just as sad about it as I am."

I never knew why she was so sad about going to Bremerton. It seemed to me that the area, despite the rain, was beautiful and summers far nicer than some of the other places we'd lived. Momma didn't like being what she called "displaced." I never understood that either.

"The ferry is docking," Piper said as she opened the car door. She and Geena had gone for a little walk while I remained in the car.

Geena climbed into the front seat while Piper got in back. "They said it will take an hour to get over to Bremerton. Couldn't we have just driven it?"

"With traffic and the distance it would have taken longer," I told her. The cars began to disembark the ferry heading into Seattle. It would only be a few minutes before we'd be able to drive onto the *Kitsap* and head to Bremerton.

"I always liked the ferry ride," Piper said. "I used to pretend it was a great ship taking me far away."

The cars began to inch forward and in no time at all they had us loaded. The marine highway was extremely efficient, I had to give them that much.

"Are you coming upstairs with me?" Geena asked. "I want to get something to drink."

I looked at her for a moment and shook my head. She looked nothing like a lawyer or professional of any sort. Instead, wearing black skinny jeans tucked into ankle boots, a mottled red-print tee, and blazer, Geena looked more fashion model than studious lawyer material. She wrapped a black scarf around her throat and turned to Piper.

"How about you?"

"Sure, I'll come," Piper said, opening the door with care. "If I can squeeze out. They sure park us in here tight."

"I'm just gonna sit here and doze," I told them. "You can bring me some coffee."

I reclined the seat and settled back. Frankly, I had a twinge of guilt for not going with them. I'd always felt a strange need to protect them—to watch over them. Dad used to say it was because I was so sensitive, but I couldn't shake the feeling that it was something more. Why should a child feel it was her responsibility to take care of her siblings—of her family? I couldn't remember ever being free from that thought. Now, as we headed ever so slowly from the harbor, the sensation of guilt coupled with duty left me feeling exhausted and wary. The days to come were ones I dreaded. But like a fatal attraction I was drawn to see them through.

Funny, the thought of "fatal attractions" brought me back to Mark. We had worked together for so long now that we could very nearly read each other's minds when it came to the projects at hand. I couldn't help but think of the time when he took me with him to Long Island, where we met with some Kennedy cousin or in-law. She wanted to write a book about being a nobody in a family of somebodies. Mark and I listened to her thoughts on what she wanted to write and almost immediately had the same idea for how the book might come together. That happened a lot.

We liked a lot of the same books—the same foods. I had little trouble talking to him about anything . . . so long as it wasn't personal. We could discuss history, politics, movies, and of course books, and never feel a moment's unease. But just let the conversation drift into personal experiences . . . family . . . relationships, and I was lost. I tried to imagine myself explaining my trepidation about this trip. How could I open the crypt to the family skeletons and not expect Mark to go running in the opposite direction? He was a good man, but he wasn't perfect. No one was. Well . . . Mark would try to remind me that God was perfect, but even God turned away that night fifteen years ago.

Closing my eyes, I tried not to think of those last days at the summer house, but I couldn't help it. I could see it all as if it were yesterday.

"What's Daddy doing?" Geena had asked.

We girls were gathered on the upstairs landing that overlooked the open downstairs living area. "He's making Momma her cocoa," I told them.

"I want some," Piper said, her six-year-old voice a little louder than I would have liked.

Of course, given the fact that Momma was playing her rock music as loud as the stereo would allow, I didn't figure Dad would hear us.

"We're supposed to be asleep," eight-year-old Geena said.

Just then our father crossed the room to switch off the music. I fully expected our mother to complain, but there wasn't as much as a word. I couldn't tell if she was even still in the living room. Maybe she'd gone to bed.

Without the music playing, however, I could hear another sound. It was our father and he was muttering and talking to himself. He was also crying. At least that was what it sounded like. I heard him sniffing and saw him wipe the back of his hand against his eyes.

"Why is Daddy crying?" Geena asked in a hushed whisper.

So it wasn't my imagination. He really was crying. I'd never seen this before and it scared me. Something must have been very wrong if he was that upset.

"I have to do this for the girls." His words were as clear as those Geena had just spoken. I shook my head and leaned closer to the rail.

"It's for them. They will be safe."

He took a prescription bottle from his

pocket and opened it. I was mesmerized by the scene. What was he doing? What did he have to do for the girls—for us? I suppressed a yawn and watched as he crushed the pills and sprinkled them in the hot chocolate.

"What's he doing?" Piper asked.

I pushed her back and put my finger to my lips. Returning my attention to the scene below, I watched as our father mixed the medication into the drink. I was old enough to know that something was desperately wrong. I wanted to go to Daddy and offer him whatever comfort I could, but instead I sat frozen in place.

"It has to be this way. I must be strong and see this through," our father said. He put the spoon aside and squared his shoulders. He stood completely still for a few moments. I guessed that he was calming himself and getting his tears under control.

"Tony? What happened to the music?" our mother questioned. She sounded far off, and I figured she was probably in the master bedroom. "Tony, you know how important it is."

"I was afraid it would wake the girls," Daddy called back. "I fixed your hot chocolate while you were showering. It's ready if you want it."

Momma said something I couldn't understand and Daddy picked up the cup and moved out of sight. I punched Geena lightly.

"We need to go back to bed."

I hoped that Daddy wouldn't hear us scurrying across the floor. I waited until Geena and Piper disappeared into their rooms before heading into mine. What was going on? What had we just witnessed?

The scene faded from my thoughts and I tried to open my eyes, but my lids felt like they were weighted down. I could hear my mother humming as she often did. She told me this was to keep the FBI from reading her mind. She said they were trying to find her— to use her against her will to help them solve a crime. I couldn't remember the first time she'd told me this, but it seemed I'd always known it.

Now I was walking down the stone steps to the beach. My mother's humming grew louder. I called to her—at least I think I did. Everything seemed so confused and obscured. A hazy darkness seemed to settle over my vision as I lifted my gaze to the water.

"Bailee?"

I opened my eyes to find Geena tapping on the window and calling my name. I unlocked the door and she slid onto the seat.

"Here's your coffee. It tastes pretty strong so I put quite a bit—" She stopped in mid-sentence. "Are you all right?"

I shook the scene from my mind,

straightened, and put the seatback upright. "Why wouldn't I be?"

"You look like you just saw a ghost."

I cast a quick glance behind her. "Where's Piper?"

"Restroom. What's wrong?"

I shook my head. "I was just thinking back to that night." I took the coffee from Geena. "I closed my eyes and that's what came to mind."

"I suppose it's only natural." She looked out the front windshield to the back of the SUV in front of us. "Why do you think Dad's arranged this?"

"No idea." I sipped the coffee and grimaced. It was strong even with the cream Geena had thoughtfully added.

Geena turned to lean back against the door. She fixed me with a hard stare. "You don't suppose he's going to tell us the truth, do you?"

It had crossed my mind. "I don't know. I suppose better late than never, but I can't imagine he would."

"Piper thinks he might. We were talking about it on the way to the airport."

I tried to put it all in perspective. "But why now? Why after all this time would he finally be willing to talk to us?"

"Maybe he's feeling guilty. Maybe he plans to come clean."

I couldn't imagine the family secrets being laid out on the table—not even for us. Piper popped out several vehicles ahead. She seemed to have lost track of where our car was. I leaned out the open window and waved.

"Over here, Piper!" I called. She heard me and made her way over.

"He didn't sound guilty," I said, turning back to Geena. "He sounded strange—not at all like himself."

"I know what you mean. He did lack that businesslike determination when I talked to him on the phone. He almost sounded—"

"I couldn't remember what kind of car we rented," Piper declared as she got into the back seat. Neither Geena nor I said a word. She looked at us and the smile faded from her expression. "You're talking about it, aren't you?"

"*It?* Have we really reduced that night to nothing more than *It*?"

Piper crossed her arms and sat back. She looked irritated. "I don't know why we have to be quiet about that night. It's been fifteen years. We ought to be able to ask Dad to explain what happened."

"We ought to be able to do a lot of things," I replied, feeling more frustration than I cared to admit. Piper had been so young and all I had wanted to do was protect her.

I still felt like that was my number one job in the family.

Geena, ever the realist, glanced over her shoulder at Piper. "Our father killed our mother. What's to explain?"

CHAPTER 3

For several minutes none of us said a word. It was as if the truth, spoken aloud, had somehow caused us all to go mute. Pain in my hands made me realize I had gripped the steering wheel as if it were a life preserver. I loosened my hold, but it didn't do much to relax me.

"Look, I know we made a promise to never talk about it—to never ask Daddy about it," Piper began, "but I can't help but think enough time has passed. We're all grown, after all."

"I doubt any amount of time is enough when a murder was committed." Geena turned to me. "But I do agree with Piper. Enough is enough. We have to confront him. We have a right to know what happened that night and why."

"But we know what happened," I said, shaking my head. "Confronting Dad won't change that, and it very well might ruin our relationship with him."

"Relationship?" Piper asked. "I have more of a relationship with his checkbook than with him."

I shrugged. "Well, it will put us all in an awkward position."

"More awkward than what we've already known?" Geena asked. "Come on, I think we all know this family can't get much more dysfunctional."

"Things can always get worse," I muttered.

Piper surprised me with her growing irritation. "But I would like to know the truth. Look, Dad probably wants to tell us as much as we want to know. Can you even imagine carrying something like this around for all these years? I think it would be a relief to share the story."

I felt my stomach lurch. I was either becoming seasick or talking about that night was getting to me. I sipped my coffee and closed my eyes. Coming here had been a bad idea. A really bad idea. And I found myself simply wishing I could talk . . . not to my therapist, but to Mark.

Where had that idea come from? Was it now, when I felt time and memories ganging up on me, that I would admit my longing for Mark Delahunt's comfort? I chided myself silently. Next thing you knew I'd be thinking about God as well. Better to put an end to such thinking here and now.

People were returning to the cars around us, and all I could think of was how glad I'd be to leave this ferry. The walls had closed in on me.

"I think we should just go slow with this," I finally replied.

Geena rummaged through her handbag and pulled out a stick of gum. "Dad said he wanted all of us here for some announcement. It could be he does want to talk about that night, but it could also be that he has something else in mind. Let's just wait and see what happens."

But that was just the problem, I thought. I hated surprises. Hated anything out of the norm. I had come to depend on my schedule and order over the years to keep me on an even keel.

Geena secured her seatbelt. "We've spent a lifetime keeping this to ourselves. What's a few more days or years?" Sarcasm laced her words.

I noted the bitterness in her tone, but I said nothing. I had no desire to get into this further. In fact, I wished fervently that I could forget we'd ever brought the subject up.

Geena had already plugged in our address on the GPS, while I maneuvered through the ferry traffic to disembark. Lights glittered from the buildings and reflected on the black waters of Sinclair Inlet. It felt hauntingly familiar. I followed the other cars onto Washington Avenue without another word.

This was a huge mistake, I told myself. Over the years I'd learned to live with our family secrets—our life of unspeakable questions. What in the world was Dad thinking to bring us all here now? I felt my chest tighten.

"At the next street make a right onto the Manette Bridge," Geena instructed about the time the GPS announced the same.

I suddenly felt exhausted. A sort of oppression had settled over me—weighing me down, stealing all of my residual energy. I heard the siren before I saw the flashing lights of the ambulance pop around the corner ahead of us. I braked hard and waited for it to pass, but in my mind I saw the ambulance in the tree-lined driveway of our summer home.

I could still hear the paramedics calling out numbers, orders, concerns.

"She's not breathing. We're going to need to intubate."

"She's not responding."

"There's no heartbeat. Charging the paddles. Clear!"

"You can go now." Geena's voice came through the muddled images in my mind.

I looked at her for a moment. From her expression I knew she had no idea where my thoughts had taken me. I nodded and made a quick glance over my shoulder before pulling out.

For the first time in years, I really found myself wishing that I had faith in God. Mark always seemed so strong in his beliefs, but I couldn't help but equate God to a sense of betrayal and church to the scorn my mother had faced—that we all had faced.

"I don't remember any of this," Piper announced from behind me as I turned onto the bridge.

"I know what you mean," Geena said. "Most of it is a blur. But wait! Look on the other side of the water—there's a restaurant there. I remember going there a long time ago. Oh, what was it called—the Boat House?"

"The Boat Shed," I replied mechanically.

"That's it!" Geena seemed so excited.

I found myself sharing aloud what my therapist had said. "Dinah thinks that coming here is a good idea. She said there will most likely be many visuals that will help with unlocking memories, and in turn, help with healing." Why didn't I believe her?

Geena ignored my comment and continued to give directions. "You're going to angle over and get on Eleventh Street."

I had never driven this route, but I had ridden it many times before. Our house was on the east side of Bremerton, facing the water. Dad had purchased the house long ago as an investment and getaway for the family. Momma hated the area's rainy weather, but she always seemed to like the seclusion this beach house offered. She told me once that it was safe here. I never really understood what we were safe from.

"At Trenton, turn left. Then you'll stay on that for a mile or so," Geena instructed.

"Do you suppose any of it will look familiar to us?" Piper questioned.

I felt fairly confident that far too much would look familiar. "I think we'll be able to gauge that better in the light of day," I answered.

It seemed appropriate that we should return to this place under cover of darkness. It was rather like naughty children sneaking back into their rooms—like we had done that fateful night. I sensed, more than remembered, that we were getting very close. I followed Geena's directions, turning first right and then left again. When Geena declared with the GPS that we were arriving at our destination on the right, I was already starting to turn. How could I have known? I was just a little girl the last time we'd made this turn.

Our house was set on a rocky ledge that rose about fifteen feet from the shore. The drive to our home was narrow and steep, and dropped down considerably from the higher roadway. We were canopied by trees of various types, their branches stretching at awkward angles along the way. From the road there was no indication of a house below. For all intents and purposes, it looked like an abandoned, heavily forested piece of property. Exactly the reason our father had chosen it.

"This is really creepy," Piper said from the back seat. "The trees are snuffing out all of the light."

"Not that there was much to begin with," Geena interjected.

The last of the streetlights faded from view as the driveway curved and declined in a steep grade toward the bay. I couldn't see the house or the water yet. The thickness of cedars, firs, yews, and alders blended as one in the limited illumination of the car's headlights. I didn't remember it seeming so frightening.

We passed a small building to the right. I figured it must have been the guest cottage Dad had contracted a few years back when tourism in the area really began to build. There had always been a small building there, but it wasn't used for guests until Dad had it rebuilt. Now caretakers rented the cottage and beach house out to vacationers. Dad said it was quite profitable; he was actually thinking of acquiring additional properties.

"Sure glad the rain hasn't made it too muddy," Piper said.

"Dad had the drive packed with rock," Geena threw out. "He said it was nearly as solid as asphalt and that we shouldn't have any trouble."

We rounded the last bend to see lights shining from the house. Dad had said he'd arrange with the caretakers to have the place readied for our arrival. I supposed that meant leaving the lights on for us.

I pulled to a stop outside the garage and turned off the engine. For a moment none of us moved. I figured we all had that same strange sense of returning to the scene of a horrible accident.

Glancing up at the house, I remembered someone describing it as a two-story Alpine saltbox style. You found a lot of saltbox houses back east. They had been a popular Colonial period design. Here, however, I thought the house looked displaced. Perhaps that's why Dad had purchased it. Maybe it had reminded him of his childhood in New England.

"Well, the car won't unpack itself," Geena said, opening the car door.

Piper quickly followed suit, leaving me to decide whether to remain seated or do likewise. I moved rather stiffly to open the door. My senses were assaulted by the damp, earthy scents. We gathered our things from the trunk and hurried up the stone walkway to the front door.

"I have the key," Piper offered. "Dad gave it to me just before he flew out on business." She edged past Geena to unlock the door.

We might have hesitated to enter, but the rain was now falling in earnest, sending us quickly inside. We maneuvered in just far enough to close the door behind us, however. I momentarily forgot about Piper and Geena as my eyes caught sight of the surroundings. Despite at least two remodeling jobs on the main house; the place had an odd feeling of familiarity.

Looking past the entryway, I could see the large great room. Without thinking, I set aside my luggage and walked forward, soaking it all in. The high vaulted ceilings, the stone wall and fireplace, the dark wood floors. To the right was the staircase and above, the landing where we girls had spied on our mother and father.

"I don't like to think of strangers renting this place," Geena said, coming to stand alongside me. "I know Dad kept the master bedroom off-limits to the tourists, but I still feel as though people were intruding here."

Piper moved around the room touching the furniture. None of it was the same stuff we'd known. She turned and looked at me and shook her head.

"I really can't remember much of anything. I know my room was upstairs. I remember sitting on the stairs all those times we snuck out of bed." She went to the window. "I remember the stone steps to the beach and all the trees." Piper pulled back from the glass. "I wish I could remember more."

No you don't, I thought. *Be glad you don't remember.* How I wished I could forget more than I already had. I glanced once more to the stairs. I could almost see three little girls crouched there in silence. Dinah told me that burying memories was my way of protecting myself. So why couldn't I forget that night along with the other things I'd put away from my mind?

"I wonder if anyone thought to stock the fridge," Geena said, heading across the room to the kitchen.

Here more than anywhere the house looked different. The kitchen had been anything but grand when we'd been little, but now it looked like something a professional chef would have designed. A large granite-topped island separated the kitchen from the rest of the great room. Large stainless-steel appliances had been purchased to replace the old standard white ones, and rich cherry cabinets lined the far wall.

Geena opened the refrigerator and gave a nod. "There's some sodas, bottled water, and what looks like everything we need for sandwiches."

"There's bread and a big bowl of fresh fruit over by the sink," Piper said, pointing.

"Guess we'll make it until we get a chance to go shopping tomorrow." Geena popped the top on a can of soda.

I felt the strain of the day begin to over-whelm me. "I think I'm just going to go to bed."

Heading back to where I'd dropped my bags, I retrieved them and walked to the stairs. I paused for a moment and glanced upward. The landing was empty except for a plant stand, which hugged the corner where the stairs turned.

"I guess we should turn in," Geena said. "It is pretty late."

Only Piper seemed at all disappointed. She took up a handful of grapes. "I suppose," she said, shrugging, "we can talk more tomorrow."

Heading on up, I left the conversation at that. I really didn't want to explain how I felt or listen to Piper or Geena bring up the past. At the top of the stairs, I flipped on the hall light and noted the open doors of the bedrooms and bath. It seemed quite welcoming, but still I hesitated.

"Bailee?"

When I turned I momentarily saw my mother, but then Piper smiled—once again my younger sister. "You're blocking the road."

"Sorry about that." I turned left to take the only bedroom that faced the front of the house. I felt Geena and Piper breeze by me and head to their own rooms as I switched on the bedroom light.

The room had been completely renovated to replace my twelve-year-old decorating skills. I remembered Dad letting me get bold-colored curtains that had some sort of bubble-like valance. I'd had a twin bed and single dresser where now a beautifully accessorized queen-sized bed invited me to rest. In the corner was an oversized upholstered chair with an ottoman. Gone were the bright colors and in their place were relaxing pale greens and blues. The room seemed airy and light.

I closed the door, anxious to be alone with my thoughts. Leaving my bags by the bed, I walked to the window and lifted up the edge of the blind. We'd failed to turn off the outside lights and I could see the front yard and driveway. Without warning I was transported back in time—twelve years old, watching the ambulance attendants carry my mother away.

Her face was so pale, and she didn't move so much as an inch. At least I couldn't see her move from my vantage point. I wanted to go to her—to reassure myself that she wasn't dead, but in my heart I knew otherwise. Daddy had said it was for the best—that he had to do this for us. I was old enough to understand—at least I told myself I was.

"Where are they taking Momma?" Piper asked.

I turned, expecting to find her standing behind me, but the room was empty. My cell phone began vibrating just then, so I pulled it from my pocket. Mark was calling.

"Hello?"

"Bailee, are you doing alright? Have you arrived in Seattle?" I had a sense of being rescued from myself as he spoke.

"Arrived and departed. We're in Bremerton at the house now."

"Is it all that you remembered?"

His voice lured me into calm. "Not really." I crawled onto the bed and piled pillows behind me with one hand as I held the phone with the other. "Dad had the place remodeled, so it's not really the same."

"What about the area outside?"

"Too dark to tell much." I leaned back

against the mound of pillows and remembered that he was three hours ahead of me. "It's got to be past two in the morning there."

"You were on my mind, so I got up. Figured I'd risk you still being awake."

Against my will, his words comforted me. "I guess you figured right."

"So what's the plan now that you're there?"

I thought about all that Geena and Piper had told me. "Dad said he'd arrive in a couple of days. Last-minute business in Chicago. I guess after that, we'll hear what he has to tell us."

"Any thoughts on what that might be?"

I couldn't believe I was talking so casually about my family. "None." I knew it was a lie.

Neither of us said anything for a few moments. The awkwardness was back, and I felt compelled to end the call. "I need to get some sleep," I told him.

"Yeah, me too. Look, if you need to talk . . . I'm here. And Bailee . . ."

"Yes?"

"I'll be praying."

I bit my lip to keep from saying something sarcastic. After I composed myself I thanked him and hung up. It wasn't that I didn't appreciate his concern, but the entire matter put me in a strange situation. As my supervisor we worked closely together, and he was slated to take over the business one day. Still, we both knew the relationship was more than professional. At least . . . it could be.

Cradling the phone to my chest, I closed my eyes. I could almost hear Mark asking again, "So what's the plan now that you're there?"

That was the million-dollar question.

I thought back to shortly after I'd started working for Masters and Delahunt. Mark had joined the business only the year before, but he had a real knack for recognizing talent. He had managed to land at least six of the company's bestselling authors of that year, something his father was proud to announce at the first in-house meeting I had been invited to attend.

"We are small, but growing," Mr. Delahunt had said. He beamed a smile at Mark. "I guess we all have Mark to thank for his tireless search for quality books. I'm proud of you, son."

I couldn't imagine what it felt like to have that kind of genuine approval. Mark and his father were close; I'd been able to observe them together when no one else was around, and they genuinely seemed to enjoy each other's company. I'd never experienced that. My father avoided having a real relationship with me . . . with my sisters. I always presumed it was his memories of the past, and perhaps his worries for the future that kept us apart. I tried to tell myself, even as a young girl, that it was normal—necessary, even, for him to survive what he'd done. Spending time with his children would only serve to remind him of the fact that he'd robbed them of their mother.

After that first meeting at M&D, I'd sat for a moment going over my notes. The other editors and staff were vacating the conference room as quickly as they'd entered, but I lingered. For reasons I couldn't explain, I felt safe there. The walls were lined with dark mahogany shelves, and books were strategically positioned to draw attention to the accomplishments of M&D's publishing efforts.

"So how are you liking it here?" Mark had asked.

I was surprised to find him still in the room. I must have looked it too, because he put his most reassuring smile in place and apologized.

"Sorry. I didn't mean to startle you."

"No, that's quite all right. I thought everyone had gone." I collected my wits and my notes. "I was just going."

"No need. Stay as long as you like, Bailee. Right? Your name is Bailee."

"Yes. Bailee Cooper." I extended my hand. We hadn't been formally introduced, but it didn't matter. Mark acted as though we were lifelong friends.

"I was impressed when Dad showed me your letters of recommendation. Seems you made a great many professors very happy with your work."

"I hope I'll make Masters and Delahunt happy as well." I tried to look away, but found myself caught in his unflinching gaze.

Mark smiled. "Well, for now you have only to make this Delahunt happy. I'm your boss—well, sort of. As a freelancer you're really your own boss, but I'll be the one you report to and get projects from. I'll be reviewing your work and assisting you as you learn the ropes."

"Well, I hope you'll find me a quick study."

He laughed. "I'm sure I will. Say, it's nearly noon. Let's grab a bite to eat, and I'll tell you more about your job."

It was the first of many lunch and dinner dates we shared. It was only after a couple of months that I realized no one else had lunch dates like we did. It was Mark's assistant who actually spilled the beans one day. She made a comment about how she always knew to clear Mark's calendar when I came to town. I asked if that was standard procedure with all of the freelance editors, and Sandy laughed.

"Honey, there aren't any other freelancers who come into the office like you do. We're lucky to see our other out-of-town staff on a quarterly basis."

I had been stunned. Mark told me that he needed me to come into the office at least twice a month for a couple of days each visit. The company paid for it and put me up at one of several nice hotels, so I never really thought about it. But after that, I thought about it a great deal. I finally confronted Mark about all the lunches and dinners.

"Okay, so I selfishly enjoy your company." He didn't seem at all apologetic.

"Mark, I'm not looking for a relationship," I told him firmly. "I want to focus on getting my career up and running. I'm sure you understand."

I can still remember the way he looked at me. His eyes seemed to devour me. Why hadn't I seen that before? How could I have been so completely naïve about this "business arrangement" of ours? But I couldn't be too hard on myself. I really didn't have a lot of experience to draw from. It taught me a good lesson, however: Keep my distance.

⁓

I woke up the next morning with the phone discarded beside me and the comforter pulled up around me. I glanced at my watch. It was past ten. Funny, I hadn't figured to be able to sleep at all in this house, and here half a day was nearly gone.

Stretching, I pushed off the bed. A surprising sense of refreshment came over me. Maybe my therapist was right. Maybe being here would release something pent up inside of me. Perhaps the past could truly be set aside. A quick shower and change of clothes later, I was anxious to see exactly what could be accomplished.

"I wondered if you were ever coming down," Geena said as I came into the kitchen.

"How'd you two sleep?"

Piper shrugged. She seemed to be in a mood. Geena handed me a cup of coffee. "Good enough. We were just discussing what to do today."

"And what did you come up with?" The coffee smelled wonderful, and I realized I was quite hungry. Glancing around the room, an idea came to mind. "Why don't we go have lunch somewhere?"

"Sounds good to me. I definitely didn't want to cook." Geena pulled on a white and blue jacket. "It's kind of chilly outside."

"The air's always a little cooler around the water." I glanced at my youngest sister. "What about it, Piper? Some lunch sound good?"

"I suppose."

I looked at her for a moment. There were

dark circles under her eyes. "Something wrong?"

"Why does everybody keep asking me that?" she snapped. "Nothing is wrong. I'm just tired. If we're going to go get something to eat, let's go." She stormed out of the room.

Geena and I exchanged a glance. "She's been touchy all morning. I invited her to jog with me earlier, and she bit my head off."

A worrisome thought flickered through my mind. Was Piper starting to take after our mother?

"I think she's jetlagged," Geena added, grabbing her purse. "You ready?"

Nodding, I found my bag and car keys. There was no sense in stewing over Piper's mental state. At least not at this moment. I'd have a much better time making sense of everything once I'd eaten something and gotten a few more cups of coffee down.

We all piled into the rental and hit the road. I drove around the area and headed back to Bremerton proper. After several minutes of silence and no luck in agreeing on a place to eat, Geena plugged in the GPS and did a search.

"There's a Pancake House out Kitsap Way," she announced.

I made a command decision as the oldest. "I have no idea how to get there. Tell me where to go."

Piper snorted from the back seat. "That's a first."

Her comment was the first indication she might be loosening up a little, so I decided to take it as a good sign, even if it was aimed at me.

It wasn't long before we were seated at the restaurant with steaming cups of coffee and enough cream to start our own dairy line.

"Man, when you ask for a lot of cream, you really mean for them to bring a lot of cream," Piper declared.

Geena laughed. "Well, why not. I happen to like my coffee pale."

Without warning, Piper leaned forward. "I've decided that I'm going to confront Dad whether you two do or not."

I looked at her for a moment, and her blue eyes narrowed. "And don't try to talk me out of it. It's time I understood what was going on in this family. All of my life I've felt like . . . well . . . that I wasn't in on the joke."

"Some joke," Geena said, shaking her head. "The Cooper Family Comedy Hour."

"I couldn't sleep last night for thinking about it." Piper lowered her voice only slightly when the waitress passed by our table. "I don't remember much of anything. I can't remember our mother. It's like the first six years of my life were erased."

"Maybe that's a good thing," I said, not realizing how heartless it sounded. I immediately regretted my words. "I didn't mean for that to sound so harsh." I could see that Piper was taking it all wrong, and I held up my hand hoping to silence any outburst. "Look," I said, "I know you want answers, Piper. But I don't think we even know what questions to ask in this situation."

"I do." She looked at me matter-of-factly. "I want to ask Dad why he killed Mom."

"Shhh," Geena warned. "This isn't exactly the place to make such a declaration."

"Our entire life has been like that," Piper replied. She leaned back and folded her arms across her chest. "There's never a good place or a good time. We're always trying to protect someone. . . . Well, no more."

"Here's the breakfast special with hash browns," our teenage waitress announced. She put the plate in front of Geena. "And here's the vegetarian omelet." She looked at Piper and then to me as if trying to remember who had placed the order.

"That's mine," I told her.

She nodded and put the order on the table. "And that leaves the pancakes for you." She put the dish before Piper. "I'll be right back with toast for you two," she said, nodding at Geena and me. "Can I bring anything else?"

"I think some more coffee would be great," I replied.

Once the waitress returned to deposit the toast and fill our coffee cups, Piper seemed to have calmed once again. She toyed with her pancakes for a few minutes, adding butter and syrup, before finally looking up.

"I think it's time we were honest," she said simply. Shoveling a mouthful of pancakes into her mouth, she gave a shrug, as if that was all that she needed to say.

"Honesty would have been great a long time ago," Geena said, putting her fork down, "but now I'm not so sure."

I looked at her. "Since when did the truth go out of vogue?"

"Since I became acquainted with the law. If we confront Dad about . . . you know what," she said, looking around in a nervous manner, "it also means we'll have to testify against him."

"Testify? Who said anything about testifying?" Piper's voice grew hushed. "I can't believe you'd even say that."

"If we're really going to open this Pandora's box of Cooper family fun," Geena said in a sarcastic tone, "we have to realize it won't stop here. Once a secret is let out, there are consequences. Long overdue ones, I'll give you that much."

"I don't want anything to happen to Dad," Piper said, looking quite appalled. She put down her fork. "I can't believe you would even suggest something like that."

"He's responsible for . . ." Geena glanced around again and shook her head. "We can't pretend we didn't see and hear what we did. We were children then—frightened and scared of losing the only anchor we had left to us. Now we're adults. We deserve answers."

"Answers, yes." Piper looked at me for support. "But that's all. Just answers."

Geena fixed Piper with a steely look. "Unfortunately, I can't turn my back on my responsibility to the legal system. Believe me, I've tried. As I've gotten closer and closer to taking the bar, I've become only too aware of the obligation we have to share the truth. A woman died because a man decided to end her life. Yes, it happened to be our mother and father, but the law is the law."

"I never thought of it as being a legal matter," Piper declared. "I only wanted to know the truth." She eyed her plate and picked up a piece of syrup-soaked pancake with her fingers. Popping it into her mouth, Piper quickly wiped her fingers on her napkin.

I shook my head. "Answers have a way of being complicated." I thought of all the things I'd questioned in life, and how one answer had led me to another question and then another. "There is no simple way to handle this, no simple answer. If we do this—if we confront him—there's no going back. Everything will change."

"Maybe it needs to change," Geena said in such a soft voice I barely heard her.

I heaved a sigh. "Maybe it does."

CHAPTER 4

"Bailee, wake up. Bailee, they're coming!"
I opened my eyes to see my mother pulling back my covers. "Bailee, the men are coming."

I scooted to the edge of the bed and swung my legs over the side. The floor looked far away, but I pushed off the mattress and jumped. Momma hurried to the door and motioned me to follow.

"We have to hide you. We have to hide the baby."

I couldn't find my shoes and the floor was cold. "Mommy, wait." I shivered and reached for my cover.

"Leave it, Bailee. We have to hurry." Her expression betrayed her fear and a chill ran up my spine. Men were coming to hurt us—to steal us away from our family. Momma said so, and she was never wrong.

I grabbed my dolly and ran after her.

Momma picked up the baby and looked around the corner before heading out the back of the house. It was so cold and my feet were bare. I hesitated at the door.

"Mommy?"

"Come on," she commanded.

I crossed the yard to a building far behind the house. Inside it wasn't much warmer, but at least I was out of the wind. Momma looked frantically around the room and motioned for me to get inside an abandoned cardboard box. I did as she told me. It was scary when she closed the lid and put something atop the box. I pushed at the top, but Momma told me to sit down and be quiet. I clutched my doll close to keep from crying.

"I have to hide the baby," she told me.

I discovered a hole on the side of the box and peered out. Momma was putting the baby in a dark bag. I couldn't really see too well, but the baby remained sleeping and didn't make a sound.

"Stay quiet," she commanded. "I'll be back for you in a little while—when it's safe."

———

I awoke with a start, unable to shake the heavy cloak of dread that wrapped around me. I looked around the room. Afternoon sun filtered through the blinds and tracked across the room in a pattern of slots and lines. I was safe.

Safety had been the biggest concern in my childhood. There were repeated episodes of Momma hiding us away from imagined threats, and sometimes a memory returned to me in a dream, like just now. I couldn't remember when the exact event had taken place, but I knew it had really happened.

This was my reality: the past suddenly slipping into the present like that. Long-forgotten events returning to be displayed, just like a museum rotating artifacts.

I yawned. When Geena and Piper had gone grocery shopping, I had decided to take a nap. I glanced at the clock and saw that I'd only slept about a half hour. The house remained quiet; I figured my sisters were still gone.

My feet touched the floor beside the bed and my thoughts unwittingly went back to the dream. I was quite small in the dream; young enough, anyway, that Geena was a baby. At least I thought the baby was Geena. It could have been Piper.

I rubbed my temples for a moment, feelings of fear still clinging to me. "Those things can't hurt me anymore," I said aloud. Besides, maybe it wasn't real. The setting wasn't at all familiar to me. I couldn't remember living someplace where we'd had a detached garage or outbuilding.

Glancing at the window, I crossed the room

to see if the rental car was back. It wasn't. I stared out at the driveway and yard for several minutes, remembering how I'd stood at this window and watched them take away my mother all those years ago. I'd stood here looking and waiting for my father to bring her back.

Of course, that never happened. I remembered Dad sitting us girls down and telling us that Momma wasn't coming home. I thought maybe she hadn't really died, but instead had gone away on one of her jobs for the FBI. She often had to leave for a few days—sometimes weeks at a time. I didn't really understand what she did, but I was always worried when she was gone. It was a mixed sense of panic, dreading the bad men coming while she was gone, and an uncomfortable sense of anticipation. Years later I had learned the truth. During those absences Momma had been under psychiatric care.

I went downstairs and without planning it, ended up standing in front of the master bedroom door. Our father had locked this door to keep out the vacation renters, but Geena told me the key was on the ring with the other keys.

Searching the kitchen, I found where Geena had discarded the keys. Apparently she'd thought the place safe enough to leave it unlocked for a quick trip to the grocery store.

It made me thankful I'd secured the bedroom lock before going to sleep. I took the keys back to the master bedroom and opened the door. It was dark inside, so I flipped on the light.

To my surprise the room sat just as it had fifteen years earlier. The vanity where my mother often sat to put on her makeup was still in the far corner opposite the queen bed. I could almost conjure the image of my mother sitting there combing her hair.

Why had Dad left the room like this? Did he want to remember? Was that why he kept it locked away from visitors? The replication Tiffany lamp beckoned my touch. I remembered my mother buying this at one of the thrift stores downtown. It had a couple of bad chips, but she didn't care—she thought it was the most beautiful lamp she'd ever seen. I suddenly remembered that Dad had a similar lamp on his desk at home—only that one was real.

There'd been a lot of unusual, almost eerie happenings in this house. Children being hidden away from supposed dangers. Loud music being played to thwart spies from reading our thoughts. My mother having conversations with people who didn't exist.

I ran my finger over one of the chipped places on the lamp and thought of the day she'd brought it home.

"Isn't it pretty?" she asked me.

"It's like a lamp a princess would have," I told her. At six years of age, I fancied that one day I would be a princess and live in a castle. And when I did, I wanted just such a lamp.

Shaking my head, I turned to look at the rest of the room. It was rather dusty and smelled stale. If Dad was going to sleep in here tomorrow night, it could do with a cleaning. I walked to the window and unlocked it. It stuck, but after a couple of tries, I managed to get the window up. A fresh breeze blew in from the beach, but the cloudy day suggested more rain.

After retrieving a dustrag and cleaning spray, I went to work wiping down all the wood surfaces, including the vanity. I tried not to disturb things too much, moving only what was necessary to clean. But as I ran my hand along her things, I couldn't help but wonder if my mother had done the same chore. Dad had hired a full-time housekeeper and nanny when Piper was little. He told me that he wanted Mom to have free time to do whatever she wanted, but Mom said they were spies to keep track of her. Now I realized it was just Dad's way of trying to keep Mom, and the rest of us, out of trouble. Unfortunately, Mom wanted no part of it. She would inevitably make life so miserable for the hired help that they'd quit without notice, often leaving before my father even returned from wherever it was he'd gone.

I remembered one particularly kind older woman. Her name wasn't one I could recall, but she made the best chocolate chip peanut butter cookies. Momma, however, said the treats were poisoned and forbade the woman to bake anything more. Momma told me in secret that the woman had plans to hurt us, frightening me deeply. It was bad enough to have my mother confident that intruders were coming to steal us away; the idea that someone living on our property might be seeking to do us harm kept me awake at night.

By the time I'd finished cleaning and straightening up, a light rain had begun to fall. I went to close the window and caught sight of the ferry crossing to Seattle. On a good day we could see the city from our beach, but this definitely wasn't one of those days. When we were little we'd made many trips by ferry to Seattle. Sometimes we left the car at home and just went on foot. We would walk all over town, usually ending up at Pike Place Market—which was like a circus and giant carnival all in one. I could remember the smells of popcorn, bakeries, and fish. Street performers, musicians, and jugglers.

With the window back in place and the room looking presentable, I went to the kitchen and searched for something to eat. About that time, however, Geena and Piper came home. I heard them arguing all the way up the walk and into the house.

"You can't file charges against our own father," Piper was saying.

"I wouldn't be the one filing anything," Geena countered. "I merely said that if questioned about what we know, I would have to tell the truth and charges would most likely be filed."

Piper looked at me and tossed a couple of plastic sacks on the island. "Do you hear her? She wants to see our father in prison."

Geena rolled her eyes. "He killed our mother. He should face the truth and deal honestly with us. If there was any history of Mom having problems with mental illness, then those records could be used to support what happened."

"How would that support murder?" Piper asked. "Listen to yourself. You're the one who'll soon graduate law school. I won't be party to this. I want to talk to Dad about what happened that night. That's all." She looked at me with a pleading expression. "Can't we just talk about it without it having to turn into a murder trial?"

I felt sorry for my sister. Actually, I felt sorry for both of them. "Look, I think we can talk to Dad about this without having to do anything more. Maybe if he knows that we know, he'll turn himself in." But I knew my words sounded lame. Did I really want the truth to become public knowledge? Did I want our family to be victims of the next national campaign to expose dysfunctional families?

"If he hasn't done so in fifteen years," Geena began, "what makes you think he would now?"

Taking up one of the bags Piper had discarded, I began to pull out the items one by one. "I don't know. Maybe he's only remained silent because of us. To give some semblance of a family. I'm sure Dad doesn't want to give up the rest of his life to sit in a prison cell. Still, I think he worries about our good thoughts more than what the world thinks."

"This isn't a popularity issue. Whether we think bad or good of him, it is a legal problem." Geena sat down on one of the bar stools. "Look, I've had this on my mind since I started law school. Ethically, I feel obligated to say something. I have for a long time."

"I can't believe you would betray your own father that way," Piper said. She sounded close to tears. Reaching mindlessly for a box of snack cakes, she tore into it like a person long deprived of food. Her action made me frown. For someone as thin as she was, it was odd that she always seemed to be eating during times of confrontation. Was she bulimic?

With all of the grocery items out of the sacks and lined up in front of me, I tried to think of something to say or do that might lessen the severity of the moment. I didn't want to think of Piper having an eating disorder, nor of our father going to prison. There had to be something I could do or say to quell the intensity of the matter. Nothing of real value came to mind, however.

"Dad gets here tomorrow," I finally said. "Let's see what he says or does. We can decide what to do based on that." I knew it was a stalling tactic, but it was the best I could do.

⁓

It rained the rest of the day and into the evening. I put together sandwiches for us to eat for supper while Geena built a fire in the living room hearth. When we finally settled down with our food and drinks in front of the flames, it seemed the tension had calmed considerably from our earlier discussion. Piper was less than animated now, but that wasn't entirely unusual. Piper often withdrew and seemed to crave—even need—the quiet.

"So have you decided what you're going

to do now that you've graduated?" Geena asked Piper.

She shrugged and took a drink of her cola. "I have an internship I can take. It would put me in a good place for potentially becoming full time with an international fashion buyer."

"That's exciting news," I said. It was the first I had heard about such a possibility. "Does it appeal to you?"

Piper turned to face me, and I was struck by the vulnerability in her clear eyes. "It appeals about as much as anything. It would require a great deal of travel. Maybe even a move to London."

"And that's a bad thing?" Geena asked. "I love London. It would be great to have you there—a perfect excuse for us to come and visit."

I watched Piper give another little shrug before turning her attention to the food on her plate. "I don't know," she said before taking a bite.

"Travel can be exhausting," I said. "I have to decide about taking a job in New York City, and if I do, I have to figure out whether I'll move or commute."

"That's a long commute to do every day," Geena commented.

"It is," I agreed. "Although I wouldn't have

to make it every day. I could work part-time at home. But they're offering me a really nice sublet in the city. I could even live there full time."

"And you haven't jumped at the chance? Do you know how hard it is to get decent housing in New York?"

"I do know. I just don't know that I want to live there. I mean, you and Piper are in Boston. You're my family."

Geena shook her head. "I don't intend to be there for the rest of my life, and Piper already has a chance to leave. You certainly don't have to think about us."

Her words hurt me, but I didn't want to admit it. "I like thinking about you. I thought we were close."

"Of course we are." Geena's expression suggested I'd said something stupid. "That doesn't mean we spend the rest of our lives living under the same roof or even in the same town."

I knew that much was true, but I couldn't deny that I felt responsible for them in a strange way. Ever since we'd been young it had been my job to keep track of them. Momma had given me that job—to help her so that they wouldn't be stolen away from us.

"Do you remember when Mom was worried about that serial killer?" Geena asked, as if reading my mind.

"Why do you ask?"

She laughed. "I don't know; it just came to mind. I guess I have this memory of us hiding in a safe room or something. Do you remember that?"

I gave a slow nod. "Mom used to have us hide in different places when we were little."

"A serial killer?" Piper asked.

"Yes. About the time you were born there was a serial killer on the loose who targeted children. We were living in Texas," I added, "and even though the murders were taking place in the Midwest, Momma was terrified for us. The man was especially fond of little girls." I didn't bother to mention that our mother's paranoia had started long before that particular turn of events.

"I remember I could never get very far out of her sight." Geena took another bite of her food.

Or mine, I thought. I didn't say it though.

"Did they ever catch the guy?" Piper asked.

"Yeah, but not until long after Mom was gone," I said.

"She used to say she was helping the FBI hunt down the killer," Geena told Piper. "Remember, I told you that a long time ago."

Piper nodded. "But what if she really did help?"

"She had Dad convinced for a while. She

kept talking about all that she was doing and it sounded real enough," Geena said. "I suppose she might have gone to the FBI and tried to help them. I can't imagine how, but maybe she thought there was something she could offer. Frankly, I think she just told us that stuff so we'd feel safe."

My mind began to race, my mother's words echoing in my head. She was adamant that we be on our guard. Every stranger was a possible threat. Every man had the potential to be a killer. As a result, I lived in fear. My therapist often said it was one of the reasons I found it impossible to connect and commit to another human being—especially a man.

"Momma was so saddened by the stories in the paper," I said without thought. "I remember her sharing them with me and crying. She said it wasn't just the serial killer who stole children, however." I looked at my sisters and shook my head. "She said the FBI had been doing it for a long, long time and no one had the guts to challenge them on it."

Piper looked at her plate and pushed it back. "Why would she say things like that?"

"Because she was afraid it was true," Geena replied. "Mom had problems like that. She was afraid of a lot of things."

"Aren't we all?" Piper said.

She was right, but I didn't want to comment. I wanted the conversation to move to other topics. Instead, Geena forced the subject to become more personal for me.

"Does being afraid keep you from agreeing to get serious about Mark Delahunt?"

I looked at her in surprise. "Why do you ask that?"

A hint of a smile crept onto her face. "Don't you think it's time someone did? I mean, he's quite the catch, if you ask me."

"I didn't."

Geena laughed. "You are so touchy about anything related to him. I think you care a great deal about him."

"Maybe I do, but that doesn't mean it's open for discussion."

"We're supposed to be close, right? You expect us to freely discuss our love lives," Geena replied.

"Or lack thereof," Piper added.

"But I'm your big sister. I'm supposed to ask about those kinds of things," I protested.

"Oh really?" Geena looked at me with a raised brow. "Where's that one written down? Is there a secret handbook for firstborns that I don't know about?"

The conversation was getting completely out of hand and I knew there was only one way to get the topic off of my dating or not

86

dating Mark. "Look," I said, "Dad gets here in twenty-four hours. We need to decide what we're going to do." It was a cheap shot, but I knew I had to take it. "Are we going to ask him for the truth?"

CHAPTER 5

The next day we waited rather impatiently. With spaghetti simmering on the stove, we watched the clock, feeling the tension mount as we anticipated Dad's arrival. We'd all agreed that we would talk to him about the past and clear the air once and for all. We just weren't sure how to go about such a task. Should we eat first and then bring it up? Should we just get right to it and use food as a distraction when things got rough? Unfortunately, there wasn't a manual that told you how to go about confronting your father for murdering your mother.

Piper had suggested we make Dad a special meal, and so the spaghetti supper was born. Geena and I had long ago mastered a recipe that everyone seemed to like, so we went to work on that while Piper put together a salad and garlic bread.

By the time Dad arrived, the rain had

stopped. He came into the house and stood for a moment just looking around. We hadn't seen him since Piper's graduation and that had been for only a few hours. He was always traveling for business, it seemed.

"Well, the remodel was money well invested," he said, turning to where the three of us girls stood. "You have any trouble getting here?" He put his suitcases by the stairs.

"No. We pretty much drove right to it, thanks to the GPS," Geena answered.

"And the caretakers had it clean and fully stocked," I added.

"I don't remember much about this place or town," Piper offered with a sigh. "I feel like it's all new to me."

He nodded but changed the subject. "What smells so good?"

"We made a special dinner . . . spaghetti," Piper said, smiling. "We used the very best ingredients—fresh everything. Come and sit."

Why did I have the feeling we were coaxing an old dog to the vet to be put down? Dad's whole demeanor was foreign to me. He was still the same no-nonsense sort of man, but there was something about him that I couldn't quite figure out. I'd had that feeling at Piper's graduation as well, but there hadn't been time to investigate it—maybe now there was.

"I'm starved," he said, taking a seat. "Seems

that flight out here gets longer every time I take it, and I was only coming from Chicago." He took up his napkin and looked at it for a moment. "These must be new."

I glanced at the orange, green, and white-striped cloth and nodded. "Maybe they were added during the remodel."

"You're probably right." He glanced around again. "Doesn't look much like it used to."

Geena went to the kitchen and returned with the spaghetti, while Piper brought freshly toasted garlic bread.

"I know this might seem strange, but if you don't mind," Dad said as we joined him at the table, "I'd like to offer a prayer."

The three of us fixed him with an identical look of shock. Our father had never been known for his spiritual convictions.

He smiled, knowing he'd taken us by surprise. "I'll explain in a minute." He bowed his head and began to pray.

Geena and Piper closed their eyes, but I just sat there, too stunned to act. Our mother had been devoted to church, but not so much our dad. To hear him pray and act as though this were an everyday occurrence was more than I could ignore.

"Amen." He ended the prayer and reached for the salad. "This all looks wonderful. I sure am glad you all could come here. We're going to have a great time."

"You didn't exactly give us much of a choice," Geena said, taking the words right out of my mouth.

He looked a little sheepish. "I know, and for that I apologize. I was just . . . well . . . enthusiastic about my news. I didn't want any of you to miss it, and I didn't want to just share it at home like it was nothing special."

"So what is this all about?" I asked. "You have to admit that coming back to this house wasn't exactly something any of us anticipated. And now you open the evening in prayer. I'd say there's a lot of explaining that needs to follow."

Dad smiled, not in the leastwise offended, and passed the salad to Piper. "I've just got a lot to share with you girls, and this seemed like the right place and time."

We passed the food around and once our plates were full, looked again to Dad for a continuation of his explanation.

"Is there coffee?" he asked, as if he didn't notice our interest.

Geena nodded and got to her feet. "I'll get it."

"Thanks." He twirled spaghetti onto his fork and then stuffed it in his mouth.

I leaned back in my chair and toyed with

a piece of garlic toast. I watched Dad to see if I could discern anything out of order. The only thing that seemed different about him was a new haircut. Had he actually spiked his graying hair?

"So you've been gone an awful lot this year," Piper said. "Does that have something to do with this sudden urge to vacation in Bremerton?"

Her tone was sarcastic, but Dad didn't seem to mind. He continued eating and nodded. In between bites, he spoke. "It is. I'm really sorry that I was gone so much. Of course, you gals are grown women now and hardly need your father hanging around."

Piper frowned. "You haven't hung around since Mom died."

I couldn't help but suck in air rather notice-ably. Geena looked at me and shrugged. I supposed it was inevitable—the game was on. There was no turning back now. Piper had rattled the box of secrets and was determined to lift the lid.

Dad put his fork down and looked at her. "You're right, of course. I haven't been a good father to you since that day." He picked up a piece of toasted bread and sobered even more. "No, I was never a good father, period. I don't blame you for being upset with me. I suppose that's why I wanted you three to be the first to know about some changes I've made in my life."

Piper sat back and folded her arms. "Like what? Praying before meals?"

I didn't fault Piper for her words—she wasn't saying anything the rest of us weren't thinking. But as I looked at Dad, I found myself actually becoming rather annoyed. All of my life I'd felt like I had to make excuses for this man, for the fact that he hadn't bothered to be around for our upbringing.

Dad dropped his gaze, and when he looked up again at us, his expression was mixed. Regretful, yes. But it also possessed a measure of determination. "I've gotten my life on track with God."

You could have heard a pin drop on a pile of pillow stuffing. Geena narrowed her eyes. "Exactly what is that supposed to mean?"

He took another bite before answering, in no hurry to accommodate his stupefied daughters. Since when had God even entered into the picture? In our family, church and God had been something Momma instigated, and because of that, it just as quickly left when she died. Now I was truly starting to feel angry. How dare he come to us after years of all but ignoring us emotionally, to tell us that he'd found God? I suppose next he'd be seeking forgiveness and expecting us to overlook his absence.

"I want to tell you more about that in a little bit. First, however, there's something else you need to know," Dad continued. "I know this will come as a shock, but I hope you will hear me out."

"This doesn't sound like good news," I said, feeling great trepidation. "You said you had something good to tell us."

He grinned. "It is good news. At least to me. I'm hopeful it will be for you as well, because it's something that makes me really happy."

"So tell us already," Geena demanded.

Our gathering was beginning to feel like an interrogation, and not with the list of questions that we had figured to deal out.

"I've remarried."

I felt as if I couldn't breathe. I looked at him to gauge his seriousness and could see that he was telling it to us straight.

"You remarried?" Piper was the first to speak. "Just like that?"

Dad had the audacity to chuckle. "No, not exactly. I've known Judith for some time now. She's worked with me for years."

"Judith? The same Judith who manages your office in Chicago?" Geena questioned.

"The same. Judith and I have been friends for a long time," he continued. "I hope you'll welcome her, spend some time getting to know her." He picked up his garlic toast again. "Our love for each other grew out of a solid friendship. It's unlike anything I've ever known."

"Not even with Mom?" Piper asked.

He frowned. "Your mother . . . well . . ." He looked at Piper. "Never mind."

His tone left me chilled. To hear him now made me feel that perhaps we should let things drop. Maybe it was best that he didn't want to talk about her after all these years. Maybe we had it good and just didn't realize it. Fear was starting to replace my anger.

I thought back to the day I'd overheard our housekeeper, Mrs. Brighton, on the phone. I never knew who she was speaking with, but her comment to the listener held me in place until the end of the conversation.

"The poor kids. Their mother killed herself a year or so ago. It's tragic to be sure. Their poor father never wants to even speak her name. I've never seen anyone grieve so hard."

The words echoed in my mind even as I came to realize that Piper had gotten to her feet. I tried to focus on the matter at hand.

"You didn't even bother to let us in on this." Piper leaned on the table. "Now you want us to spend time with her? Get to know her? Should I call her Mommy?"

"Piper, calm yourself." Geena turned to Dad. "It is a shock, you have to admit. We came here figuring you might want to tell us something else."

"Like what?"

I shook my head and jumped up. "Look, like Geena said, this is a shock. I think we all need time to digest it."

"Well, that's why I came out here today. Judith is arriving tomorrow morning at SeaTac. I'll pick her up and be back in time for lunch. I'm hoping we can go somewhere nice. Maybe up to the Yacht Club in Silverdale."

"I can't believe you can just act as if this is all perfectly fine." Piper shook her head and knocked her chair backward in order to leave. "This family has issues to talk about. This family has spent a lifetime with secrets and heartache. We didn't need a new mother. We needed answers." She ran out before Dad could even reply.

He looked at Geena and then at me. "What was that all about? What kind of answers is she looking for?"

Geena got to her feet. "I'd better go see if I can calm her down."

I felt usurped. Overseeing Geena and Piper's well-being was my job. Instead, Geena left me to face Dad on my own. What was I supposed to do now? I couldn't very well just blurt out the fact that we knew he'd overdosed our mother and we wanted to discuss it.

"I knew this would be a surprise for everyone, but I certainly didn't expect hostility." Dad sighed. "I suppose you're mad at me too?"

I shook my head. "I'm not sure what I'm feeling. Confused might be the best way to describe it."

He frowned. "Why confused?"

"You said you would never remarry."

"That was because I felt you girls needed me to remain single."

His answer threw me. "Why would you think that?"

He gave up trying to eat and looked at me. "I figured I needed to be devoted to your welfare."

"And being gone three hundred days out of the year accomplished that? Sending us to boarding schools met that need?" Now I was getting mad again. I thought of the things my counselor had said about confronting the past. I tried to calm myself. "Dad, you were always gone—or we were."

"True, but I sent you to the best schools. I worked harder and longer hours to make sure you wanted for nothing. I tried to spend as much time as I could at home in the summer when you girls were there."

"We lived with housekeepers and nannies," I said, my sense of disbelief quite evident. "Yes, our schooling was the best, but we were alone except for each other. Had you not insisted they room us together in the early years, we would have run away. We were left alone far too much, and the one person we wanted—needed—was you."

He looked hurt, but what I'd said was the truth. He shook his head slowly and glanced upward. "I know I wasn't a good father. I hope you'll forgive me for that."

"It's got nothing to do with forgiveness. We lost our mother—we were three little girls whose lives had been completely turned upside down. But instead of getting us counseling or even just encouraging us to talk to you—you sent us away." I was frighteningly calm and to the point. "We were alone and terrified."

Dad reached out a hand toward me, then dropped it. It hung limply at his side. "I'm so very sorry. I never intended for you to be hurt that way. God knows you had already endured so much."

"What's with all this forgiveness and God stuff?" I asked. "You were never concerned about these things when we were growing up."

"I know, and I'm sorrier about that than anything else."

Sorrier than for killing our mother?

I didn't ask the question aloud, but I wanted to. I thought of Mark and something he'd once said about God making us into something new. I hadn't given it much thought at the time because religious nonsense wasn't of interest. Now, however, I found myself wishing I knew more. Was religion why Dad had a different look? Was he trying to be something—someone—new? How could he possibly do that without dealing with who he was and what he did in the past?

"Look, none of this makes sense. You told me a long time ago that the only things we needed in life were determination and drive. You said that we needed to set a goal and keep our eyes on the mark."

"And now I'm going to tell you that I was wrong," he said matter-of-factly. "You need to put your eyes on Jesus."

I wasn't about to sit and listen to this rhetoric. "I'm not interested in that." I looked at him without a shred of compassion. "I want to know why you've never been honest with us about Mom."

He paled and looked more than a little disturbed. "I don't know what it is you expect me to say."

"For one, you might like to explain to us about mom's mental illness. Didn't you suppose we had a right to know?"

"How did you hear about that?" he asked.

I shook my head. "That's all that concerns

you? How I found out? Not that I should have been told years ago? Not that we all should have been put into therapy after our mother's death? What about the fact that maybe with a counselor or psychiatrist seeing us on a regular basis, we wouldn't have all of these secrets between us . . . that maybe I wouldn't lay awake at night, wondering if one of us might follow in our mother's footsteps."

Dad was clearly disturbed—shocked even. It seemed only fair after his little announcement of remarrying, yet I suddenly felt very guilty for having ruined his happiness.

"I never wanted you to know," he finally said. He sounded so tired.

"But why not?" I asked. "We have a right to know the risks to our own health. We have a right to know a lot of other things too."

He looked at me and nodded. "I suppose you do."

CHAPTER 6

Answers weren't forthcoming that night. Geena and Piper were nowhere to be found, and I definitely didn't want to hold a conversation about Mom's death on my own. By the time my sisters returned and found me in my bedroom, it was nearly ten and Dad had already gone to bed.

I suggested to my sisters that we do likewise, but Piper wanted no part of that. "How can we just go to bed? I couldn't sleep if I had to. He's remarried, just like that? Frankly, the fact that he never even told us he was considering it makes it all very suspicious."

"Suspicious?" I questioned. "Of what?"

Piper waved her arms as if to emphasize the importance. "Of everything. How could he be carrying on with Judith all this time and not let us know it was getting serious? How could he just remarry without talking to us about it? What if he plans to repeat the past?"

My mind whirled. She was right. How could he be carrying on with Judith all this time and not let us know it was getting serious? How could he just remarry without talking to us about it? What if *he* has some sort of mental disorder? I'd never considered that he could be just as troubled as Momma. "You mean as in overdosing Judith?"

"Exactly," Piper replied, flipping her bobbed brown hair as she snapped her head toward Geena. "We both think it's possible, and why not. He did it once."

I shook my head. "I don't think that even makes sense. There was a strong reason for doing what he did. He did it for us."

"What about insurance money?" Geena asked. "Did Mom have a lot of it? Did Dad stand to gain financially?"

I tried to remember if I'd ever seen any life insurance policies. "I have no idea. You are making him really sinister, Geena. I figured he was doing what he did to save us."

"Save us from what?" Piper asked.

"Our mother and . . ." I let the words fade. I wasn't ready yet to talk about her problems. I really wanted to talk to Dad about it first. I wanted him to tell us the truth in his own words—from his firsthand knowledge. He would have been the one the doctors talked to. He would have received all of the intricate details of mom's condition.

"That's why I want him to come clean about the past," Geena threw out, "even if it means he has to face punishment for what he did."

"I'm starting to feel the same way," Piper said, surprising me.

"You two really want to see Dad go to jail?"

"No," Geena replied. "I want to see this family set free of the past. If it takes that—then we'll just have to accept the price."

I hesitated a moment. I wasn't at all sure how Dad's going to prison would set us free. But right now I wanted nothing more than to let someone else take charge. Geena and Piper were grown women after all. It wasn't my place to watch over them anymore. Frankly, like my therapist said, it was never my place. I had been playing guardian to them at the cost of my own childhood. A childhood that had already been robbed by a mother disconnected from reality.

"I think we should get Dad up and make him talk about this," Geena continued. "He plans to go get Judith in the morning, and we should have this out before she arrives."

"She shouldn't come here at all," Piper said.

I silently agreed. "Maybe we should be the ones to leave."

Geena raised a brow. "And run away from the truth?"

I considered all of the things that I knew that they didn't. The truth they wanted so much to know was going to change their lives forever. I feared none of us was really prepared for this.

"Is Dad downstairs?" Piper asked, heading for the door.

"No, actually he set himself up in the guest cottage. He thought we might be more comfortable that way," I replied. The two-bedroom cottage was plenty big for a family of four and would amply accommodate Dad and Judith.

"Why don't we just plan to talk to him in the morning?" I suggested. "We can meet over breakfast."

"I suppose that'll work," Geena said, glancing at her watch. "He's always up early."

I nodded. "At least by five thirty. Why don't we plan to get up around that time too. We can explain that we need to talk and try again to get to the bottom of this mess."

❧

Five thirty in the morning was a time for complete lunatics, I decided. Maybe that's why it seemed appropriate for our discussion.

Geena had taken on breakfast preparations, while Piper said she'd go to the cottage and get Dad.

"I have this under control," Geena commented over her shoulder. "You might as well just take your cup of coffee and go sit down."

I yawned and grabbed my cup. Wandering out to the dining room, I found I couldn't get Mark out of my mind. I'd thought about him off and on all night . . . and to be honest, I thought about him a lot of the time. I tried to tell myself it was just because of our work projects and the fact that he wanted me to take the position in New York City. But it was a poor excuse. I found myself doing the one thing I'd sworn never to do—call him for a purely personal reason.

"Hey there, I was just thinking about you," he answered after just one ring.

I felt stumped as to what to say next. "I . . . ah . . . well. . . ." I stopped stammering and tried to think about what I wanted to say. Mark gave me the time. "I guess I just needed a friend."

"You've got it. What's going on?"

He made it sound so simple and casual—like we did this all the time. He couldn't possibly realize the importance of this one small action. I left my coffee on the dining room table and walked out on the deck. The sun peeked out above the horizon, radiating beams against a nearly clear sky. It looked as though it would be a beautiful day.

"Remember I told you," I began, "that my life has a lot of baggage."

"Sure. Remember I told you that everybody's life does?"

"Right." I recalled that only too well. "My father has remarried." I hadn't meant to just blurt it out, but of all the things on my mind, it seemed the safest.

"That's great news, I hope."

"Not exactly. See, we didn't even know he was seeing someone."

"And you're all jealous that a new woman has come into the picture?" he asked in a teasing manner.

"No. That's not it at all." I sighed and took a seat at the deck table. "I can't really explain."

"Can't or won't?"

"Okay, I won't explain. It's too personal. Too deep and very painful." I couldn't believe I was saying all of this.

"That'll make our conversation harder, but not impossible," Mark replied. "Why don't we back up. What do you need in a friend right now?"

I honestly couldn't tell him. I had spent my life being careful not to cultivate relationships.

If friendship was a garden, I had worked 24/7 to pour ground kill on my plot.

"I guess I just wanted . . . well, I needed someone outside of the family. Just needed to step away from the mess and focus on something else. Tell me what's happening in New York."

He chuckled. "Well, I miss you. How's that for starters?"

I shook my head and leaned forward to plant my elbows on the table. "That's a lousy start. How's the workload? Did you get the Armstrong contract completed? What about Mary Simpson's historical on the life of Sarah Polk? Did she get the manuscript turned in?"

"Yes and yes."

I was more than a little frustrated with his lack of detail. "And what about the Beijing Book Fair? Who's planning to attend this year?"

"Dad is taking a team of five. Daniel, Leo, Justine, and Michelle, and he's stealing Sandy from me to act as assistant to them all. It seems she speaks Mandarin fluently. Should come in handy."

"I should say so."

I knew this conversation wasn't at all what I needed or wanted. I wrestled inside my mind. Trust did not come easily to me, and even though Mark had only proved worthy of my confidence, I held myself in check.

"What's your weather like?" Mark asked since I remained silent.

"This morning is beautiful. But they are too few and far between." I glanced around and studied the yard for a moment. "The flowers are blooming—the scents are incredible. I like what the caretakers have done with the landscaping. There are a ton of honeysuckle bushes and roses. Everything is blooming early, it seems. Even the hydrangeas are starting. I'd forgotten how much I love the vegetation here."

"Are you planning to garden while you're there?" he asked.

"I have no green thumb. I kill houseplants."

"I'll try to remember that when I send you flowers." He sounded amused nevertheless. "So what are your plans for the day? Unloading baggage?"

He caught me unaware and I actually laughed. "Don't I wish. I mean, that is the plan, but it was also the plan last night."

"And things got away from you?"

"Completely out of control."

"And do you think today will go any better?"

I felt strangely at ease with this man. "I hope so. We're planning a talk with our father this morning."

"I'll keep you in my prayers."

"Funny you should mention that. My dad

says he's gotten his life in order with God. What do you suppose he really means by that?" I already figured I knew the answer, but at least it would give Mark something to talk about other than me.

"I think you should ask him," Mark said without missing a beat.

Not exactly the answer I had hoped for. I was about to comment on my interpretation of such a statement when I heard Piper ranting about something in the house.

"Look, my sister is back with Dad. I need to go. Thanks for being there."

"What are friends for?" he said. I could hear the smile in his voice.

"To tell you the truth, I'm not exactly sure. I've never really had one."

I closed my cell phone and went inside. Dad was nowhere to be seen, but Piper was going off about something.

I slipped the cell phone into my jeans. "What's wrong?" I picked up my coffee and sipped it, thankful it was still fairly warm.

"He's gone already," Piper declared. "Dad must have taken the first ferry out, because he's not there."

"So much for having a discussion in private," Geena said, spatula in hand. "So now what? Do we wait until we have him alone? Do we talk to him in front of Judith?"

I had only known Judith as a voice on the telephone, speaking with her only the few times I'd had to call Dad in New York or when Judith had been calling to reach him at home. That was the sum total of my relationship with the woman. I knew she and Dad worked together and had for some time, but other than that, I didn't know much.

"It's hardly the kind of subject matter you want to discuss in front of a stranger." I saw that Geena had cut up fresh strawberries and cantaloupe, and was now finishing up a stack of pancakes. "But she's not going to be a stranger for long," I said. I drank the last of my coffee and walked to the pot for a refill. "We might as well eat and figure out what we want to do."

"I can't believe he'd just leave like that," Piper muttered. She pushed past me to get to the refrigerator. "He clearly doesn't care about what we think."

"Maybe he got a call and she's coming in on an earlier flight," I offered, trying hard to be the voice of reason.

"He should have let us know." Piper took out the orange juice and slammed the door closed. "He shouldn't have remarried."

"Maybe not," Geena agreed, "but we can't change that now. The question is . . . can we speak freely in front of our new stepmother?"

I made my way to the table. "Surely we'll have some time alone with Dad. I wouldn't want to discuss any of this with Judith. She may be his wife, but she probably doesn't know all of the problems mom had."

"Do we even know what kind of problems mom had?" Geena asked, bringing the pancakes. Piper followed with the orange juice, while Geena made another trip for the fruit and a can of whipped cream.

I wanted to confess all that I knew, but I still hesitated. "Mom clearly had depression," I said. "I remember times when she would just hole up in her room and cry for hours on end." And I was left to take care of my siblings—even when I was much too young to be able to do the job properly.

"Did she get . . . help . . . treatment for it?" Piper asked hesitantly.

I knew I had to tread carefully. "I think she tried to work through it. There were other things that bothered her as well."

"Like being paranoid over a serial killer coming to take your children?" Geena asked.

"Exactly. Mom . . . Mom had a lot of struggles."

The phone rang, stealing our attention. Piper went to answer it while I helped myself to breakfast. I thought of Dad praying over the food, but didn't offer to repeat it. I wasn't sure I even knew how. I realized, strangely enough, that I often talked to God internally, but my comments weren't at all in an attitude of thanksgiving.

"Yeah, we noticed," I heard Piper say. "And when do you plan to be back?"

I focused on my food, hesitant to eavesdrop on this conversation. I couldn't answer for Geena, but a strange sensation came over me. It was like nothing I'd ever known. I looked at Piper and for a moment was transported back in time.

"Bailee, go watch your sisters," Momma had commanded.

I hadn't wanted to go. I wanted to listen to her talk on the phone. But I was scared for some reason. . . .

The image passed, and I simply sat there, staring at Piper as she hung up the phone.

"Dad says there's been a delay with Judith's flight. She'll be in later this evening, so he's just going to stay over in Seattle and handle some business."

"Rather than come here and have to face us," Geena said before stuffing her mouth with pancakes and fruit.

"He said he plans to sit down and talk to us when he gets back. In fact, he asked that we definitely set aside the time. He figures around nine tonight."

I nodded. "That's fine by me. I have some work to keep me busy." I began to eat in earnest as Geena and Piper discussed how to spend their day.

"I have a book to read," Piper said.

"As do I," Geena replied. "But I think I'd rather go shopping. You wanna come?"

"Where?" Piper questioned.

"I thought maybe we could look for vintage clothes. There are several consignment stores that advertise a nice selection. I found them online before we left Boston."

Piper shrugged and speared a piece of cantaloupe. "Sounds better than the book idea."

"I wouldn't mind some clamming either," Geena added. "I have a great chowder recipe to try. One of my many suitors gave it to me." She laughed, but her comment gave me a start.

"Many suitors? How many guys are you dating?" I tried to keep the sound of my voice casual.

"Well, I have three I'm just casually dating." Geena smiled mischievously. "Though I could probably string along a half dozen or more. They think I'm hot." She laughed and Piper did as well.

"Well, you do have that nice runner's bod. I can see why the men would be crazy for you. They sure don't look at me that way."

"Oh, I think they're after me for my mind," Geena teased. "They probably realize I'm going to be an important lawyer one day and make tons of money."

Piper shook her head. "They're crazy for your long hair and the way you do your eyes all smoky and dark. You always look like you have something really intriguing to say."

"That's what I mean," Geena said. "It's my intellect they're after." She giggled and cut into her pancake. "I'm just irresistible."

"Sounds like you have the day planned," I said, pushing aside the niggling unease I felt at her declaration. "At least enough to keep you busy until tonight."

"Yeah, until tonight," Piper murmured.

We all looked up at the same time. I wanted to believe it would all work out—to reassure them of the same. But I didn't have the words.

CHAPTER 7

D ad called around five to tell us that storms had further delayed Judith's flight. Initially a change in aircraft and a problem engine caused her delay, but now thunderstorms and threats of tornadoes in Chicago were keeping her grounded.

"He said it's some of the most violent storms the area has seen," Geena declared after hanging up the phone. "He's gonna get a room near the airport and just wait for her at SeaTac. He thought she'd still get out tonight, but she won't arrive until late."

"I guess we can save the chowder until tomorrow," Geena offered.

I found I had lost my appetite with worry at the thought of confronting our father. Now that the discussion was postponed once again, I decided I might actually like to eat. However, I had toyed all evening with the idea of telling my sisters the truth about our mother's mental illness, and now I had the opportunity.

Piper was sitting curled up with her book and Geena was focusing on a crossword puzzle. "I want to use this time to tell you both something," I interrupted. "It has to do with our mother."

Geena eyed me curiously, but Piper actually looked excited. No doubt once she heard what I had to say, she'd be less so.

I pulled up an ottoman and sat in front of them. "I started to say something earlier, but I wanted some time to think about it. I also called my therapist while you two were out. She felt it was important to move forward, so that's what I'm doing."

"So what is this all about?" Geena asked.

"When we talked earlier today, we spoke of Momma and her mental state—her problems. I've known something about them for some time, but I've never said anything. I felt it was my place to . . ." I didn't know exactly how to finish that sentence, but Piper did it for me.

"Keep the secrets?"

"Yes. . . . I suppose that's the best way to put it. I felt it was my place to keep the family secrets in hopes of protecting you two."

"And now?" Piper eyed me quite seriously. "Now is it time to be honest about them?"

"I think so. I think it was time years ago,

but perhaps we wouldn't have been mature enough to deal with it. I know when I first found out the truth, it was very disturbing." Now both of them were frowning. Geena's brows had knit together as though she was actually angry. When she didn't comment, I continued.

"When I was thirteen, I overheard our housekeeper on the telephone. She was talking about how sad it was for us—how much our father was mourning Momma's death. Then I heard her mention that Momma had . . . that she was—" I paused and drew a deep breath—"schizophrenic."

Geena's eyes widened. "You're kidding. You've known something like this all these years and said nothing?"

"What exactly does it mean to be schizophrenic?" Piper asked.

"It's a severe mental illness," Geena replied. "Genetic, if I recall correctly."

"It can be," I said. "But it doesn't have to be."

"What kind of mental illness?" Piper put her book aside. "Like really, truly crazy?"

"Our mother was a paranoid schizophrenic who had delusions and depression," I began. "She feared 'bad men' were going to take us away. She said the legal authorities were after her—trying to read her mind—trying to steal us away. She also believed other men were constantly eyeing her with desire or sexual intentions." My sisters' eyes were wide. "She was always trying to hide us, but things got even worse about the time you were born, Piper. She heard about that serial killer and something seemed to snap."

"But that was real," Geena interjected. "I've seen the old newspaper articles on it. That serial killer was a real person, killing children—mostly girls."

"Yes, he was real," I agreed. "But our mother was not involved with helping the FBI to catch him. Neither was the FBI using us as bait. No one was coming to steal us away from her, yet she would wake us up out of a sound sleep to hide us away from supposed intruders."

Geena shook her head. "I thought it was all a game. You know, like the fire drills at school."

"It wasn't a game to Momma. She honestly believed we were in danger. She also believed that most every man who caught sight of her was crazy for her. She believed herself to be irresistible." I hadn't meant to use Geena's word from the previous evening. If she remembered it, she didn't show any sign. But I couldn't help but recognize the parallel between the two. My stomach clenched.

"Do either of you remember how she acted

in church?" I stood up, suddenly unable to sit still anymore. I turned away, and I could barely speak over the lump lodged in my throat. "She'd stand up during the service and declare that the pastor or one of the deacons or other men in the congregation wanted to have an affair with her. She claimed she was confessing her sins and theirs—although nothing had ever taken place."

"I do remember once when a kid in my Sunday school class said my mom had made his mom cry," Geena said. "But I was only six or so. We didn't go to church a whole lot after that."

"No, we didn't. We couldn't." My voice hardened. "The 'good Christians' of the congregation didn't know how to deal with the mentally ill. Mom frightened them, talking about working for the FBI and giving gruesome details about the killings. The pastor asked Dad to keep mom home so she wouldn't disturb the congregation anymore."

"Why didn't Dad go to church with us?" Piper asked.

"He always said he knew there was a God, but that was enough. He figured if God was truly all-knowing and all-powerful, then there wasn't anything he could do to change God's mind about the future. He didn't believe God would be swayed by our begging, so why pray."

"I've felt that way too," Piper said. "I think that's why I'm so surprised that he's changed his mind now. How could a person completely switch the way he looks at something—especially that important?"

"I don't know," Geena murmured. She let the crossword puzzle book slip from her lap. "I still can't believe you've kept this from us. What else do you know, Bailee? Tell us everything. Start at the beginning."

I suppressed a shudder. I couldn't possibly begin to share everything. "Momma sometimes woke us up in the middle of the night. She would load us into the car, and we'd drive all night. She said we were escaping the FBI." I studied my sisters for a moment. "Geena, you must remember some of those drives."

"I do, vaguely. But like I said, Momma always made it seem like a big game to me."

"I remember once when we did get up in the night to go for a drive," Piper suddenly said, as if it were all just coming back to her. "It was just before we came here the last time. I think we were living in California."

I nodded and tucked my feet up under me. "We were. We lived just north of San Francisco. Dad was handling a major consulting job in the city. We had a housekeeper, as well as a nanny. Mom hated them both—she said they were spies. Anyway, one night when Dad was away, she waited until the housekeeper had gone home for the night and the nanny was asleep, then loaded us up in the car."

"Why would they leave us alone with her if she was so bad off? Why wouldn't someone stay awake? Why wouldn't the nanny keep us with her?"

Piper's questions were some I'd asked myself, but I didn't really have a solid answer. I only had guesses. "Momma could appear quite . . . normal. Quite healthy. In fact, there were times when I was even convinced that the bad times were behind us. The staff was fairly new. They didn't know how she could be. Dad had probably warned them or said something to let them know she had problems, but when she acted normal there was no reason to believe she was a threat to anyone. Especially for a person who wasn't familiar with schizophrenia."

"So Mom had us leave in the night. What happened?" Piper asked. "Because I don't remember. I think I fell asleep in the car and when I woke up the next day, I was back in my bed."

"Mom drugged you." I waited for their reaction.

"Drugged? Both of us?" Geena's tone betrayed her disbelief.

"Yes. I didn't realize that was what was happening at the time, but later I figured it out. She would give you something to make you sleep. She'd put it in a cookie or pastry."

Geena's eyes widened. "I remember her giving us something to eat every time we went for a ride."

"Exactly." I could see they were starting to understand. "I didn't know at first that she was doing this. She didn't give me the treat—she said I had to wait. She said it was my responsibility to take care of you two, that I needed to make sure you were safe and that nothing bad could happen to you. She always offered me one of the cookies when we got home—after I'd helped her get you two to bed. Sometimes I ate it and sometimes I didn't."

Geena shook her head. "No wonder you've always watched over us like an armed guard at a bank."

I didn't comment on that. There wasn't time, because Piper was already moving on with her questions. "But why did she drug us? Why did she take us out in the dead of night? How could she possibly believe there was a real danger? The only danger to us was her."

"I don't know what to say." I looked at my sisters and then let my gaze travel beyond them to the back of the room. "I began snooping around to learn what schizophrenia was after overhearing Mrs. Brighton on the phone. I didn't like the information I found—it sounded so hopeless."

"It is rather hopeless," Geena interjected. "There isn't a cure."

"That doesn't make it hopeless," I said. "There are medications that really help."

"But a person has to be willing to get help," she countered. "Obviously our mother wasn't one of those people."

"Sometimes she got treatment. Remember the times when she was supposedly off working with the FBI?"

I saw the understanding in Geena's expression as she half stated, half asked, "She went to a loony bin during those times?"

I nodded. "Or the hospital. Dad tried to force help on her, but she didn't want it. I read some old records that Dad had hidden in his office. Mom didn't trust doctors or medicine. She was paranoid about getting any kind of help. For a time she allowed Dad to help her with medicine and food, but after a while she believed everyone was trying to hurt her. Even Dad."

"And he was," Geena responded.

"At least that last night," Piper declared. She reached for one of the sofa pillows and hugged it close.

"Well, you seem to know everything; what

else did Mom do to us?" Geena asked. Her emotionless expression gave me the distinct impression she blamed me for our mother's problems, like if I would have said something, she might not have gotten worse. But it was no more than I'd told myself. Blaming myself for Mom's death—for her problems in life—was something I was quite good at doing.

"She used to hide us in various places. Boxes, closets, trunks, you name it. She felt it was the only way to keep us safe." I tried to keep my voice even. "Once she put all three of us in the trunk of the car. Piper was a tiny baby and I held her in my arms."

Geena's eyes widened. "I can't stand small spaces."

I knew that same fear. I didn't even like to use the elevator at my condo. "There were times when . . . when her actions endangered our lives. She put Piper in a garbage bag once. I was able to get her out of it before she suffocated, but it was close."

"Mom nearly killed me? When did that happen?"

"When you were an infant." I felt my body tremble. "It wasn't the only time. She did it with Geena too. Sometimes I still have nightmares about it. She tried to hide us once in the water. It was so cold that we all had hypothermia."

"Why didn't Dad do something about it? Why did he let her go on like that?" Piper asked, her voice rising.

Now came my moment to confess. "I don't think he knew—after all, he wasn't around all that much, and when he was, I think he ignored Mom's idiosyncrasies. As for why I didn't tell him . . . Momma told me I couldn't say anything . . . to anyone." I bit my lip. I was just a little girl, and my mother's word was gospel. "I'm sorry that I wasn't smarter about things. I should have said something."

"Yes, you should have," Piper agreed. "You could have stopped it from happening."

Her reproachful tone hit me hard. Could I have stopped it?

"She was just a child—just like you and me," Geena countered, surprising me. Perhaps she didn't blame me after all. "We all could have said something at the time. Bailee can't be held responsible. But Dad can. He should have known better. If the doctors told him Mom was schizo, then he should never have allowed us to be left alone with her."

"And when you knew why she acted that way," Piper said, narrowing her eyes at me, "you should have told us. You should have told Dad about the things that were happening even if you were scared. That way he could have protected us."

"He tried to provide for our safety," I argued. "That was the reason for the house-keepers and nannies. It was the reason he tried to work less during the summer—probably the reason we came here."

"And the reason we moved so often," Piper declared. "I always thought it was because of his job, but it was because of Mom, wasn't it? Because she made things difficult." Her words were clearly edged with anger.

"Most likely," I admitted. "She sometimes caused problems with neighbors, as well as the church folks. I think Dad felt the need to relocate and start over in hopes of pretending things could eventually get better. I think he hoped that sooner or later Mom would find the right blend of medications and actually take them on a regular basis. But she didn't. She was convinced the doctors meant to do her harm."

"Why didn't Dad have her put away?" Piper asked. "He obviously knew how danger-ous she'd become—at least there at the end. Why didn't he do something like that instead of . . . kill her?"

Geena spoke before I could. "Because it's not that easy to put someone away. The years of ridding yourself of crazy relatives is long past. There were so many false cases—situ-ations where folks just wanted to put away wealthy relatives so they could take over their estates, for example, that laws were changed. You can't just force a person into treatment anymore."

"But couldn't the courts have done it?" Piper asked, her voice cracking.

"Dad tried." They both looked at me. "He tried to have her committed several times. From what I saw, however, the court interviews were never more than fifteen or twenty minutes and Mom appeared perfectly rational. One judge even commented that she was the epitome of reason and sanity and he wondered if the husband wasn't the one with issues."

Piper shook her head. "Well, you're just full of knowledge."

Geena gave me a rebuking look. I could see they were both more than a little angry. "Believe me, I really wanted to say something much sooner, but I was . . . well, I was afraid. Afraid you'd be angry at me. And obviously you are."

Ignoring my excuse, Geena spoke. "I've studied this from a legal perspective. I can easily see the situation happening just the way you've described. That's why there are so many mentally unstable people out on the streets. It's why some family members just walk away, never to be heard from again. Mental health can't seem to strike a happy medium."

"So crazy people are just allowed to call the shots and in turn risk the lives of children and others?" Piper asked.

I'd asked the same questions most of my life, but I simply said, "They have rights too."

Geena was less concerned. "Unfortunately, their inability to understand what's happening to them, or to convince themselves that medications can be useful in keeping them on even footing, tends to send them veering across the line where their rights end and ours begin."

Piper looked like she might well be sick. "Well, if Mom was crazy—if she was schizophrenic like you say and did all those horrible things—someone should have considered what she was doing to us . . . what a danger she was to us."

"Someone did," Geena said, meeting my gaze.

For several minutes none of us said another word. I could see that they were thinking the same thing I was. Maybe we shouldn't say anything about our father's deed. Maybe it was best to bury this in the past and leave it there. After all, if he'd tried to get Mom help, and I knew he had, then maybe he had been as desperate to protect us as the courts were to protect Mom. Maybe it really came down to his believing there was no other alternative.

My heart ached at the thought of him struggling to figure out how to keep his children safe from the woman he loved—the mother of those same children. If he divorced her and left Mom to her own devices, she would most likely have died anyway. And, she probably would have found a way to take one of us—if not all of us—with her. If he'd put down ultimatums, it might only have caused Mom to do something rash. I couldn't think of a single solution that didn't involve the potential for further danger to us.

"I have to do this for the girls. It's for them. They will be safe." His words echoed over and over in my mind.

Tears came to my eyes. I hadn't allowed such a show of emotion in a long, long time. I had thought, in fact, that I was cried out. I refused to give in to my sorrow and blinked back the drops. How could we move forward with our plan to talk to him? How could we betray the only one who had done what he could to protect us?

My mind rebelled against my heart. It was murder. It was wrong—even for such a necessary and noble purpose. How could I condemn my father for doing the only thing left for him to do? How could I not condemn him for such a heinous act?

CHAPTER 8

By three in the morning I still couldn't sleep. I paced my room like a caged animal and found it impossible to relax. I opened a window and drew in a deep breath. Outside, the moon's reflection in the water beckoned me. I pulled on sweats and sneakers and headed downstairs and out of the house.

I took the stone steps down to the beachfront, careful to hold on to the rail. Dad had built it when we were children, telling all of us that the slippery surface could prove deadly and that we must always use the railing. Old habits weren't easily put aside.

A damp, chilly breeze made me glad I'd grabbed a jacket just before exiting the back door. As I reached the beach, I zipped the coat up and stood for a long time just staring out at the water. The setting reminded me of Mark. He'd once asked me to take a moonlight dinner cruise with him in Boston Harbor. He'd said it was purely business, but I'd declined, thinking it sounded dangerously romantic. In this day and age of sexual harassment lawsuits, I was surprised that Mark continued to express an interest in me. Maybe he knew I wasn't the suing type. Or perhaps he saw the longing in my eyes.

Jamming my hands down into the pockets of my jacket, I walked for a short distance, listening to the water lap against the shore and dock. I remembered a time when Dad had rented a boat for us. We had spent the entire day on Puget Sound. Momma had refused to come for some reason, but Dad wouldn't be deterred. He loaded us girls in our life jackets and away we went. That day would stand out as one of the few childhood memories that made me happy.

I had been eleven that summer, and I wanted nothing more than to get in that boat and float away to some far-off place. I didn't want to come back to the house or to the routine of school and Mom's problems. I hadn't realized until now just how depressed I'd been. I'd always pictured myself as having it together—feeling very grown up and wise. Now, however, I knew those feelings had merely been cover-ups for the truth. I was terrified and tired, and those things had led me to depression.

Why depression? Why not anger or anxiety?

"But I was angry and anxious too," I reasoned. Somewhere down the beach I heard a dog bark, but otherwise I was completely alone. I stopped again and focused on the sky. The stars were visible, but I knew very little about them. I used to imagine that I could connect all of them together and make some incredible picture. Of course, that's exactly what I had tried to do with my family as well.

"I really wanted to believe we could be a happy family. I wanted the perfect life—the happy mother and father, the well-adjusted children." If only I could have connected all the dots.

A sense of weariness washed over me. I felt really old. I had been born old, I thought. There was never a time when I remembered acting or feeling like a little child. I felt the weight of responsibility for so much, so early. People had always commented on what a serious child I was. In fact, I remember once sitting at a birthday party watching a magic show. The man was doing his best to keep the audience in stitches of laughter, but I wasn't impressed. I was bored. I knew the magic wasn't real. It seemed I'd known that all of my life.

I walked back toward the house. I'd left the back light on to find my way. It illuminated the deck and yard below just enough to paint shadowy figures across the width of our property. The tall yews and cedar rose up like towering guardians, keepers of the land who sheltered us away from view and maintained our secrets. It gave me a chill. If I walked into the water—slipped beneath the blackness—no one would ever know. I would simply be . . . gone. The trees would bear witness, but never evidence.

Frowning, I questioned where those thoughts had come from. I wasn't suicidal. I didn't have any intention of ending my life. I just wanted the past to die once and for all. Was that really too much to ask?

I climbed the steps to the deck and plopped down on a cushioned chair near the rail. Gazing heavenward, I shook my head. "What am I supposed to do?"

Only the sounds of the night echoed back. I hugged my arms to my chest and felt overwhelmed with a sense of loss. Tears came unbidden, and though I wanted nothing more than to buck up and be strong, I had no strength left.

I mourned my lost childhood and the mother I might have known. I thought of girls I'd gone to school with and how much I'd envied their lives. Their mothers took them on shopping trips and weekend lunch dates.

Their mothers showed up for school functions and shared in their daughter's accomplishments. More important—they wanted their mothers to be there.

Anger replaced my sorrow. I thought of Piper's accusation that I could have put an end to it. I gazed upward. "God, you could have stopped it from happening, but you didn't."

This time, instead of the silence, I heard an audible voice. "Yes, I could have, but I didn't. What will you do with me now?"

I jumped up and looked around me. The voice had been so startlingly clear—so real. Yet there was no one there. The idea struck me that someone might be playing a trick on me. Someone might have been walking on the beach just like I had been. They might have heard me talking to myself.

But I wasn't talking to myself. I had actually uttered a sort of prayer. Had God answered me?

I reconsidered my words. God could have stopped the hideousness that was my childhood. He could have given me a normal life, with a mother who wasn't crazy. But He didn't. He let it happen. He didn't intervene and He didn't heal.

"What will you do with me now?" the voice had asked.

Was it really possible that God had spoken to me? Did He do that? Talk to everyday people who were accusing Him? To a woman who had given up on Him years ago? Or was I crazy too?

I thought of my father and Mark. They both claimed a life that now included time spent with God. Mark talked about God like He was a personal friend—someone who might answer the phone anytime I called. How could that be? Why would the God of the universe even want to take time for me and my questions?

What will you do with me now?

The question whispered in my heart. I hesitantly retook my seat and looked up once again. "Are you really there?"

I shook my head and stared at the water again. "I suppose that was a stupid question."

"There are no stupid questions when they are about me."

Again the voice seemed so real I couldn't pretend I hadn't heard it. Was I losing my mind? Was this a sign that I had inherited my mother's schizophrenia?

Fear gripped me. I had always told myself that if I made it to thirty without any signs of mental illness, I would probably be safe. Now I was hearing voices.

∽

"Hey, Bailee," Mark announced on the other end of the phone. I struggled to wake up as he continued. "I have a new project for you if you're still interested." I yawned and looked at the clock. It was nearly eight. I should have been up an hour ago, but then again I hadn't gotten to sleep until nearly five.

"Of course I'm interested."

"You sound tired. Did I wake you?"

"Yeah, but it's no big deal. I was awake until . . . well . . . I was restless."

"Wanna talk about it?" His voice soothed me.

"First tell me about the project."

"I emailed it to you already. I knew you'd say yes. It's nothing difficult—one of those tell-alls by the former nanny of the latest Hollywood 'It' couple. Nothing but a straightforward copy edit."

I suppressed another yawn and got out of bed. "When's it due?"

"I'd like it back by a week from next Wednesday. Can you manage that?"

"No problem." It would mean less time to spend with my new stepmother and father, but that didn't bother me. Without giving it a second thought, I asked Mark the question that burned in my mind. "Does God talk to people?"

"Of course He does." The matter-of-fact answer silenced me, so Mark continued. "Why do you ask? Is He talking to you?"

"Would it surprise you if I said yes?"

"Not at all."

His utter ease with the idea almost irked me. "Mark, I'm serious. I'm either hearing voices or God answered me when I asked Him something."

There was a moment of silence on the other end of the phone. Maybe Mark was stunned by the fact that I'd talked to God. Maybe he was worried just as I was that I had somehow lost my mind.

"It's been my experience that God always meets people where they are—when they need Him most. Can I ask you something?"

I shrugged and walked to my window. "Why not?" I pulled back the curtain. Raising the blinds, I gazed out on the cloudy skies. Looked like rain.

"What did you ask God?"

I frowned. I didn't really want to have to explain, but it was my own fault for having started this conversation. "It wasn't really a question. It was more of a statement."

He chuckled. "So what did you state?"

For a moment I toyed with ending the conversation. Finally I decided to give him a brief explanation. "I had been thinking of something that happened when I was young. I reminded God that He could have stopped it, but He didn't."

"And what did you hear Him say?" Mark's voice was tender.

"He agreed with me," I said, barely able to vocalize the answer. "And . . . He . . . well, He asked me a question." I suddenly felt really silly. "Look, let's just forget it."

"Why?"

How could I possibly explain without giving him the details of my life? Details that I would just as soon forget.

"Bailee?"

"I'm here." I didn't know what else to say.

He seemed to understand. "I really care about you. I want to help if I can."

"I know," I whispered.

"You don't have to tell me what happened or what God asked you, but isn't it time to face the truth?"

I nearly dropped the phone. "What do you mean, the truth?"

"You've reached out to God, and He's reaching back. It might not look like what you thought it would, but it's there just the same."

"How can you be sure it's God and not just me losing my mind?"

"I suppose I would base it on whether what He says lines up with who He is and what He says in the Bible."

"He told me I was right and that He could

have stopped it. And then He asked what I would do with Him now," I blurted.

"And what was your answer?"

I couldn't believe that I'd just told Mark something so extreme and he wasn't even questioning the validity. I looked at the floor and wondered how to reply. If I was honest, I would have to tell him that I didn't have an answer.

"I think the hardest thing I've ever had to face," Mark began, "is the realization that God can do anything, and yet sometimes—"

"Does nothing," I murmured.

"Or so it seems." He was full of compassion as he continued. "It seems that God sits idle while the innocent suffer."

"Yes." I wanted to say more, but I knew to do so would require an explanation that I wasn't yet ready to give.

"But He doesn't, you know. He has given man free will and allows us to make our choices. But He is never idle, and we are never alone. Even in those moments when we believe we are."

"Bailee!"

It was Geena calling from the hallway. "I have to go," I told Mark. "My sisters need me." I hung up without waiting for him to answer and went to the door.

"What is it?" I asked, opening the door.

"It's Piper. She's missing."

CHAPTER 9

I couldn't begin to imagine where Piper had gone. She'd taken the rental car, however, so there was nothing for Geena and me to do but wait.

"She was very angry last night," Geena said as she stirred creamer into her coffee. "You should have been honest with us a long time ago."

"It wasn't for a lack of wanting to," I assured her. "I just worried that it would only add more questions, more fears. I didn't want you and Piper sitting around dreading the possibilities."

"Like you were?" she questioned.

I met Geena's grim expression and couldn't hide my own worry. "Yes . . . I suppose so."

"Schizophrenia explains an awful lot," Geena continued. "At least from what little I know. The few things I can remember—the things we've actually discussed—all seem to fit into a giant puzzle now." She took a long drink from her mug before continuing.

"If schizophrenia was the reason Mom acted as she did, then I truly feel sorry for Dad. If she wouldn't take her meds or get help, he must have had a real nightmare on his hands. Especially since he probably got very little help from the mental health community."

"Dad didn't know the half of what we went through," I muttered.

"Piper came to me in tears last night. She asked me if depression was a sign of schizophrenia. You've seen how she's struggled . . . she figures it must be her inheritance from Mom."

"She could overcome her depression if she'd get some help. Good grief, she lost her mother when she was six. Knew that her father was responsible for the death. Then he wrapped himself up in business, leaving us at one boarding school or another . . . or in the care of hired help. Piper never had a moment of continuity in her life until we moved to Newton, but by then the damage was done."

"We never fit in at boarding school," Geena offered. "Piper especially seemed confused and alone."

"I know, but there was never anything I could do about it. At least Dad kept us at the same school—and for a time, in the same room." I remembered when the day came to split us up. Piper had spent weeks begging Dad to reconsider, but when the day came, Piper didn't cry or pitch a fit. Instead, she sat in perfect resignation. Wasn't it Thoreau who once said, "What is called resignation is confirmed desperation"? Piper had been desperate, but I found myself useless, unable to help her. God knew that I had tried. I had pled my case to the head mistresses and to Dad, but both said that the separation would be good in the long run. I disagreed then, and I've never changed my mind.

I understood that we had to separate and do our individual tasks related to school. No one would expect a fourth grader to sit in an eighth grader's class. But most children went home at night to their parents and siblings. They had dinner around the table or at least some form of togetherness. At least that was how I imagined it. Not so for the Cooper sisters.

∾

Late in the morning we heard a car pull up to the house. Geena beat me to the window and announced our sister had returned. Piper stalked into the house and threw a sheaf of papers along with the car keys onto the table.

"There you are," she announced.

"Everything you would ever want to know about schizophrenia." She picked up one sheet and began to pace. "Where should I start? Should we discuss the angle of it being a psychotic disorder—an abnormal state of the mind in which thought processes are disrupted?" She tossed the page down and picked up another.

"Why don't we take a moment to reflect on the fact that there are positive, negative, and cognitive symptoms. Better still, let's pin down what doctors generally look for first—delusions, hallucinations, disorganized speech and behavior. And those are just the positive symptoms."

"Piper, calm down. Bailee and I both know something of schizophrenia," Geena declared.

I felt sorry for Piper but wasn't sure what to say. She turned on her heel and went to the table to grab another piece of paper and continued to pace. "Well, until this morning, I didn't know much of anything about it, so please bear with me as I detail for you the five types of schizophrenia.

"There's our number one contestant—Paranoid Schizophrenia, which offers us delusions and hallucinations, not to mention that those patients generally focus on being pursued, betrayed, or plotted against. Sound familiar?" Her sarcasm was like a knife in my heart.

"How about behind door number two?" She looked to Geena and then to me. "That's right, we have Disorganized Type Schizophrenia. It doesn't seem to have the degree of delusions and hallucinations that Paranoid Schizophrenia offers, but it does allow for some negative symptoms that are not found as often in number one. You might ask what the negative symptoms are, and I'm glad you did."

Our petite little sister marched to the table once again and riffled through the papers until she found what she wanted. "Negative symptoms include the flattened effect, where folks have trouble showing emotions."

"Well, that certainly isn't your problem," Geena interrupted, her tone sarcastic. "Look, we get it. You're angry. I was angry too. Bailee didn't keep this from us to be mean. She thought she was protecting us."

Piper shook her head. "Don't interrupt. We're learning about important family history here."

I shuddered and said nothing as Geena took a seat beside me and Piper continued. "Other negative symptoms would also include anhedonia—this is where patients fail to experience or express pleasure in things they once found enjoyable. Add to this reduced speech and a lack of initiative, and you could very well be describing me for the last two years."

"Oh, stop it," Geena demanded. "You aren't suffering from schizophrenia and you definitely don't have reduced speech."

Piper zeroed in on me and came to where I sat. "What about it, Big Sis? You're the keeper of such information. Have you determined yet whether I suffer from our mother's mental illness?"

"I never meant to hurt you," I said, unable to think of anything else.

"Well, you failed," she said matter-of-factly and walked away.

"Piper, I always intended to tell you. I just wanted to wait for the right time."

She turned and looked at me. "And how did you determine when that might be? When we started showing symptoms? It's hereditary, you know."

"It *can* be. It doesn't have to be. Scientists credit drug usage as the main cause of increased cases," I countered. "There's only about a ten percent chance in people who had one parent suffering the disorder."

"Is that supposed to make me feel better?" she asked in disbelief. "You've known about this for years and said nothing."

I couldn't muster a response. I'd always imagined this moment of disclosure, but I figured my sisters would be grateful. Once I was able to explain my reasoning, I figured they would be touched—appreciative. That was far from what I was seeing now. Something authoritarian rose up in me.

"I was wrong." I looked at Piper and put on my role of big sister. "I'm sorry. I truly am sorry." Glancing over to Geena, I added, "You both have a right to be angry. However, I want to remind you that Dad will be here today with our new stepmother. I want to resolve this now."

Piper crossed her arms. "Good for you."

Her lack of understanding made me angry. "This is the thanks I get for doing what I could to keep you safe from harm? I spent my entire life watching over you and seeing to your needs before my own."

"Nobody asked you to," Piper said, taking a step forward. "Nobody."

I nodded. "You're right. They didn't ask. They demanded." I felt rage begin to bubble up from down deep inside. I felt unappreciated and scorned for my devotion. "They demanded."

"Who demanded?" Geena asked. "Who forced that on you, Bailee?"

"Our mother," I said, shaking my head. "She always demanded that I keep track of the two of you—that I help her account for your safety."

"From dangers that didn't even exist," Piper interjected.

In a flash I found myself taken back in time to a moment when our mother had tried to teach us to swim in the Port Orchard Strait. I had no idea where our father or the house-keeper was, but Piper was nearly two. She couldn't possibly remember the event, but she'd gotten too cold in the water and was sick for nearly three weeks afterwards. Dad had been very worried about her recovery, but I had never told him the cause of Piper's sickness. Would the dangers have stopped if I'd been honest?

"But Bailee is right," Geena said, bringing me back to the present. "Dad will be back before we know it, and Judith will be with him. Dad is the one who should have told us the truth. My question, however, is do we approach him about this with a stranger in our house?"

Piper calmed a bit. "I don't see as how we have a choice."

I could only imagine the scene we would create. "Maybe we can convince Dad to speak with us privately. After all, they plan to stay in the cottage."

The phone rang as if on cue. Geena was closest and picked it up after the first ring. "Hello?"

I could tell that it was Dad. I saw Piper slump to a chair as though all of her gusto was now spent. Geena nodded and looked to me. "We'll see you when you get here." She hung up the phone.

"The ferry just docked and they'll be here in a few minutes. Dad wants us to join them for lunch."

"I guess we can talk when we get back then. Hopefully Judith will want to rest—maybe take a nap. We can let her know that we want to talk privately with Dad. She'll understand."

"What if after confronting Dad, he decides to turn himself in?" Piper asked.

"I hardly think that's going to happen," I replied. "He's had fifteen years."

Confusion muddled my thoughts. Geena had been determined to get a confession and see Dad face the consequences for the past. Piper had been terrified of what that might mean. But after all I'd shared, what did they think now? I was starting to feel a sense of exhaustion.

I remember Dad talking to my grandma Cooper when I was about seven. She told my dad that love sometimes required sacrifice, and often that sacrifice would be uncomfortable—even painful. It seemed this was one of those times.

I checked the clock on the wall. They would

arrive in a matter of minutes. Not only would we face an alteration to our family in the form of a new stepmother, but we would confront the past head-on. We would ask the question that had consumed us since our mother died. Were we strong enough to hear the answer?

CHAPTER 10

My first impressions of Judith were quite positive. She entered the house at Dad's side and smiled at each of us and called us by name. Her demeanor, calm and gentle, expressed an ease about her that made me relax. Her brunette hair just grazed her shoulders, framing the delicate features of her slender face. I couldn't tell what her age might be; there were wrinkles around her eyes and mouth, but a youthfulness in her spirit suggested she was just a woman who liked to smile a lot.

"I've seen photographs of you girls for so long, I feel I know you already," she declared.

"That must be nice," Piper said in a snide manner before slouching into a stuffed chair near the fireplace.

Judith threw her a sympathetic look. "I know I have you all at a disadvantage. I told your father it was hardly fair to dump me into the equation like this. I had thought it would be easier back in Boston."

Geena extended her hand. "It would come as a surprise no matter the location. Dad has never said so much as a word about dating anyone."

Dad spoke up to defend himself. "I didn't know my love life was any of your concern." He smiled good-naturedly and put his arm around Judith's shoulders. "I specifically remember you girls telling me that as adult women you weren't obligated to tell me the details of your romantic interests. I presumed that the same courtesies were extended to me." He turned to his new wife. "Judith, it would seem that I've brought you into the lion's den."

"Hardly that," Geena countered. "We were just surprised."

"That's putting it mildly," Piper muttered.

I drew in a deep breath and steadied myself. "So were you able to fly out last night?" I hoped this would change the focus of our conversation and lighten the mood.

Judith appeared to understand my intention. "By the time the last of the storms rolled through, I had already opted to stay the night and fly in this morning."

I nodded. "Our weather has been mild. Rain, but nothing too harsh." I looked at Dad and could see his brow had relaxed. "We fixed some clam chowder but decided to save it for another time."

"Judith and I will be here for at least a week. We hope all of you will stay at least that long."

"Seems strange that you're actually taking a vacation," Geena said. "We've been after you to do this for a long time."

Dad glanced at Judith. "She convinced me that I needed to learn to relax. Apparently I work entirely too much."

"This is ridiculous," Piper interjected with a huff.

"Piper, congratulations on your graduation from college," Judith said in an attempt to soothe my sister. "Do you have plans for the future?"

Crossing her arms, Piper gave the older woman a hard stare. "I plan to seek the truth."

I motioned to the living room. "Would you like to sit down, or should we just go right to lunch?"

"I'm not going anywhere until I get some answers," Piper said, surprising us all. She all but exploded out of the chair and crossed the room to the table. She picked up her papers and thrust them at Dad. "Maybe you could start here."

Dad's smile faded even before he looked at the information. "What in the world has gotten into you?"

Piper generally took his side in any family discussion or argument, so for her to appear so hostile now was a great shift in character. She stared hard at Dad as if silently daring him to deny what she already knew.

He glanced at the papers and then held them up for Judith to see. "So . . . you know about your mother. I suppose you told them?" he asked, looking at me.

"Bailee should have told us a long time ago. She's known since she was a teenager," Piper declared. She looked at me in an almost apologetic manner before going back to her chair.

Dad exchanged a glance with Judith, then turned to me. "How did you find out?"

His tone betrayed his hurt. "I overheard Mrs. Brighton talking about it on the phone one day. That set me off on a journey to learn as much as I could. I suppose the only real question I have is why you didn't just tell us. It's not like it would have changed anything."

"I was advised against it," Dad said, looking at the papers as if he might see something important there. "I was told it wasn't in your best interest."

"Who in their right mind would tell you that?" Geena asked. "We had a right to know. We can inherit mental illness."

"Yes, but you didn't," he countered.

"How can you be sure?" Piper threw out. "How can anyone be sure?"

Dad put the papers aside and led Judith to the sofa. I followed, not knowing what else to do, and took a seat in the rocking chair. Geena pulled up the ottoman. We waited for Dad to continue, but instead, Judith began to speak.

"I've had personal experience with this type of mental illness."

All I could think of was that Dad had somehow married another woman with the same problems Mom had endured.

She continued. "Your dad and I met sixteen or seventeen years ago."

"You were running after her while married to Momma?" Piper accused.

Dad tensed. "I most certainly did not."

Judith patted his hand and he relaxed. She smiled at him and continued. "No, we didn't begin a romantic relationship until earlier this year. We met back then at a group therapy session. A support group, really." She turned to face Geena and me. "It was for families who had loved ones with schizophrenia. It was quite new and neither of us had any idea what to expect."

I was stunned. "You went to therapy, Dad?"

"Yes. I didn't know how to deal with your

mother. I didn't know how to help her—especially when she wouldn't help herself."

"I would have liked to have known how to help her too." Bitterness clung to my words.

"But there was no reason to involve you girls," Dad said. "It wasn't up to you to figure out such weighted problems."

I felt the knife turn a little deeper. My therapist had told me many times that my mother's problems were not my responsibility and that I should never have been forced to act as her guardian during those times when she had bad spells. Now, however, the very person who placed that responsibility upon me was sitting here saying the same thing. I forced myself to calm down.

"Look, Dad, we would just as soon talk to you about this . . . alone. Judith shouldn't have to be in the middle of this."

"It's too late for that," he replied. "Judith has been in the middle, as you call it, for a long time. Like she said, we met in therapy. Her husband was also schizophrenic."

"And your children?" Piper asked.

"We didn't have children," Judith answered in a soft voice.

Piper smirked. "Well, how lucky for you."

Judith flinched.

I'd never seen my little sister act like this. Fact was, I'd never seen Piper have this much enthusiasm for anything. Now, however, she was like a pit bull unleashed on a poor unsuspecting kitten.

"Piper, that was uncalled for," our father declared.

I turned to Judith. "I'm sorry for the hostilities here. You see, I made the mistake of keeping our mother's illness from my sisters until last night."

Judith nodded. "It's not your fault or theirs. Your feelings are valid and you all have a right to be angry. Your father should have told you years ago about her condition."

"I suppose I should have," Dad began, "but I didn't see how it would help."

Geena fidgeted with the tail of her button down shirt. "It might have helped us to better understand some of the things that happened."

Dad turned his attention back to me. "Did it? Does it help you now to know the truth? Did it help you these last years, Bailee?"

I shook my head. "Not completely. It gave me something to focus on, but . . ." I fell silent. I realized that knowing of my mother's mental illness had never made the circumstance of the past any better. It didn't resolve anything for me—it only created more questions, more worries.

"Your mother's sickness had to be

frightening to all of you," Judith said. "Your father told me there were times when you were put in danger."

I looked at him and could feel the heat of his betrayal stain my cheeks. "You knew about those times? You knew and did nothing?"

"Oh, he did plenty," Piper snarked.

I waved my hand to silence her. "You knew Mom put our lives in danger, yet you left us alone with her? You knew we could be harmed but didn't stop it?"

"I did what I could. I hired people to help—to watch her and be there for you. I tried to get the doctors to help me, help her." He lowered his head. "Your mother thought it was a big conspiracy to see her out of the picture."

"And was it?" Geena asked.

His head snapped up. "No. It was never that. I wanted her to get better. I loved her and wanted our family to be together. But her mind told her otherwise. Her mind told her that everyone was against her—that we wanted to hurt her. She was convinced that doctors were spies for the government, that medication was poison."

He got up and walked to the fireplace. "I tried to convince her that she could beat this thing. When she was on medication and feeling better, I would try to explain to her what was happening. She didn't believe me. I think explaining only served to make things worse. I suppose I thought it would do the same with you girls. I mean, if you knew the truth . . ." His words faded.

If only he had known the truth, I thought. That was the thing I wasn't sure about now, however. How much had he known? Did he realize how many times she'd nearly caused our deaths?

"We know the truth," Piper said. "We've known it for a long, long time."

I looked at her. My fingers tingled, knowing the time had come for the truth. Geena went to sit beside Piper on the arm of the chair.

"She's right, Dad," Geena added. "We know."

"Know what?" he asked.

"We know what really happened—to Mom." Geena said, crossing her arms. "We're tired of playing games." Apparently Piper's anger was spreading.

Our father and Judith exchanged a look that resembled a cross between disgust and surprise. Dad's eyes narrowed. "What are you talking about?"

"Mom," Geena said, then hesitated. "Her death."

Dad moved back to the sofa and reclaimed a seat beside Judith. He looked dazed, lost. I almost felt sorry for him and wished we'd never started this. Almost. I didn't really want to cause Dad pain . . . but I did want answers.

For several moments no one said a word. That it should be Judith who encouraged him to tell the truth was almost offensive.

"Apparently they know the worst of it, Tony. It's time you all sorted through the details of this and talked about what really happened."

Piper was livid. "How can you act as though it's nothing more important than explaining how the vacuum runs? Our mother died a horrible death and you sit there with the knowledge of it? You knew and married our father anyway?"

Judith looked puzzled. "Why shouldn't I have? I had heard Tony—your father—speak about your mother's death in our sessions. It was an awful death, but it has nothing to do with the way I feel about him."

"How can you say that? It makes you, in a fashion, an accessory to murder," Geena declared. She shook her head. "Surely you don't think it was right?"

Dad inched forward on the sofa. "What are you talking about?"

"Oh, come on," Piper said, her voice breaking. She began to cry. "Don't lie to us anymore. We deserve to have the truth."

"We already know that," Geena said,

putting her hand on Piper's shoulder. "What we want to know is why. Why was that the only solution to the problem?"

I watched Dad carefully. He seemed genuinely confused. He met my gaze and shook his head. "What are they talking about?"

Squaring my shoulders, I felt the weight of responsibility once again settle upon me. "We were watching that night."

"What night?"

I looked at Dad, unwilling to turn away. "Mom's last night."

"Watching what?" he asked.

"We were watching from right up there," Piper said, pointing to the landing on the stairs. "We saw everything." She wiped angrily at her tears.

"I don't know what you think you saw, but maybe you could explain."

"Dad, we didn't say anything because . . . well . . . we didn't know what to say. We knew you were doing it for us," I offered. "We felt obligated to keep the secret."

Geena had apparently had enough. She got to her feet and fixed her hands to her waist. "We saw you mixing drugs into Mom's hot chocolate. We know you overdosed her—killed her. We know you did it for us, because we heard you say as much. We've lived with this knowledge for fifteen years. Fifteen years of pretending our father wasn't a murderer—no matter the reason."

Judith's mouth dropped open. She turned, eyes wide, to look at Dad. "Tony," she whispered his name. "Oh, Tony."

Dad didn't react at all like I had figured. He sat staring at us as if we'd suddenly changed into objects he couldn't begin to recognize. I felt a tingling run up my spine. What had we just done?

CHAPTER 11

Without a word, Dad got to his feet and walked out of the house. The sound of the door slamming closed echoed for a moment and left me feeling horribly empty.

"Where does he think he's going?" Piper got to her feet and looked at me as though I had the answer.

"He's obviously upset." I looked at Judith. "Maybe we should go after him."

"I don't think that would be the best idea," she said. "I know this is hard for all of you, but I think you should give your father some time alone. He certainly wasn't expecting this."

"Maybe he should have." Piper turned on me at that point. "This is all your fault. You made us promise not to tell Dad what we knew. You said it was the only way to protect him and us. Now look what's happened."

I was stunned. How could she turn this

back on me? Piper stepped directly in front of me and pointed her quivering finger.

"You're to blame. You didn't tell us about Mom's problems, and you told us we couldn't talk to Dad about what he did." She began to cry and Geena went to comfort her. I felt completely displaced. How had I become the enemy?

"I hate you!" Piper ripped away from Geena and ran for the stairs. Her sobs could be heard until she closed herself into her bedroom.

"I'll go talk to her." Geena quickly followed Piper's retreat.

That left only Judith and me. We sat in silence for some time before I got to my feet. "I need to find Dad. He owes me some answers."

"I wish you wouldn't press him just now," Judith said.

I don't know why, but I sat back down. I tried to think of what I wanted to say. My sisters were angry, my father completely taken off guard, and my new stepmother was already imposing her will on the family. Well, I supposed the word *imposing* was rather harsh. She no doubt only wanted to protect her husband.

"He needs time to think. This was a hard trip for him," Judith said. "We talked a long time about this before he asked you girls to come here."

Easing back in the chair, I focused on her

concerned expression, which seemed to ease my sense of urgency. I wanted to ask her a million questions, but I felt them all stick in my throat.

"Your father was wrong not to tell you about the mental illness," Judith offered. "I tried to tell him that on more than one occasion. He was torn, however. He had been advised by child psychologists to only give information as questions were asked. You have to remember how great the changes have been in counseling and therapy over these last fifteen years. For every counselor or psychiatrist, you have the same number of opinions for treatment."

"But you knew all about Mom and her death." I narrowed my gaze. "Tell me your thoughts on it."

"I can't. Not until your father is able to talk to you and your sisters. It's not my place." She seemed to consider something for a moment. "I can say, however, that I know what it is to experience the problems schizophrenia causes. I know how necessary it seems to keep things hidden. Worse still, I know how alienating it can be. Few understand and because of that, they're frightened."

"How long was your husband sick?"

Judith looked past me to the fireplace. "He wasn't diagnosed until his late twenties. However, he was sick a lot longer. I just didn't know it. He seemed just fine. He held a good job, had friends, and was brilliant." She gave a sad smile. "I thought we had a good life."

"What happened to show you otherwise?"

She looked back at me. "For years Kevin—that was my husband's name—went to work and came home each evening, played poker with the boys on Tuesday nights, and took me out on Fridays. Caleb Carson worked in the same office—they were developing new designs for aircraft. He and Kevin were the best of friends. They helped each other on various projects and arranged their travel schedules together so that they could get in the odd game of golf. The only problem was that Caleb wasn't real—he was one of Kevin's hallucinations."

I couldn't hide my surprise. "He wasn't real? How could you not know?"

She shrugged. "I know it sounds ridiculous, but there was never any reason to question Caleb's existence. Kevin's work was very confidential and I wasn't allowed to visit his office. If we met for lunch, it was always at a restaurant or maybe just outside the building, but never inside past security. I often asked Kevin to invite Caleb to join us for dinner or a weekend church event, but there was always some reason why he couldn't attend."

She glanced toward the door, as if to make

certain Dad hadn't returned. "Your father knows all about this, and I know all about your mother; but we seldom talk about it anymore. We both kind of wore out the topic a long time ago."

"I wish he would have talked to us. I wish he would have been there for us. It might have made life a whole lot easier."

Nodding, Judith agreed. "That's what I kept telling him. I told him that you girls needed to know about your mother. You needed to remember the good things about her and understand the bad, and why she did the things she did."

"There's so much I wish I understood." I shook my head and chewed on my lower lip. How was it that I felt so comfortable talking to this stranger?

Judith tucked her hair behind her ears. "I know how you feel. At least I know how it feels to want to understand the mental illness of a loved one. I also know how having a loved one with schizophrenia alienates you from the rest of the world. Even in places where it shouldn't—like church."

"That's for sure. My mother had a tendency to make a scene, and people were . . . well, I think they were afraid of her."

Judith smiled. "Maybe not so much of her, but of her sickness. I found that folks were often afraid they would catch Kevin's illness or that he was possessed. Others were just uncomfortable in dealing with his strange comments, his turning to speak to someone who wasn't there, or his paranoia."

This was something I connected with. "Our mother was delusional. She created ugly situations at church with accusations, and the next thing I knew we were leaving to attend elsewhere. The same thing happened with school and teachers or the principal." The memories rushed back as if it had been only yesterday. "I was glad Dad moved us so often. I didn't want anyone to see her or know her. I went out of my way to try and hide her." I let out a big breath. "I'm so ashamed to admit that."

A look of compassion and comprehension passed over Judith's expression. She closed her eyes for a moment. "I loved my husband dearly, but there came a time when I just wanted to put him away." She opened her eyes. "Of course, I couldn't really do that. He was hospitalized briefly at a very good private institution. I thought he made fantastic progress there as well. He seemed happy to have adjusted to a new medication and was well on the way to getting back on track with his life."

"What happened?" I asked.

"Budget cuts and downsizing. When

Kevin's favorite doctor left to relocate to the West Coast, my husband no longer had any interest in continuing the therapy or medication. He walked away, and though I tried to convince him otherwise, that was the end of it. It was all downhill after that. When we learned that Kevin had cancer, it was even worse. He refused all treatments, convinced that we were trying to kill him. Of course, with the cancer left unchecked, it did exactly that."

"I'm sorry." And I truly was. It was impossible to listen to this woman's story without feeling a tremendous amount of sympathy for her. I had spent a lifetime putting people at arm's length, but Judith waltzed into my life and disarmed all of my natural defenses.

"So are you active in church now?" Judith asked, surprising me with the topic.

"No. I have no use for church." It wasn't hard to admit the truth, but there was a niggling suspicion in the back of my mind that this wouldn't be the end of the matter.

"Why is that?"

I drew in a deep breath. I'd been right. This conversation was taking a most uncomfortable turn. I got up and walked over to the window, hoping I might spy Dad somewhere on the property. I tried to focus on something other than the question. The skies looked to be clearing. Maybe the day would turn out nice after all.

"I'm sorry. That was a very personal thing to ask."

I turned and leaned against the windowsill. "It is. It's also a little difficult right now."

"Because of your dad?"

I laughed, surprising us both. "Hardly. No, I'm glad Dad has found comfort in God—he certainly never found it in his children. If God can help him, more power to him. My problem is that I can't find comfort in God. In fact, I don't even know where to look." Judith started to speak, but I held up my hand. "Please let it drop. I need to check on my sisters. If Dad comes back, I'd appreciate it if you'd let us know."

She simply nodded. I was relieved to reach the stairs and not hear her explain how wonderful God was. I thought again about the question I'd heard in the quiet of the night. What would I do with God? Where did He fit into the picture?

Making my way upstairs, I wasn't at all sure I could come up with an answer. God had seemed so distant for so many years that I felt awkward even contemplating what to do with Him now. What if it was simply too late to do anything with God? Did that happen? Did people just miss their opportunities to figure out who God was and how He figured into their life?

I stood outside of Piper's room for a moment. I could hear Geena's voice, but I couldn't really make out what she was saying. The closed door between us felt like a tangible barrier—my sisters together on one side, me alone on the other.

I raised my hand to knock, then thought better of it. I couldn't deal with rejection at the moment. So instead of interrupting them, I went to my room.

For all the time we'd had this summer house, I had never really felt at home. I glanced around my bedroom. I wanted to feel a sense of belonging, but this house didn't offer that. No place really did. Not my condo in Boston. Not the Cooper home in Newton. Where did I belong? Where did I matter? What was my purpose?

Stretching out on the bed, I stared up at the ceiling. I thought of my work and of Mark. I took great pride in what I did. I loved words and stories about people. I was fascinated by the turn of a phrase. To me, words were just as much an expression of art as any painting or sculpture. Maybe it was time to think about moving away from my family. Maybe New York City held the key to my future.

"I'm only twenty-seven. It's not like I don't have options."

I thought of my sisters and how hard I'd

tried to be mother and father to them. *"As a big sister,"* my mother had told me, *"you are responsible to keep them safe."*

I'd mentioned this to my therapist. She had asked me the expected question. "How did that make you feel? How do you feel about it now?"

It made me feel neurotic, I'd told her. I couldn't sleep well at night. I couldn't let go of the idea that something might happen to one of my sisters and that it would be my fault. I closed my eyes and tried to remember that moment so long ago when my mother had given me charge of my siblings.

"Bailee, you are older and you have to help me keep the little ones from harm. That killer wants to find them—find you too. You have to do exactly what I tell you, and you have to watch over them at all times."

I felt myself drifting as a drowsy wave washed over me. For some reason I saw myself alone in a room where light barely filtered in from a half-covered window. It was a garage or shed of some type.

It seemed I was crawling out of a hiding place. A box. Yes, I could see that it was a small room where someone had stored gardening equipment and tools. I was very young and cold. My feet were bare, and in the back of my mind I knew this was going to get me into trouble.

"Bailee, it's safe to come out now."

It was my mother. She was standing at the door peering out. She'd only opened it enough to see at an angle toward the house.

"Are the bad men gone?"

She turned and smiled at me. "Yes. Go get the baby."

I frowned. "Where? Where's the baby?"

She pointed to a pile of dark blankets. "I hid the baby over there."

I looked again but could see nothing of an infant. I hurried over, my bare feet nearly frozen. The ground was earth-packed and cold. I pulled away the blankets but still didn't see the baby. I moved quicker, straining my tiny arm muscles with burdens never intended for a child. The blankets barely budged.

"I can't get the baby, Momma."

The sense of panic that gripped me was like nothing I'd ever known.

CHAPTER 12

It was nearly an hour later when Judith came to get us. Dad had returned and wanted to talk. He asked that we join them downstairs. I felt anxious as I entered the living room. I could see Dad sitting alone by the fireplace. He looked so much older than his forty-nine years. Had we done that to him? I wanted to go to him and comfort him, but something in his body language told me my touch would not be welcomed.

I retook the seat I'd had earlier and waited. My sisters soon came down and sat on the sofa, and Judith took the oversized chair. For several minutes we sat in an uncomfortable silence, as if we were all awaiting yet another guest. Finally Dad cleared his throat.

"I can't believe I'm having this conversation with you," he began. "I can't believe for the last fifteen years you've believed me to be a murderer and said nothing."

"But, Dad," I interrupted, "we . . . love you." The words came hard. "We knew you were only concerned about us. Mom was crazy and dangerous. We heard you say you were doing it for us, and we felt obligated in return to do this for you."

His face was incredulous. "Do what?" he asked. He looked to Geena and Piper. "What was it you felt you had to do?"

"Keep quiet," Geena replied.

"Keep the family secret," Piper added, twisting the edge of her shirt like a nervous child.

He looked back to me and shook his head. "You believed a lie."

I wasn't at all sure what he was getting at. I leaned forward. "Dad, we saw it. We saw you mix the pills into Mom's drink. We heard what you said—we saw you crying. We know you did it for us."

"No! I didn't do . . . it . . . for you. I didn't do it for anyone because I didn't do it. At least I didn't do what you think I did." He was carefully holding his temper in check.

"Don't lie to us," Piper said, her face contorting. "I don't want to be lied to."

Dad got to his feet. "I'm not lying. What you saw wasn't what you believed it to be. What you saw was my poor attempt to keep your mother on the medication the doctor gave her before we left on our trip."

I shook my head. "Why would you have been upset then? Why were you crying? If you were simply doing a task that you knew would be helpful to Mom, why be upset about it?"

He looked to Judith and she nodded. Drawing a deep breath, Dad continued. "I was emotional because I felt so helpless. I had argued with her about taking the medicine and she told me she didn't need it—that it wasn't really helping. She was convinced that it was a poison the FBI was using to end her life because she wasn't cooperating with them."

Walking to the fireplace, he turned away from us and gripped the mantel with both hands. "I told her the medicine would help her to think clearer—to be calmer. She said that was just what they wanted us to believe, but she knew better. I was beside myself. I knew that without the medicine she was going to get worse. Probably even with the medicine.

"Your mother was determined to have it her way. I was in tears because I'd reached the end of my rope. I wanted to walk away from the entire situation, but I loved her so much." Dad straightened and turned back to face us. "How could you possibly believe me capable of killing her?"

Piper began to cry again. Geena reached over and pulled her against her shoulder.

"Then what happened to her?" Geena asked

the question that was on my mind. "If your medication that night didn't kill her, why did the paramedics come and take her to the hospital?"

"Because she'd taken other pills. A prescription I hadn't known about. She had what she thought was a medication that would keep the authorities from finding her. She just couldn't shake the idea that there were people pursuing her. She thought if she could muffle the voices in her head, her thoughts would be clouded to them. The only problem was that the pills very nearly stopped her heart. She was unresponsive when I found her the next morning. I called an ambulance, and they barely got her to the hospital in time."

I was confused now. If she'd killed herself with an overdose of medication, what did he mean she barely got there in time? I opened my mouth to ask, but Dad continued.

"They pumped her stomach in the emergency room and countered the overdose with their own medications. She regained consciousness and the doctor figured it was a close call. He took me out to the nurses' station, and we discussed what had happened. He wanted to know if I thought it was a suicide attempt, because if so, he could send her to the psych ward for observation."

"Stop it!" Geena demanded. "Stop lying to us. We know what happened. We saw it."

I was stunned by her venomous reaction.

"I'm so tired of the lies and secrets this family has perpetuated," she continued. "We've lived through fifteen years of it and I'm done. If you can't be honest with us, then I'm leaving."

"I am being honest with you," Dad replied. "I'm telling you exactly what happened."

"If she didn't overdose, then how did Mom die?" Geena threw back.

Dad looked at Judith. For several moments their gazes locked us out. It was as if everything had ceased for Dad . . . except for Judith. When he looked back at us there were tears in his eyes.

"I was talking to the doctor about what to do when the nurse went to change your mother's IV bag. She came back a moment later, declaring that the patient was missing. We began to search for your mother, but she seemed to have just up and disappeared. The police were summoned and the hospital went on full alert. The exits were sealed, but I figured it was too late, she'd already fled. Then we got a call that a patient was up on the roof. I knew it was your mother."

"The roof?" I questioned. "The roof of the hospital?"

He nodded. "We never were exactly sure how she got there. It wasn't like there weren't precautions in place to keep people from going there, but your mother always had a way of slipping into places unnoticed. They called me to talk to her because she was clearly distraught. I was taken to the roof and I started across the expanse to where she was standing near the edge."

My stomach churned madly. I felt sick, both fearing and knowing the outcome.

Dad's voice cracked. "I . . . I tried to . . . to talk to her. I remember saying, 'Natalie, I need you—your children need you. Come back and let the doctors help you to feel better.'" He shook his head. "She said I was . . . was . . . with them. That I wanted to hurt her. She said she'd found the medicine residue in the cup of cocoa when she poured it in the sink and knew I was working with the government to shut her up."

Tears poured down his face. "She thought I wanted her dead. You thought it too."

I bit my lip to keep from crying myself. I saw that Geena and Piper were already in tears, but I desperately wanted to keep the wall of emotions that was pounding at my defenses from crashing over me.

Dad gave a shudder. "I tried to creep close enough . . . to . . . to take hold of her. She could see what I was doing and warned me to stay back all while backing closer to the edge. She said she had to find you girls because men were coming to take you away. I promised her that wasn't true, but she wouldn't believe me. Before I could . . . before I could. . . ." He dissolved in tears and Judith came to him immediately.

"Before he could reach her, your mother jumped to her death," Judith announced. She wrapped her arms around Dad's shoulders and led him to the chair she'd just abandoned. Dad did nothing to fight her. He went willingly and collapsed. Sobbing like a small child, my father's pent up emotions spilled out for all to witness.

"I tried," I heard him say from the muffling of his hands. "I tried."

With trembling hands he pulled a yellowed piece of newspaper from his shirt pocket. He handed it to Judith, who in turn brought it to me. The headline read, *Woman Jumps to Her Death From Local Hospital Roof.*

I scanned the newspaper article, then handed it back to Judith, who then took it to my sisters. I couldn't think clearly. I fell back against the chair and tried to process the information. I could still see the words.

Thirty-two year old Natalie Cooper jumped to her death. . . .

The words warred against all that I had believed to be true. Why had Dad lied to us?

He'd told us she died from the overdose. Or did he? I strained to remember, but my thoughts were overrun with accusations and rebukes. *How could you believe your father to be capable of murder? How could you love someone and think something so horrible of him?*

"I thought I was right to keep the ugliness of her death from you. We weren't even able to let you say good-bye to her," Dad said, fighting for control of his emotions. "She was too . . . too . . . disfigured."

Piper buried her face against Geena while I swallowed back bile. Maybe Dad was right. Maybe the ugly truth was too much. Would it have been easier to go on believing Mom died from an overdose? But how could it be—especially when we believed that overdose came from our father's hand?

Judith refolded the article and returned it to Dad. He held it for several moments and then stuffed it back into his pocket. "I should have told you the truth a long time ago."

"Yes, you should have," I muttered. "You should have told us the truth. You deceived us."

"How was that deceit? I didn't know what you believed. I didn't know you girls were watching that night—that you thought I was staging a murder. I can't believe you thought I would do such a thing. Despite her problems,

I loved your mother. I only wanted her to get well." He got up and looked at Judith. "I'm going back to the cottage."

She nodded and Dad slowly walked from the room. Judith waited until he was gone to address us. "You have no idea how this has tormented him all these years."

"He has no idea how it tormented us," Piper countered, looking up. She pushed away from Geena and got to her feet. "We thought he killed her. We saw him and heard him, and it's never been more than a thought away." Then singling me out, Piper added, "This is all your fault. You made us swear to keep the secret. You told us that we'd lose Dad if we said anything, and now we've probably lost him because we didn't say something."

"I was talking about him being taken away—to jail. Then we would have been sent to foster care," I defended. "I'm just as angry at him as you are at me. I didn't lie to you, but you need someone to blame. So blame me," I said, slamming my hands against my thighs. "Blame me that our mother is dead. Blame me that Dad was never around when we were growing up. Blame me for whatever you want. I'm sure Dad will do the same."

"Your father isn't that way," Judith interjected. "He loves you, Bailee. He loves each of you. He would never turn his back on you.

He's hurt, but that doesn't keep him from loving you. Give him some time to pray and rest in God."

"What good is that going to do?" I asked. "God didn't seem too concerned up until now." I was growing angrier by the minute. "God hasn't seemed to worry too much about any of us and the pain we've endured."

"She's right about that," Geena said, rising. "I've never bought into religious nonsense. I've never had any reason to believe God cares, and if anything, this just proves that He doesn't."

Judith shook her head. "Whether you want to believe it or not, God loved you enough to send His son to die for you. Jesus came to intercede on your behalf—on the behalf of all mankind. He didn't have to die for anyone—He chose to because He wanted you to be reconciled to His Father." She looked directly at me. "I know you're hurting, but God is there for you. He's always been there for you . . . and He always will be. The fact that you don't believe it changes nothing."

She left us, following Dad from the house without another word. I figured she was headed back to the cottage as well, and frankly I was glad. I didn't want to hear any more about God and His love for me.

What will you do with me now?

The voice reverberated in my head. I pressed my fingers to my temples.

———

I tried to edit to get my mind off the situation, but it wasn't working. I felt awash in guilt and sorrow. Each time I thought of how our father had kept the truth from us all these years, I felt a growing rage inside of me. Yet at the same time I knew it had to be a shock to him to know we thought he had murdered our mother and said nothing. I couldn't keep the vision of Dad's hurt expression from my mind. It was the ultimate betrayal, I decided. To have your children believe such heinous things about you must be the worst thing a parent could feel. To be misjudged and held responsible for something over which you had no control.

Putting aside my laptop, I decided that I had to get out of the house. I grabbed my purse and the car keys and went in search of Geena and Piper. I found them on the back deck.

"Look, I know you're both mad at me, but I'm driving into town. Would you like to come along?"

They looked like I felt—drained and unable to contemplate the events of the day. Geena drew in a long breath and let it out slowly.

"I am hungry," she said. "I don't know how

I can even think of eating, but that's all I want right now."

Nodding, I agreed. "I figured something to eat would help me as well. What about you, Piper?"

"I just want to be left alone," she told us.

A part of me wanted to argue with her, but instead I asked, "Do you want us to bring you back anything?"

She shook her head and walked toward the stone stairs. "I'm going to walk on the beach."

Geena and I watched her go, then went into the house. "Let me get my purse and I'll meet you at the car." Geena quickly headed upstairs without waiting for my comment.

I walked to the car, trying hard not to calculate what Dad might be thinking at that moment. I hoped that Judith was able to comfort him, but at the same time I wondered if he cared about our damaged emotions.

"I never meant to hurt him—none of us did," I muttered aloud. Could a person's misery be eased by the very one responsible? It posed a serious question in my mind. I wanted Dad to comfort me—to make me feel better, yet I blamed him for the sorrow I felt. Could it be the same for him?

Geena soon joined me and I questioned her. "Do you think that a person who causes someone pain can also ease the pain they cause? Like us with Dad? Or him with us?"

I put the car in gear and headed up the steep tree-lined drive. Geena sat contemplating my question, and for a few minutes I thought perhaps she'd never answer. She finally frowned and shrugged.

"Sometimes the only person who *can* help is the one who is in pain."

We crept by the cottage and saw that the car was gone. Apparently Dad and Judith had decided to head to town as well. I thought for a moment on Geena's words.

"What exactly do you mean?"

She looked straight ahead. "I think that our own determination to be free from pain is the key to that recovery. Some people like to hold on to their pain. Not for the feeling of anguish, but because it's all that's familiar. Like holding a long, long grudge. It's a known element—something recognizable. There's a warped sort of comfort in that."

"But I don't want to hang on to the things that hurt me. I don't want to hate Dad," I said. "I want to be able to enjoy my life—to live it to the fullest—to know happiness."

"To my way of thinking, those are all choices we make for ourselves. We can cradle the hurt and pain—wrap it around us like a shield to keep ourselves safe from attack—or we can let it die."

"Let it die," I murmured. Could a person really let their pain die? Could they stop feeding it and nourishing it with reminders and accusations of the past?

"What would that look like?" I asked Geena. "To let the pain die?"

She shrugged again. "I think it would look different for each person. I can't take your pain for you, neither can I kill it. Just as you can't remove my pain or isolate it from me. We can't stop Piper or Dad from feeling miserable over the problems in their lives, but we can be supportive and understanding when that pain interjects itself into our relationship. We can also be very impatient and damaging."

"Piper hates me now, doesn't she?"

"Piper hates her life," Geena replied.

"How can you be sure?"

"Do you hate Dad? I mean, really hate him? He didn't tell us the truth either."

"No, I don't really hate him," I admitted. "I'm hurt by him. I'm angry that he left us alone so much—that he refused to have a real relationship with us until we were adults. Now he acts like just because he has plans for the future and a desire to be religious that we should just forget about all of that and accept that he wants to be close."

"I can't speak for Dad, nor for Piper. I do know that with her it's something entirely different. It's not you. In fact, it's never been about you or me. She grew up without a mother and she's never gotten over it. She's done things to herself and with others that she regrets, all in a desperate search to ease her misery."

"We were all in that boat," I countered.

"Yes, but we were smart enough to get counseling—at least when we got old enough to get it for ourselves. Dad should have seen our need and provided it for us as children, but we can't go back and remake the past. Although God knows we've tried enough times."

"You're right. I hadn't really thought of it that way until just now."

"Sometimes I think it's very black and white," Geena continued. "Maybe that's the lawyer in me. There's a right and a wrong. The shades of gray only serve to complicate the truth of the matter."

"Which is what?" I came to a stop sign and waited until she answered.

"That each person has the ability to control whether they will accept or reject the hurt offered them."

"That surely doesn't absolve others from the responsibility they have to treat people right—to do the right thing. It doesn't excuse bad behavior or deception."

She shook her head. "Of course it doesn't, but we don't have control over what another person does or how they feel. We only have control over how we respond to it—what we do with it. At least that's the way I see it. We need to take charge of our lives or someone else will."

"And you don't think God or the Bible has anything to do with how our behavior should be?"

Geena rolled her eyes and looked away. I took that as my cue to move on down the street, and to another topic.

"So where do you want to eat?"

"Let's go to the Yacht Club Broiler in Silverdale. I read about it online and Dad mentioned going there for lunch. Sounds really good."

I nodded. "Plug it in and we'll do it." At the GPS's instruction, I headed for Highway 303 and tried to forget that I still longed for an answer to my question about God. Geena obviously wasn't the one to give me any help.

CHAPTER 13

We came home some hours later. Geena brought Piper a cheeseburger just in case she had regained her appetite and I brought a take-home box with most of my dinner. Funny, I'd been half starved when we'd started out, but by the time the meal arrived, I only picked at the food on my plate. When we reached our driveway, I saw that Dad's rental car was back. I wondered if he would consider talking to me about what had happened.

Why hadn't he been honest with us about Mom? I could understand hiding the details from us when we were children; however, as a young woman I would have been able to deal with the truth. Dad could have brought us all together when Piper was sixteen or so and explained it. He could have taken me aside and sworn me to secrecy when I turned eighteen.

More secrets? Why did that always seem like a logical choice for our family?

Geena and I made our way into the house. Everything was quiet. I put my food away and because there was a bit of a chill in the damp evening air, I went to my room for a sweater. I had already decided to walk on the beach and talk to Mark, but I knew the temperature would only continue to drop as the sun faded from the sky.

Slipping out the back door, I made my way to the stone steps and spied my father some twenty yards down the beach. I felt a sudden awkwardness. I still had anger to contend with, but I also felt a new sense of loss. Being the oldest, I'd always felt as though I were on some sort of selective team. He and I dealing with Mom—trying to keep balance in a family that seemed perpetually off-kilter. Would he be offended if I joined him? Could I be civil if we spoke?

I gritted my teeth. If I was ever going to get answers—figure out why I couldn't move forward in life—then I needed to confront him. But not with rage or my damaged feelings. I needed to be able to approach this logically and calmly.

I tucked the phone back into my pocket and walked slowly to where he stood. He saw me but said nothing. I turned to look out on the water and wondered if he would ever trust me again. Why did that worry me more than whether I could trust him?

"I never meant to think so badly of you," I said in a whisper. "I should have known better."

He looked at me for a moment, then turned back to the water. "Yes, you should have."

His words offered no comfort. I suppose I shouldn't have expected them to, but somewhere deep inside that was exactly what I'd hoped for. I wanted him to assure me that it was a simple childish mistake. That it didn't matter. I wanted him to convince me that despite the pain I'd caused him, he still loved me and wouldn't hold it against me.

"You should have explained the truth to us," I said matter-of-factly.

He looked at me for a moment and nodded. "Yes. I should have." He turned back to the water, and I tried to figure out where to go from there.

"I didn't understand," I began again. "I was a child, and it seemed reasonable to my child's mind to believe what I saw and heard." I thought of God and how we must seem to Him. We often believed the worst of God— blaming Him for things He should have or could have done. Didn't I feel that way right now, in fact?

"I'm really sorry, Dad. I never meant to hurt you."

"Bailee, I didn't think you planned it out. God knows I didn't mean to further your pain or that of your sisters," he replied. "But that doesn't stop the pain from existing. I've tried to do right by you girls. I know I deserted you by putting you in boarding school and hiring housekeepers and nannies, but I also knew I wasn't able to be a decent father to you. I had failed you in so many ways—failed your mother too. No one knew this better than I did."

"All we really wanted . . . was you." I felt as if I were twelve years old again. "We'd already lost Mom. We felt so alone."

"I never wanted that."

I felt my anger surfacing. How was it that he could make me feel like I owed him an apology for feeling alone . . . for being afraid?

"So why couldn't you have been there for us? Why did you desert us?" I knew my voice betrayed my frayed emotions. Still, I forced myself not to apologize.

His expression was stoic in the fading light. "I did the best I could with what I had, but what I had was never enough." He stuffed his hands in his pockets and shook his head. "I wanted to do better. I wanted to be the man you needed me to be, but I had nothing left to give." He looked at me with an apologetic expression. "I'm not saying I was right or that it should explain away everything. I'm saying it because it's the truth. I didn't mean to make you girls suffer for my inability to deal with the loss."

Tears came unbidden. I wanted to hide them away, but instead I kept my focus fixed on Dad. "And that's all we get?"

He looked at me oddly. "What do you want me to say . . . to do? It's not like I can go back in time and do things over. I hate what happened. I hate the way I acted. I hope you'll forgive me, but I can't change any of it."

"You could at least sound like you wish you could," I said, squaring my shoulders.

"And you think I don't wish that every day of my life?"

Now he was angry. The set of his jaw reminded me of times when he'd had to deal with unpleasant business complications. Was that all we girls were to him? A complication of the past that he'd just as soon be done with? Maybe that was why he'd remarried. Maybe that was what he meant by getting "right" with God. He was making a new start. One that clearly didn't include us.

"You wish we'd never been born, don't you?"

His face contorted. "How can you even say

such a thing? I only wish things could have been different for you . . . for your mother. I wish I could wave a magic wand and give this family normalcy. But I can't. Not any more than you can."

My mind took off in a different direction. "Momma was a good person—she should have gotten the help she needed."

"She had plenty of help, Bailee. She didn't want it. She rejected the advice of doctors and she disregarded the medications they provided. I wanted to believe the love between us could keep her focused on the plan, but it wasn't enough. Love wasn't enough. At least not that kind of love."

"What do you mean?"

He fell silent for a moment. A short ways down the beach, gulls screeched over some tidbit of food. The water lapped gently against the shoreline, soothing some of the tension from the moment. A stiff breeze blew across the water, and I tightened my hold on the sweater.

Dad finally ran his fingers through the spiked ends of his hair. "God's love would have been enough to see us through, but we didn't have any interest in that. At least I didn't. Your mother spoke of it from time to time, but I figured it was just her sickness. She said she heard God speaking to her."

I swallowed hard at that. I wanted to tell Dad about thinking God was talking to me, but I wasn't really ready to admit that my childhood Sunday school lessons might be valid for my adult life.

"God would have made a difference in how I treated her. It would have changed how I parented you girls," he continued. "That much I do know for certain. I was afraid of what I saw happening. I felt alone and unsure. It was easier to be gone from the situation and pretend it wasn't all that bad rather than deal with it."

"If only we could have escaped it," I murmured.

"I wished that for you too."

"So why didn't you . . ." I paused. I didn't want to blame him, so I fell silent. The question on my mind would have sounded like an accusation and done neither of us any good.

Dad understood my heart. "Why didn't I get you away from her? Why didn't I take you to safety?"

I nodded.

"Your mother was very keen. She had her fears and hallucinations, but she was a smart woman with a high IQ. I couldn't just pretend with her. Fooling her wasn't an option. Her paranoia kept her constantly ahead of the game, while her delusions clouded the truth.

"Added to this, I didn't want to frighten her. Once when I mentioned the idea of sending you girls to boarding school, she freaked out on me. I feared mentioning it again—thought she might take you girls and run. Knowing her as I did, I worried that I might never find you if she did that. So I tried to bide my time. I tried to make sure that someone was always aware of what was happening—that you were safe."

"But we weren't." I looked at the ground. "Dad, I never told you half the things she did. She told me I couldn't say a word to anyone." I looked up to find him scrutinizing me. "She scared me. I loved her so much, but she scared me."

"I'm so sorry, Bailee. I didn't know. You should have said something."

"We both should have," I admitted. "But I thought keeping quiet was the right thing to do."

"Bailee, I can't say that what happened here today hasn't left me shaken. I always thought I had the confidence and support of my children. Judith reminded me that God has a plan, even in this—but I'm hurt and I won't lie and say otherwise."

"But what kind of plan?" I stiffened. "What possible good comes out of such things?"

"Well, the truth for one. We've put an end

to the lie that you've believed all these years. That's progress, isn't it?"

I thought about it for a moment. "But it really doesn't change anything."

He looked at me oddly. "How can you say that?"

For a moment I thought I should just drop it—to change the subject to something, anything else. I was afraid of my emotions and of what I might say or do. In so many ways I felt like I was talking to a total stranger.

"It's . . . well . . . it's just that . . . this was only one of the secrets. Our whole life has been about secrets. I feel . . . I can't help it, but I know there are things that I can't remember. I know that there are things that happened to me that I need to understand."

"What kind of things?" His look was both questioning and uncertain. Maybe he feared I was becoming as delusional as Mom had been.

I shook my head. "I don't know. I've spent a lot of time in therapy, Dad. My counselor says I've blocked out an awful lot. There are long ribbons of my life that I can't remember. There are also spaces of time that I can't seem to forget. She says I have some of the earliest memories she's ever seen in a person, but at the same time there are stretches of years that are simply blank."

"There's a lot of things I don't remember from my childhood," Dad replied. He scratched his chin where a stubble of whiskers served as reminder that he was on vacation. "I never saw them as important."

"Well, they are to me. I need to remember. I need to know why I choose to remember some things and not others. I need to understand."

"And does your therapist think that's possible?"

"She does under the right conditions."

He shoved his hands back into his pockets. "And what conditions are those?"

"There's no textbook way to know for sure. I need to feel safe. That's the most important thing." I paused and gazed at the pebbles beneath my feet. "Dad, I haven't felt safe for most of my life."

He took a step back. My statement had clearly surprised him. "Why would you say that? Haven't I provided a good home? You've never had to worry about going hungry or not having the things you needed."

Despite my resolve to remain unemotional, tears streamed down my cheeks. "I didn't have peace of mind. I still don't. I'm twenty-seven and I know that I could still show signs of schizophrenia. That secret has haunted me for so long, Dad. That secret has probably done as much harm as knowing . . . believing that you killed Mom. I've had to bear it all alone, because I knew you didn't want me to know about it. So instead I have waited and watched like an inmate trying to learn whether the governor overturned his sentence from death to life."

"But you show no signs of the disease. Why fret over it?"

The way he made my worries sound so trivial made me resentful. "Because it could happen, Dad. Do you never worry about one of us developing it? It's known to be hereditary."

"So is heart disease. We have some of that in the family as well." He sounded irritated. "Are you stewing over that too? In the end, Bailee, there are a great many things you could worry about. Physical and mental problems, relationship issues . . . but what purpose does it serve?"

"I'd like the opportunity to decide for myself whether they deserve to be considered. I'd rather consider them and meet them head on than go on hiding my head in the sand pretending they don't exist." My voice was rising as my anger stirred. "You have a philosophy of ignoring the truth—of letting reality be hidden in secrecy and deception. I can't stand it!"

His expression went blank. "I think this conversation is over," he said, turning away from me.

I wanted to run after him, but only for the opportunity to say other hurtful things. Watching him go, I knew our relationship would never be the same. Up until now we had all played the game very carefully, but now the rules had changed.

After Dad disappeared around the house, I finally headed off on my walk. I couldn't stop the tears from coming, nor did I want to. I had this odd notion that if I could just cry enough, I would cry the pain out. If only it were true.

I maneuvered down the rocks to where I spied a fallen log and took a seat. I reached for my phone and dialed Mark's number, then clicked it off and shoved the phone back into my pocket. That only served to make me cry all the harder. I wanted to reach out to him— to have him reach back. I pulled the phone out again and hit redial. Mark answered on the second ring, but I found it impossible to speak. A sob trapped the words in the back of my throat.

"Bailee? What's wrong?"

"Everything," I finally managed to croak out. It was a good thing I didn't want to impress this man.

"Why don't you tell me what's happened?"

This was my breaking moment. This was that place on the bridge where I knew if I continued across I could never turn back. I drew a deep breath and fought to steady my voice. "Mark, my life is a mess. My family is a mess. My past is a mess."

"And?"

That single word sounded like a challenge. I wanted to counter it easily, but I knew I wouldn't be able to. This was far too complicated. "And I don't know that you can deal with this much . . . mess."

He had the good sense not to laugh. "Why don't you let me be the judge?" His voice was deep, firm, and yet . . . comforting.

"Because I've never played that role well. I've always had to be strong for everyone else. I've always had to weigh out each word . . . each deed against whether it was in everyone else's best interest."

"So I'm giving you permission to think of yourself first this time," he countered. "I'm allowing you the right to matter the most in this moment."

That touched me in a way I couldn't begin to describe. It was exactly what I longed for: to matter. To let my need be known. I considered what he'd said for several moments. He wasn't preaching at me. He wasn't demanding of me. Mark was simply giving me the right to . . . be honest.

"For years I believed a lie," I told him. "I

thought I knew the truth." I sighed and fought for words to explain. "Mark, it's such a tangle of half-truths and deceptions."

"What is, Bailee?"

I sniffed back tears. "My life. It's so complicated. So ugly." I began to cry in earnest. "I'm sorry . . . I . . . I shouldn't . . . I should go."

"Please don't."

There was something so soothing in his tone. I wanted to find solace in his words—his company—but I couldn't seem to give myself that right. Despite his dispensation of approval and permission, I didn't seem to be able to force myself to let go.

"Bailee, if you say the word, I'll come to you. I'll help you through this. I'll be there just for you."

The statement startled me. No one had ever offered to be there for me like that. Was he serious? Would he really come? Did I want him to? It was silly to even question the latter. I knew I wanted him there. I knew I wanted to let go of my fears and embrace a relationship with this man. I feared, however, that I would only ruin a good friendship.

"Bailee?"

"I'm . . . here." I struggled to speak. I felt like a frightened little girl—the same child hiding in the box—the same one searching for the lost baby.

"Tell me to come to you." His voice was low and even.

I hesitated only a moment, and then something inside me broke. "Come. Please . . . come."

CHAPTER 14

I was a small child again. It was my old nightmare—one of several. My mother was hurrying me along a tree-lined path. It could have been our driveway in Bremerton. It could have been almost anywhere. I struggled to keep up. My legs were so tired, but at her urging I found the strength to follow.

Momma was carrying a baby in her arms. I heard the baby crying, but Momma quickly hushed it. "We have to hide. We have to keep them from knowing where we are."

"Who, Momma?" I remember asking the question over and over. "Who's gonna come? Who's gonna find us?"

"It's not important. What's important is that we stop them," she declared. "They want to take you away. They want the baby."

I was never at all sure who was after us. In the years right before Momma died, it was her fears of a serial killer that drove her actions. But my child's mind crisscrossed memories and thoughts with my adult dream state. The serial killer didn't come up until years later when Piper was born. I was six by then—much older than my counterpart in the dream.

I awoke with a start and sat straight up in bed. There was a hint of light on the horizon, but it wasn't truly dawn yet. I slipped on some drawstring sweats and a bulky sweater and tiptoed downstairs.

Someone had thoughtfully put up a hammock on the deck, and I made my way to it. The canvas looked damp from dew, so I threw a blanket over it and crawled atop. I liked the way the sides rose up to hug me. It was like being wrapped in a cocoon. I felt the swaying lull me into a state of drowsy relaxation as I watched the sun creep up over the horizon. Seattle's skyline could be seen glinting in the morning light. Across the sound the city would be awakening. People would be setting out for church or breakfast or a day of leisure.

I thought again of the repeating dream. Remembering my mother's desperation. Why did that particular memory continue to haunt me? Dinah, my therapist, believed these were memories trying to break through, but I wasn't convinced. To me they seemed like strange collages of my biggest fears.

The baby, I thought. The baby was key. My inability to keep the baby safe made me feel so helpless. I didn't want to let Momma down. I didn't want her to be disappointed in me. I didn't want to fail.

But fail what? In my nightmare she was carrying the baby to safety and I was following. Although I'd been slow, I'd managed to keep up. Why then did I feel that I hadn't done my part?

I knew there were other dreams where I couldn't find the baby. Maybe it was all tied together. Maybe there had been an incident that I couldn't remember fully. But with the gentle sway of the hammock soothing me, I found my eyes growing heavy. I drifted off to sleep wishing I knew the truth and fearing it at the same time.

"It's all your fault," my mother yelled. A hard slap across the face stung me. I began to cry.

"I'm sorry, Momma. I'm sorry."

"It's all your fault."

I knew I'd done something very bad, but what? I reached out to my mother only to have her turn away, her dark brown ponytail swinging as she walked.

"Don't leave me," I cried. "Don't go."

I tried to catch up, but my legs were too tired. I couldn't walk fast enough, and soon I found it impossible to move more than a few inches at a time. My mother disappeared from view and I was left alone. Dread washed over me. Danger seemed to permeate my surroundings. I was alone and something bad was about to happen. Something bad had already happened.

Waking some time later, I caught the scent of coffee on the air and knew that someone else was finally up. I shuffled into the kitchen and saw that both Geena and Piper were poised over cups of steaming liquid. Neither said a word to me nor seemed surprised that I'd just come in from the deck entrance rather than the stairs.

I poured myself a cup of coffee and turned to face them. I supposed they were still angry at me. Maybe they felt I owed them further apology. Maybe I did.

"Are you hungry? I could fix breakfast." It was a lousy offering, but the best I could muster.

"I think you've tried to fix enough," Piper said sarcastically. She looked up and I could see the dark circles around her eyes. Perhaps I was the only one who'd actually slept last night.

Ignoring her attitude, I went to the fridge and pulled out a carton of eggs. "Well, I'm going to poach a couple of these. If you want, I can do the same for you."

"I just want yogurt," Geena said, joining me at the refrigerator. She grabbed a container and padded back to the breakfast bar.

"Nothing is ever going to be the same," Piper declared.

I met her harsh expression. "No, I suppose not, but maybe that's a good thing. After all, we've uncovered the truth."

"But how many other lies have gone unrealized?"

"I don't know," I answered honestly. "I do know that we won't make things better by treating each other like the enemy. I'm sorry for my part in all of this. I'm sorrier than you can possibly know."

"It doesn't change the fact that it happened," Piper replied.

I looked to Geena. "I suppose you hate me as much as she does."

"I didn't say I hated you." Piper got to her feet. "Don't put words in my mouth."

"Nobody hates anyone," Geena interjected. "We're just hurt and tired—maybe a little scared too."

Fear I understood. I had lived all these years waiting and watching for some sign that I was losing my mind. I worried over my sisters, agonizing over whether to tell them about the mental illness or leave it be.

I put the eggs aside. "I used to lie awake at night waiting for Momma to come get us," I said without giving it much thought. "I never slept well because I was always afraid I would miss her signals. She told me every day that it was my job to keep you two from harm. I can still hear her telling me that if I didn't take my responsibility seriously something bad would happen again."

"Again?" Geena asked. "What was she talking about?"

I shrugged. "No doubt it referenced one of the many mistakes I'd made and her subsequent punishments. I remember her hitting me—knocking me to the ground. I wanted so much to please her. I thought it would make her be happy again." I shook my head. "It isn't important now, but I didn't want it to happen to you or Piper."

"She never hit me," Piper said, her tone rather defensive. "I don't remember her hitting you. Are you sure you aren't just making it up for effect?"

"No. I don't doubt that you didn't know. She saved those occasions for when we were alone. She told me she was raising me to be responsible."

"Well, responsibility doesn't equate to lying," Piper countered. "You may have been told to take care of us, but that didn't give you the right to keep the truth from us."

"You're right. You're absolutely right." Frowning, I picked up the eggs and put them back in the refrigerator. "I'm not as hungry as I thought." Her words reminded me of how I felt about Dad.

I headed for the stairs only to have Geena call after me. "Shouldn't we talk this out?"

I turned and looked at them sitting there watching me. "Talk? What can I possibly say that will make you understand? I thought I was doing what had to be done. I was wrong. I own it." Dad had said something similar and it rushed back to me like an accusation.

"But shouldn't we make some sort of plan for dealing with what we've learned?"

Geena was ever the logical one, but nothing about this situation seemed logical. "What exactly do you mean?" I asked.

She looked at Piper, then got to her feet again. "Well, for starters, maybe we should get Dad to release mom's medical records to us so we can see for ourselves the details of her condition. We're going to have to be able to speak to our own doctors about such things."

"I'm not telling anyone about anything," Piper declared. "I'm not going to some shrink."

Geena eyed her hard. "Not even if you develop symptoms?"

Piper paled. "I hate psychiatrists." Her voice was barely audible.

As far as I knew, Piper had never gone to a psychiatrist or been forced into counseling, so I wasn't at all sure why she spoke with such negativity. I wasn't sure how to counter her comment and was glad when Geena continued.

"A good counselor is useful in figuring out the details of your emotional issues. You've told me on more than one occasion that you feel depressed more often than not, yet you won't get any help."

"Interference," Piper said. "It's not help; it's just interference. One doctor thinks one thing and another something else. You can't get a straight answer from anyone."

"You sound like someone who's tried," I said.

Piper threw me an angry glare. "Maybe I have. You might think you run my life, but you don't. There's a lot about me you don't know." She got up and brushed past me. "Neither of you know as much as you think you do. Frankly, I'm sick and tired of this family. Maybe it is time for me to move abroad. At least then I won't have you two breathing down my neck."

Piper stormed off up the stairs and Geena and I stood there watching like witnesses at the scene of an accident. I turned slowly to face my sister and could see that Geena was just as surprised as I was.

"What's gotten into her? She acts like we want to hurt her," Geena said.

"She's mad at me and taking it out on both of us."

"No, it's more than that," Geena replied. "We hit a nerve. The whole mention of counseling and psychiatrists was more than she wanted to deal with. She's got one thing right, though . . . I don't think I know her anymore. She's really changed in the last few months. I thought maybe it was just the stress of graduation, but now I think it's something more. Maybe she *is* schizophrenic."

"Maybe it's the whole turmoil of becoming an adult—moving out on her own. It's a difficult time." I knew even trying to decide about moving to New York City had me in knots. How much harder for Piper to consider moving as far as England.

My cell phone chimed in my pocket. I drew it out and saw that the text was from Mark. He would arrive in Seattle around four.

"Say, I have a favor to ask." I met Geena's raised brow. "Could you possibly stand a roommate for a little while?"

"Here? Why?"

"Mark is arriving this afternoon."

Geena looked at me in disbelief. "Your boss is coming here?"

"Not as my boss. It's a long story, but I invited him, amazingly enough."

"Well, I guess you can share my room. I'm really surprised, though. I didn't think you wanted to encourage anything with him."

I looked back at the cell phone and nodded. "I didn't either, but I think I might have been wrong."

❧

Mark made it to the passenger arrival area in record time. I pulled up and gave a quick beep on the horn. A dozen people turned to look at me, but realizing I wasn't their ride just as quickly looked away.

"I'm hungry," Mark declared, throwing his suitcase in the back seat. "How about I take you to dinner?"

I suddenly felt rather shy and out of place. Mark had asked me out to dinner on many occasions, but now I was out of excuses as to why we couldn't. I met his gaze. "All right. What are you hungry for?"

"What do you recommend?"

We kept the atmosphere light and guarded. "I have a favorite place downtown. It's near the ferry. We could have some great snow crab."

"Sounds perfect." He fastened his seatbelt. "I'm in your capable hands."

Nearly two hours later, we were finishing up our crab, potatoes, and corn on the cob. By unspoken agreement we kept the conversation on work and the various books that M&D Publishing had planned for their next catalog. Mark was animated in his discussion about a new project coming their way. Apparently they'd managed to coax a reclusive old film star into writing her memoir with Mark's help. He would ghostwrite and edit the project.

"I think the book will be a bestseller," he said, leaning back. He looked so pleased with himself that I couldn't help but smile—especially since he was sitting there with a plastic bib around his neck.

"If she lets you receive credit for the work, you should have an author photo done with the bib in place."

He glanced down and laughed. "I think I will." He turned serious. "I nearly forgot. I sent that last project of yours on to one of the other freelancers."

"You what?" I was taken by surprise. I'd never quit a project before and I hadn't asked to have this one taken off my hands.

"I just figured with all that you're going

through . . . well . . . you need some time to focus on the problems at hand. I know work is important, and believe me, I have another dozen projects lined up and waiting if you really need to work. It's your call, but I needed to turn this one around quickly, and I didn't want you stressing over it."

A part of me wanted to be angry that he'd acted without talking to me, but at the same time I was really glad he had been thoughtful enough to think of it. I took a deep breath and let it out slowly. "Thank you. I think you're right. I need the time."

He nodded. "I'm glad you agree. I was afraid you would be angry."

"Yes, well I suppose that would have been my original choice." I smiled. "I find anger balances me when I feel control stripped away."

"Maybe you should try prayer instead," he said with a grin. "It leaves you with less to apologize for."

Our server came just then and offered us the house dessert, but we declined. I couldn't have eaten another bite if my life depended on it, and Mark seemed more than a little tired.

"We should head over to the ferry." I glanced at my watch. "It's getting close to the next departure for Bremerton."

Mark insisted on paying the bill, and for

once I didn't have even the slightest interest in arguing. We walked back to where I'd parked. Mark gallantly took the remote and opened my door for me. Handing me back the keys, he grinned.

"I'd offer to drive, but I'd probably end up in Canada."

His comment made me smile. "Seattle traffic and streets aren't anywhere near as bad as Boston, much less New York City."

"That's why I always take a cab." He winked and closed the door after I took my seat behind the wheel.

I knew it was a dangerous game I was playing. I was fairly certain I'd already lost my heart to this man, and if I wasn't careful he'd soon have my mind and soul as well. I stiffened and put the car in gear. I instantly became very aware of the man beside me.

Soon we were in line for the ferry and enjoying some classical music on the radio as we waited. The car began to feel very small and I wondered why in the world I had agreed to his visit. Mark would want to point to God as the answer for everything, and if I openly trusted him with the dark truths in my past, there was a good chance I could lose his friendship.

"You're uncomfortable." His words came out of nowhere.

I nodded. "I suppose I am."

"Why?"

I gave a nervous laugh. "Why do you suppose? This isn't exactly something I do all the time."

"What? Get together with friends?"

"Yes."

He considered this for a moment. "Don't you have many friends?"

"No. I've not allowed myself that luxury."

"Why not?"

I looked at him. "Don't you remember? I'm the one whose life is a mess." I couldn't believe I'd had that breakdown with him on the phone. "Look, I'm sorry I got so emotional. Things were just . . . well . . . hard."

"I'm sorry they were hard, but not sorry that you reached out to me. Good grief, Bailee, I've been reaching out to you for so long I was beginning to despair of it doing any good. I'm glad you wanted me to come here. It saved me from turning into a stalker." He grinned and I couldn't help but smile. I could just imagine him sneaking around the trees—hiding and watching me from afar. I frowned as I realized he was watching me.

"Please don't put the wall back up," he added in a low, tender tone.

I thought about what it would mean to our relationship if I agreed. I hadn't allowed myself a close friend in . . . well . . . ever. My sisters were my only real relationships, and right now we weren't doing that well. I needed what Mark was offering, but it was hard to admit it—even to myself.

"I'm afraid," I finally said.

"I know." He reached over and gently took hold of my hand. "But you don't have to be. I won't hurt you."

My eyes narrowed. "How can you promise such a thing? Everyone gets hurt, and at one time or another everyone hurts someone. I don't want you trying to make me feel better with lies or promises you can't keep."

He nodded. "All right, how about this. I won't set out to hurt you, and I'll do my best to treat you with the respect and love you deserve."

Love? Had he really just casually mentioned love as if it were nothing more than a comment on the weather? My gaze fixed on to where his hand was touching mine. Things were moving awfully fast—weren't they?

I looked back up and found him watching me. He smiled again and I felt my heart actually skip a beat. "You won't regret this," he told me.

"But you may," I said.

The blast of a car horn behind me interrupted any comment he might have given. I yanked my hand away and looked around like a naughty child caught stealing. They were loading, and I hadn't paid attention to the line. I put the car in gear and pulled onto the ferry.

"I'm going to find the restroom," I said, shutting off the engine. I was gone before he could reply, and had I been a woman of prayer, I would have prayed that Mark would never know how much he'd stirred my heart. I would have prayed that he would never realize the longing and need he'd awakened in me.

But from the look in his eyes, I already knew better. I just didn't know what to do about it.

CHAPTER 15

Dad, this is Mark Delahunt. His grand-father and father own the publishing company I work for, and he's my—"

"Friend," Mark interrupted, thrusting his right hand toward my father.

My sisters exchanged glances.

Dad shook his hand. "Good to meet you, Mark. Call me Tony. This is my wife, Judith."

Mark smiled at Judith and shook her hand as well. "I'm pleased to meet both of you."

"What brings you out to Washington, Mark?" Judith asked.

"I had hoped to see Bailee in a more relaxed atmosphere," he told them. He threw me a smile, then continued. "Work allows us very little time to get to know each other better."

"How nice. Tony and I have worked together for a long time. I know how that can be." She smiled at my dad. "Had I not instigated some quality time away from the office, we might never have married."

Mark laughed and gave me a wink. "See, I knew I'd like these folks."

"Where are you staying?" My dad's question caused me to realize I hadn't even suggested to Mark that he could stay there with us.

"I have reservations at a hotel near the ferry."

"Oh, nonsense," Dad said. "We have a cottage at the top of the drive. You must have seen it when you came in. Anyway, there are two bedrooms—one downstairs and one up. You can take the upstairs room if you'd like. It opens into the house and also has a separate entrance outside. We often rent the cottage as two units to summer tourists."

"Sounds perfect," Mark replied. He looked at me as if awaiting my approval.

I thought to protest and tell them that he could have my room, but figured this would be the better solution. "Dad's right," I agreed. "There's plenty of space."

"Well, if you're sure it won't inconvenience anyone," Mark said.

"I'd have you stay here," Dad added. "There is a master bedroom on the first floor, but it needs cleaning and some work. Besides, it doesn't really seem appropriate to have you here with my daughters. I'm a little old-fashioned in my thinking."

I was surprised after Dad's insistence for years that the room be off-limits that he'd even consider offering it to Mark. Maybe it was a sign that he was finally able to let go of the past and his memories of Mom. Maybe it was time for all of us to do the same.

"I completely understand," Mark said without the slightest hint of protest. "I'm a little old-fashioned myself. Say, I have a shirt similar to yours only in green."

Completely taken by surprise at his comment, I looked quickly to Dad's shirt. *PSALM 103 PRAISE* was clearly embroidered on the upper left pocket of the polo top.

"So you're familiar with their ministry?" Dad asked.

Mark nodded. "I attended their East Coast seminar last April. Great stuff. Learned a lot."

I decided if there was to be a secret handshake or other strange ritual, I was leaving the room. Fortunately, Dad only nodded in agreement.

"I plan to get involved with starting a local chapter," Dad said.

"I wish I could do the same," Mark said.

Dad seemed aware that the topic wasn't of interest to me or my sisters and changed the subject. "We can talk about it later—it's getting late. Why don't you come with me and get settled in at the cottage. Tomorrow Bailee can give you the guided tour of the area."

He acted as though I had only been away from the area for a few months rather than fifteen years. Nevertheless, I nodded obediently and watched as Judith and Dad led Mark away after bidding us all good-night.

Piper and Geena looked at me expectantly. I wasn't at all sure what to tell them, though. Should I mention my breakdown on the beach? Should I tell them that Mark offered to come and support me at a time when I felt everyone else had deserted me?

"We have projects to talk about," I lied. "He thought it would be easier in person."

"How long is he staying?" Geena asked.

I hadn't even thought to ask. "Mark didn't say, but I can't imagine it will be long." At least that much was true. I figured that at best he might be here two or three days. Anything more than that would create a bind at the office, and I knew he hadn't had time to really cover his duties with additional staff.

"It won't really give us any privacy to talk," Piper declared.

I looked at her for a moment. "I didn't figure you were talking to me anyway."

"Oh, you know that's not true. Just because I'm angry and hurt doesn't mean I won't talk to you." She turned to Geena. "Besides, Geena's helped me to better understand your situation. I never really knew how much Mom demanded of you."

I was surprised and actually rather touched by Geena's endeavor to explain my position. "It's amazing that a person could be dead for over fifteen years and still have such control over one family."

We wandered into the living room as if by agreement. Lights from houses along the sound dotted the landscape like diamonds against dark velvet. The moon hadn't come up yet, but the stars were vivid in the sky.

"Why was she so hard on you?" Piper asked.

Her question took me by surprise. I turned away from the window and came back to where they were standing. "I suppose because I was the firstborn." It seemed the only logical answer. I thought about my mother for a moment. "Momma knew how much I wanted to please her. I lived for her approval. I suppose she sensed that and capitalized on it."

Piper gave a nod. "That would make sense. I'm sorry I blamed you." She seemed rather embarrassed, so I gave her a smile.

"It would seem that despite my desire to keep you and Geena safe and free from hurt,

I only managed to add to it. I'm the one who's sorry."

Geena shoved her hands deep into her jeans and narrowed her gaze. "Sometimes it feels like we'll never really understand the past. For all we've learned in the last few days, it's only served to complicate matters more. I keep thinking to put the past behind me, but it keeps springing to life. Are there any other secrets we should know about?"

I considered her question for a moment. Were there other secrets that I should explain? Wasn't that the very question I had for myself? Were there other secrets? Things I could no longer remember. Things so confidential that I buried them away and forgot them?

She looked at me oddly. I shrugged. "I don't know. I keep thinking about that. Knowing about mom's schizophrenia was the one big thing I was keeping from you. The rest have been Dad's secrets. Maybe he's the one we should ask."

"Maybe we don't want to know."

Geena and I looked at Piper. Her comment put into words what I supposed we all were thinking.

"Keeping the truth from us all these years hasn't served any good purpose," Geena said. "Our mother committed suicide when we thought our father had murdered her.

Knowing that sooner would have changed things—at least for me. Still, it's hard to understand why she was allowed to take her own life in such a manner. If that happened today, there would be all sorts of investigations and lawsuits."

"Not to say there weren't fifteen years ago," I added.

"No, I suppose not." Geena gave a shrug. "I'd like to know if Dad pursued it at all. Maybe he felt it was all his fault, but the fact that the hospital neglected to keep Mom safe is a big deal."

"So what?" Piper countered, her voice edged with anger. "What does it matter? It won't bring Mom back and it can't buy us peace of mind. What good does it do to torment Dad for answers about the past?"

Piper was back to feeling protective of our father. It didn't surprise me. He was the only parent she'd really known, and like most things in life, Piper seemed to run hot and cold in her emotions.

∞

The next day, I was surprised when Dad, Judith, and Mark all walked into the house. Dad sniffed at the air and smiled.

"Smells good in here."

"I'm making French toast," I told him.

"There's already some on the table if you're hungry."

Judith came into the kitchen. "Can I help?"

I nodded. "You can get the juice out of the fridge and onto the table."

"What about me?" Mark asked.

Since he was away from the office, he had ditched the suit and tie and was wearing a pair of khakis with a blue pullover shirt. The blue really complemented his eyes, and I couldn't deny how good he looked. He threw me a smile as if he knew what I was thinking.

"I think . . . we have it," I managed. Turning back to the stove, I flipped the French toast and reached for a plate. "I'll have this batch on the table in a minute."

Geena and Piper ambled in just as I finished up the last few pieces. We gathered like a regular family at the breakfast table. Dad said grace and before I knew it we were chatting about plans for the day.

"This coffee is fantastic. Seattle's Best, I suppose," Mark stated more than questioned.

"Bremerton's Best," Geena corrected. "Or at least Cooper's Best."

Everyone laughed except Piper. She seemed in a dark mood. I noticed she wasn't eating and wondered if she was feeling poorly. I started to ask, but Judith spoke up. "I'm going to do some painting down on the beach today. I'd love to have your company." She looked at the three of us girls and added, "It would be great to get to know you better."

I was glad for an excuse to opt out. "I promised to take Mark around." I offered no other comment and instead turned my attention to the food.

"Where do you two plan to head out to?" Dad asked.

Mark looked to me for answers. "I guess we'll play it by ear. I haven't been here since I was twelve," I reminded him.

"Take him to Poulsbo," Dad suggested. "It's a quaint little Scandinavian village on the north end of Liberty Bay. It's got some great antique stores, and I know you like that kind of thing." A faint memory came back to me. I had been there with my parents long ago.

"I like to browse antique stores too," Mark said, much to my amazement. "I have fond memories of antiquing with my mother."

"Well, you sound like a man after my own heart," Dad declared. "I've got a collection of Old West memorabilia. Spurs, barbed wire, old tools. You'll have to come see it sometime. I keep a lot of it in my office in Boston."

"I'd like that," Mark replied. "I can't say that I know much about that kind of thing. My mom was quite fond of Haviland china and Limoges pieces. I can probably tell you more about that kind of thing than a man has a right to know."

"I love Limoges," Judith interjected. "I've got a set of china that dates back to the 1880s. It's a delicate blue floral print with beautiful scalloping and gold trim."

Mark nodded. "I've seen similar pieces gracing our table at home."

"So you didn't just have it to look at," Judith commented. "That's exactly how I feel about antiques. If you aren't going to use them, what's the point of having them? They're only things, and if their only purpose is to gather dust . . . well . . . I don't need that kind of object in my life."

"I couldn't agree more," Mark said. "I want the things around me to have purpose and be of value. Utmost on that list, however, is to have people in my life." He turned a smile on me and lifted up a forkful of French toast. "Especially ones who can cook."

My cheeks grew hot, and I immediately grabbed my coffee to have something to do. I sipped at the brew for several minutes so that no one would expect me to comment. Mark had a way of making me feel so relaxed and nervous all at the same time.

We had covered a variety of casual topics by the time breakfast ended. Geena got to her feet first. "Piper and I can clean up since you fixed the food. That way you and Mark can get on the road."

I looked at Mark. "Are you ready for a day among the Scandinavians?"

He laughed. "As long as you're among their number."

"You two have fun and don't worry about us," Judith said. "I have plans after painting to put together a nice dinner for everyone. I hope you don't mind."

"I'm always happy for someone else to cook," Geena replied. "Come on, Piper. Let's get these into the dishwasher." She picked up several plates and headed to the kitchen.

Piper looked less than excited at the prospect, but picked up her own plate and cup. My eyes lingered, however, on all the food on her plate she'd barely touched.

∽

"So you seem a little better," Mark said as we drove north to Poulsbo.

"I feel a fool for having dragged you into this," I said as I turned onto the 303. "You must think me really ridiculous."

"Not at all. I know you want to be a pillar of strength—an island unto yourself," Mark answered, "but that isn't exactly how life works. At least not how it works successfully."

"Oh, and when did you become an expert on such matters?"

He chuckled. "I never presumed to be an expert on it or anything else. I just judge it by my experiences. My guess is that your experiences have taught you to avoid people and relationships. It probably started early in your life—childhood, I'd say."

His comment made me shiver. I made a pretense of turning down the A/C and refocused on the road.

"So why not just be honest with me about the past? Maybe I can help."

Irritation edged out the fear. "And if I don't want help?"

"Everybody needs help now and then. They may not want it, but needing it is entirely different. Kind of like a good storyteller needing an editor. God never intended for us to walk through life on our own, alone."

I joined the traffic of Highway 3 and set the cruise control to sixty. "Did He intend for little girls to suffer because of the mental illness of the adults in their lives?"

Mark didn't miss a beat. "No. I don't think it was God's desire at all. It's simply a part of living in a fallen world."

"A what?"

"A fallen world. A world that turned away from the perfection God intended. When Eve allowed the serpent to give her reason to doubt God, everything changed. The world became imperfect—fell away from God—because of sin. The happiness and love we could have had were corrupted."

"Please don't start in on that," I said more sternly than I'd intended. "I'm not looking for a lesson in religion, and I'm certainly not looking for love."

"I've never seen anyone look harder for love than you."

His words took my breath. I turned and looked at him. "I suppose you think you know exactly what I need."

He gave me that cocky smile. "You need to pay attention to the road," he said, gesturing.

I glanced back in time to see that we were gaining rather quickly on the back of a semi. I slowed, changed lanes, and reset the cruise control.

"So what kind of mental illness were you exposed to?" he asked.

I'd come this far and decided to bare it all. "Schizophrenia. My mother."

He nodded. "That couldn't have been easy. Which type was she?"

"Paranoid."

He seemed to consider this for a moment. "Was she delusional—hallucinating?"

"Yes."

"Did she think people, particularly government types, were out to get her?"

I felt my breath catch. "Yes. The FBI."

Again he nodded. "Refuse treatment and meds?"

"Yes." I didn't know what else to say. A part of me was relieved that he so obviously understood the situation, while another part wanted to pull the car to the side of the road so that I might run away from further discussion.

"How old were you when she was diagnosed?"

"About six. My sister Piper was born that year and things really went downhill after that. But . . ." I paused and bit at my lower lip. I focused on the tree-lined highway. "She was sick well before that."

"I can imagine. Most folks go years undiagnosed."

I shook my head and looked at him. "How do you know so much about it?"

It was Mark's turn to look a little embarrassed. "I minored in general psychology with a strong emphasis in abnormal studies."

I gave him a sidelong glance. "Yet you became an editorial director?"

"Well, I majored in English. Where better to use such a combination but in working with crazed writers and mad geniuses? I think every editor should have a degree in psychology." He winked, and I laughed in spite of myself.

"I suppose you have me there." I sobered, realizing he'd have a very clear understanding of what I was up against. "So now you understand."

"What is it you want me to understand?"

"That I can't risk a relationship with anyone. I can be your friend, but more than that and you open yourself up to all sorts of problems."

He was very quiet for several minutes. We weren't far from our destination and I wondered if maybe he would ask me to take him back to Bremerton.

"I'm not afraid to risk a relationship with a woman whose mother was mentally ill," he finally said. "However, I am afraid to set out to woo a woman who wants nothing to do with God."

That hit me hard. Maybe harder than if he'd said he couldn't deal with the schizophrenia. I had heroically thought I was saving the world from the possibilities of my own mental illness by not having a mate and children, but never had I considered that someone might reject me based on my religious views. The very idea made me defensive, which in turn made me angry.

"So why did you bother to come out here?"

"Because I felt it was what God wanted me to do." He looked at me, and I couldn't help but glance at his well-chiseled features. Why did he have to be so good-looking? "I can't lie, Bailee. I want very much to have a relationship with you, but more than that, I want you to finally realize that God wants one with you too. And frankly, His is more important."

I fought to keep from saying anything harsh. It dawned on me all at once that the reason I was so offended by his statement had more to do with the past than I had originally thought. If I blamed schizophrenia and my mother's behavior for my inability to have a decent relationship, then I didn't have to be responsible for the matter. To say otherwise— to say that my own choices and outlook on faith and God were putting a halt to someone being able to connect with me—well, that was entirely different. That made it my responsibility, and I didn't particularly care for that.

CHAPTER 16

Arriving in Poulsbo gave us a nice diversion and reason to end our very serious conversation. I was determined not to fall into another trap of hearing how much I needed to get right with God. But even while avoiding Him, God made His presence known.

While in one of the many antique stores, I found an old framed painting of Jesus knocking at a wooden door. Later in the same store, I saw an old leather Bible. Something in me suggested I buy it, but I refrained.

During our walk around town I found myself constantly inundated with plaques, wall hangings, and cards that suggested God was either with me or wanted to be. It was annoying. After a couple of hours looking around and shopping, Mark suggested we sit on a bench and watch the water for a while.

I fidgeted and tried to focus on a family to our left. The mother and father had their hands full with three rambunctious children, none of which could have been older than four or five. They seemed happy. The children were laughing at the dad's antics to entertain them with a Frisbee. The youngest stumbled and fell, and the mother quickly helped her back to her feet and kissed away her tears. How perfect they all seemed. Why hadn't God given me a family like that?

There He was again. God. Imposing His way into my thoughts—demanding that I recognize His presence.

"All right," I finally said, giving up the fight. I turned my attention back to Mark. "I don't know what to do with God. He deserted me when I needed Him most. He allowed my mother to avoid getting the help she needed. He let her commit suicide. I won't even get into how the people at church reacted to her and to us girls. And then there's the way my mother treated me."

"Free choice is pretty painful to those of us who'd make other decisions for the people we love," Mark replied.

"What's that supposed to mean?"

"God allows us to make our own choice. Your mother was no exception to that just because she had mental problems."

"But she wasn't in her right mind," I countered. "And because of that—" I leaned in close and lowered my voice—"because of that she often endangered my life and those of my siblings. Her free will or 'choice,' as you suggest, nearly cost us our own lives."

"I don't doubt it," he answered. "I am, however, really sorry that you had to endure so much. It wasn't right, Bailee. You and your sisters shouldn't have had to go through all of that. I wish it could have been different for you."

"God could have made it different." My bitterness was laid bare for him to see. "People—Christian people—could have been more loving and kind."

"Mental illness frightens most people," Mark admitted. "I've seen it firsthand at my church. A few weeks back someone brought in a couple of homeless men. They were clearly dealing with mental issues. People didn't want to sit near them or even say hello."

"For fear it might rub off," I said, remembering all too well how church congregations had treated my mother.

"One of the older men suggested to me that the men were demon-possessed."

That roused something in me that I had very nearly forgotten. "They tried to pray schizophrenia out of my mother at one church. It was awful. They said my mother was being held in bondage by the devil." I shuddered.

"They read all those stories in the Bible about Jesus casting out demons."

Mark reached out and touched my hand. "Satan has his power and there's no doubt he torments the minds of some, but not all mental illness has anything to do with demon possession. People suffer from bad choices like drug use. They fry their brains and destroy their ability to function normally. Some are born with problems that interfere with mental stability. Some are abused and mental illness develops. And, I truly believe some are demon possessed. I won't say that isn't possible."

"But they didn't help her," I said, remembering that particular church. "They prayed over her . . . badgered her . . . and finally asked her to leave. They said she was in sin and wasn't willing to be delivered from her sickness." I looked at Mark. "How could they be so cruel? How could God?"

"It wasn't God who kicked her out of church," he countered. "It wasn't God who treated her . . . you . . . cruelly. It was the choice of people whose nature was sinful and human. Just like you and me. They made mistakes, Bailee. That doesn't mean God did."

"But He could have stopped it."

A golden retriever came bounding up to us, acting as though we were lifelong friends.

Mark laughed and gave the animal a scratch behind the ears. "Hey, there."

"Sorry about that," a young woman said as she bound up to our bench. She was dressed in running shorts and a T-shirt and held out the leash as if offering an explanation. "Buddy managed to take off before I could hook him up." She snapped the leash onto her dog's collar.

"No problem," Mark told her. "I enjoyed the interruption."

The woman smiled and gave the leash a tug. "Come on, Buddy." They took off jogging down the sidewalk.

I almost hoped Mark would have forgotten my last comment, but I knew he hadn't. Maybe if I headed him off at the pass—stopped him before he could begin his barrage of questions—we could end this conversation and move on to something else.

"I told God He could have kept it all from happening, and He questioned me. I know it doesn't make sense, but God agreed that He could have kept it from happening—then He asked me what I would do with Him now. I guess that's the place I'm in. I don't know what a person does with someone who could have kept bad things from happening, but didn't."

Mark nodded. "I've been there myself. It's a hard place to be in."

"Maybe it is time you told me more about your life, then."

"Seems only fair. And I'm glad to share with you, Bailee . . . but I get the distinct feeling that what you'd really like is to get an answer for your own issues."

With my effort thwarted, I considered my response for a moment. "Sometimes there aren't answers, Mark. Perhaps it's just as well if we let it go. God is God, after all. We can't hope to understand why He does the things He does."

"And that's the end of that?"

I forced a nod. "Yes. Seems logical to me."

"And you're all right with that?"

I shrugged. "What does it matter? Whether I'm all right with it or not, God will do as He wishes. Believe me, He's never asked my permission for anything. My safety and provision aren't as important as running the world."

"But that's where you're wrong, Bailee. They are. The Bible says they are, so I believe it with all my heart. God isn't a father who leaves His children without protection. You may have had close calls—bad things may have happened—but what about being grateful for the blessings you've also had? What about cherishing the wonderful life God gave you beyond your mother and her schizophrenia? Why do a few bad years and horrible events cancel out the wonder and beauty of a lifetime of good? Why let it keep you from years of love and happiness?"

His questions troubled me. Why should a few bad years ruin the rest of my life? Why did they have that kind of power? I had no answer. I looked up and found Mark watching me. I didn't feel like fighting with him anymore. I just wanted to take comfort in his presence. I wanted to be happy that he'd come—that he cared enough about me to make a coast-to-coast trip at the drop of a hat.

"I'm sorry. I don't have an answer for you."

He smiled in his charming way. "Well, at least you're being honest with me."

I thought about that for a minute. Honesty was critical. Our relationship, be it as boss and employee, friends, or something more, necessitated honesty. I knew where secrets could lead.

"Honesty is important to me. Maybe now more than ever," I finally said. "I want to be real with you, but that means being vulnerable. And that frightens me more than I can say."

"It frightens me too, Bailee." His words were barely more than a whisper.

"You promised you wouldn't set out to hurt me," I said, remembering our conversation on the ferry to Bremerton. "I want to give you the same promise."

Smiling, he pretended to lift an imaginary glass. "To vulnerability."

"And honesty," I said.

"Now I suggest we find a place for lunch. Better yet, we could just skip to the dessert. I saw a great looking bakery on the main street. I want to get some treats to take back to your family."

I was surprised that he was willing to drop the subject, but grateful too. "I think they'd like that."

⁂

The next morning, with Mark and Dad off exploring the nearby state park, I was surprised to find Judith on the deck, painting. I watched her for several minutes, impressed by her attention to detail. She was quite good.

"How long have you painted?" I asked.

"Since I was quite young. My father was a painter—at least for a time."

"Only for a time?"

"My father had MS. His abilities went downhill as the disease took over."

"I'm sorry. When was he diagnosed?"

"They knew about it before I was born. I just sort of grew up with it." Judith dabbed the brush in a mixture of white, sand, and blue, then touched it to the shoreline in the painting. "My father was determined to live his life as normally as possible. He even endured a lot of painful experimental treatments."

"Did they help?"

"I don't think so." She put the brush in a nearby jar of solution, then turned back to me. "There were medications that seemed to ease his pain. Other times the meds only served to put him in a stupor." She motioned to the deck table and chairs. "Want to sit with me for a while?"

I nodded and pulled out a chair. The morning light was uncommonly brilliant. The sky was void of clouds and the water glimmered exquisitely against the sun's rays. I'd forgotten how peaceful it could be to just sit and watch the day pass by.

"I used to pray that he'd get better," Judith continued. "One day he just stopped painting. I asked him why, and he said it was no longer a joy to him. He encouraged me to paint for him. I promised him I would."

Judith grew thoughtful and gazed off toward the water and trees. "He got worse and in time was pretty much bedfast. I used to take my work to him and he would give me advice on what I could do to make it better."

"Did the MS kill him?"

"In a sense. He couldn't deal with the effects on his life. He couldn't handle the pain, and so he ended his life."

I gasped. "I'm sorry. I shouldn't have asked."

She shifted in her seat and leaned against the table. "It was devastating, but I always understood why he did it. After he died I went in search of a father figure, and I found it in Kevin. We married after just a few weeks of knowing each other. It was a big mistake, although I did love him. If love could have made a man healthy, then my love would have knit Kevin's mind back together."

"But love can't do that," I said sadly.

"No."

I nodded. "I always thought that my love could help my mother. I felt responsible for my mother's condition, as well as my sisters' safety. I lost my childhood somewhere in between."

Judith looked at me sadly. "I know. Your father often spoke of it and his deep regret. Your mother was wrong to put so much on your shoulders—your father too. Just because I love him doesn't mean that I can't see his mistakes. I think that's the good thing about love, however. We look beyond."

"My father knew?" I said in disbelief. "If he knew, why didn't he help us—me?"

She drew a deep breath and let it out slowly. "He knew to some degree. At least he suspected. He knew your mother could be very hard on you regarding your responsibilities. Especially after—"

"Good morning," Geena called and waved from the stone steps below.

She had apparently been out for a run on the beach. She jogged across the yard and climbed the deck stairs to join us. "I hope I haven't interrupted."

I couldn't help but wonder what Judith was going to say. I turned to her. "Judith was just telling me something."

Geena took a seat. "About our father?"

I looked to Judith. "Was it about him?"

She shook her head. "Not entirely. I was just going to say that he was aware of your mother putting pressure on you to be responsible for your siblings. Especially after the death of your brother."

Geena responded before I could. "Brother? We didn't have a brother."

I didn't have a chance to agree before Judith continued. "Oh, that's right. You weren't born yet—just Bailee."

I felt as if she'd slapped me. There was something of truth in what she said, but I couldn't put the pieces together. A brother?

"What are you talking about?" Geena looked at me. "Do you know what she's saying? Or is this something else you've kept from us?"

A growing dread settled over me. I looked at Judith in confusion. "A brother?"

Her face took on an expression of alarm. "You didn't know? How could you not?"

I shook my head. There was the slightest glimmer of a memory and then it was gone. A baby—the baby I couldn't find—the baby that one day just went away. I felt my chest tighten. What in the world was going on? I felt so helpless.

Geena put her hand on my arm as if to offer comfort, but there was no comfort for this.

"I feel terrible," Judith said, shaking her head. "I thought you knew. I presumed it was something that all of you knew." She put her hand to her mouth and issued a muffled apology.

"I'm just so sorry."

CHAPTER 17

Judith and I were standing in the dining room when Dad and Mark returned. They were laughing about something and acting as if they were lifelong friends. I sprang on them like a cheetah on prey.

"We've got problems, and I need answers."

Dad's eyes narrowed. "What's wrong? Answers about what?"

"It's my fault, Tony," my stepmother announced from behind me. "I'm sorry, but I said something about your son and didn't realize Bailee and Geena were unaware."

My father shook his head. "Bailee, you knew about the baby who died."

His tone sounded almost accusing and took me by surprise. "No. I don't know about a baby who died," I said, looking from him to Mark and back again. "What are you talking about?"

Geena and Piper had joined us by now. I

went to them. "I don't know what he's talking about. I swear. I would have told you if I did." They didn't look as though they believed me, but said nothing.

"Why don't we sit down and I'll tell you what I can," Dad said, pulling a chair out for Judith.

I wasted no time. I took a seat at the table before Judith could even respond to my Dad. I looked at Geena and Piper and motioned them to join us. They seemed reluctant to sit, but did so. Mark looked rather out of place, but I couldn't see kicking him out.

"You might as well stay, Mark."

He looked at Dad. "Would that make you uncomfortable?"

"Not at all. Please stay." Dad looked at the three of us girls. We were all lined up on the opposite side of the table, as if about to conduct some sort of post-war interrogation.

Mark sat at the end of the table between the five of us. I thought again of his psychology background. He could definitely use this family as a case study if he wanted to further his education in psychology.

"Bailee, you were very young. Only three, I think." Dad rubbed his chin. "Noah was less than a month old—just twenty days. He died from SIDS—Sudden Infant Death Syndrome. It was very hard on your mother. She stayed in bed for weeks after that. I think it only served to promote the schizophrenia, if that's possible. It definitely caused her to have a breakdown of sorts."

I closed my eyes and pressed my fingers to my temples. Why couldn't I remember my baby brother? Or maybe I did. The baby who was missing. The baby I couldn't find. It would make sense that he had been there one day and then gone. Perhaps in my child's mind I thought he was just misplaced. Maybe I blended his existence with events that happened years later with my sisters.

"But we've never talked about him? A baby brother named Noah and in all these years no one even spoke his name?" Geena said in a questioning tone. "Why did you never mention him? Why didn't Mom say anything about it?"

"As I said, your mother had a breakdown when he died. The doctor who saw her said it was typical of women who lost infants. She was depressed and despondent. They gave her Valium and something else I don't remember. She slept a lot and I hired someone to come in and take care of you, Bailee. Do you remember that?"

I shook my head. It was like a big chunk of time was missing.

"Well, like I said, you were only three." He

gave me a sympathetic smile. "And perhaps that's all the better. It was such a sad time. I was as heartbroken as your mother. I buried myself in work. I had wanted a son very much. And I don't think I figured we'd have any more children after him. Your mother seemed to have her hands full, and though I didn't know it at the time, the schizophrenia was already starting to control her life."

"But there are no pictures of him," Piper said, finally joining in. "It's like he never existed."

"I know," Dad replied. "That was how your mother wanted it. I remember saying something about Noah when Geena was born. I asked the doctor if it was likely that she might also die from SIDS, and your mother went ballistic. She ranted and threw things at me. She said I was never again to mention Noah's name. That we weren't ever going to speak about him again. I decided that if this was the only way to help her recover, then that's how we'd handle it."

"But you never said anything about him even after she was gone," Piper said, shaking her head. "Why didn't you tell us about him then?"

Dad's brows rose as he drew in a deep breath. "The details of your mother's death were just too much. I felt I needed to keep things from you girls in order to protect you. Noah's birth and death seemed too much for young girls who had lost their mother. So I kept it as my own private sorrow. As time passed, I suppose it just seemed natural to say nothing."

"Did she get any kind of help for dealing with Noah's death?" I asked.

He shook his head. "Your mother never wanted it. Said it wouldn't do any good. She promised me she'd talk to the pastor at the church where she was attending. I don't know if she ever did that or not. After Geena came along, she settled down and seemed to heal from the loss. Geena was her consolation and she genuinely seemed happy to have another child. We decided to try again for a boy and Piper was born." He smiled. "I wasn't disappointed, though. Piper was a delight and I came to realize I was quite happy with my little girls."

"Where is he buried?" Piper asked.

Dad looked to the ground. "I had him cremated and his ashes sprinkled. Your mother didn't even want a plaque put up as a memorial. He was here for just twenty short days and then he was gone."

"This is your fault," I heard my mother's voice say as clearly as if she were standing beside me. I startled and looked for her, but of

course she wasn't there. I felt my chest tighten and the air go out of me. For a moment I was dizzy and thought I might faint.

"Are you all right?" Mark asked, coming to my side.

I looked at him, then closed my eyes to stop the world from spinning. "I need some air."

He put his arm around me. "I'll take her out on the deck," I heard him tell the others. He walked me to the door and all the while I kept my eyes closed, his voice my entire focus.

"We're almost there." I heard the glass deck door slide open and felt the breeze hit my face. "Just a few more steps. Here," Mark instructed. "Sit here."

I opened my eyes and the brightness of the day hit me. How dare it be sunny when the problems of my life had left everything so dark?

"Is that better?" Mark squatted down beside me. "That had to be quite a shock. Rest for a little bit. I'll get you some water."

The moment he stepped away I was wishing for his return. I looked up to find Geena and Piper watching me from the doorway. I shook my head and whispered. "I didn't know. I swear, I didn't know."

Mark returned with the water and Dad followed him out onto the deck. "Bailee," he said softly, "I'm so sorry for this. Judith feels terrible and so do I. I never meant for it to come out like this."

I felt weary and spent. How could I ever hope to know a sense of recovery if the lies never ended? "I just don't understand how you could keep it from us. He was our brother. How . . . how could you never say anything?" The very idea of just omitting a child in the family was beyond me.

Dad took the seat beside me. "He wasn't with us long. I guess I allowed myself to pretend he'd never been with us. It hurt less, but to be honest, it still hurts. I should have gotten help with my grieving. I can see that now, but back then I was convinced that my work was the best therapy possible. In fact, the doctor himself told me it was the best possible thing for a man to do."

"This is hopeless." I shook my head. "I knew I should never have come here."

"What is hopeless?" Dad asked.

"This." I waved my hands to the people gathered beside me. "Our family. We've been doomed since the start."

"How can you say that?" he asked, looking confused.

"I say it because it's true. Our family has been built upon lie after lie." I looked at him and saw a stranger. "I don't think I even know you."

"Are there other secrets?" Geena asked from the door.

I was grateful to have the focus taken off of me. I drew a deep breath and tried to settle my racing heart.

Dad shrugged. "I suppose there are other details that were hidden. Your mother's father had a mental illness. I never knew much about him. Your mother was in foster care when we met. We went to college together and fell in love. Everything happened so quickly, and before we knew it Bailee was on the way."

He reached out to touch my shoulder. "Look, it's clear I made mistakes. We all have. I'm sorry about hiding the truth from you girls. I'm sorry that it led to you thinking the worst of me. But I want us to make a new start. I want you all to feel that you can ask anything. If you have questions—if anything comes to mind—let's make a promise that we'll talk about it. All right?"

I wanted to agree but felt too overwhelmed at the moment. I got to my feet. "I need some time to think." I pushed past Dad and the others and went into the house to retrieve my purse. A drive seemed like the logical choice of escape. I was nearly to the car when Mark appeared.

"Would you like a friend?"

I shook my head. I'd been stupid to pretend

a relationship with him might work out. "No. I don't think that's wise. In fact, I think you should probably just go home."

He frowned. "Just like that?"

What did he want from me? How could I help him understand the raging doubt that warred inside me when I couldn't comprehend it myself?

"I told you a long time ago that I had a lot of baggage." I gave a harsh laugh. "Only I didn't realize just how much there truly was."

"And you think that's a reason to stop trying—to send me away? Bailee, I can't imagine what you must be feeling, but I care about you."

"Well, don't," I said, shaking my head. "Please just don't."

∽

I drove for a long time, not even thinking of where my journey might take me. From time to time tears blinded my vision and forced me to pull over. My life was unraveling. Dinah, my therapist, had said that coming here might prove helpful. Instead, all I was finding was more damage.

I tried to forget the uneasy feeling of my mother's accusation, but it was like wearing silk on a hot humid day. It clung to me, absorbed my fears and anxieties. Had her words to me been real? Had she really blamed me for something related to my brother's death?

Why couldn't I remember something that important? I'd had a brother, and yet there was no memory of him in my mind. I conjured an image of what I thought he might have looked like, but the faceless infant offered no comfort.

I took an exit from the highway, not even mindful of where I was. It didn't really matter. I'd already decided that as soon as I got back to the house I was going to pack and leave. It seemed the only thing to do. I'd pretty much gotten what I'd come for—hadn't I?

"The truth has been told. Dad's not a murderer," I announced in the empty confines of the car. "My mother committed suicide, and I had a brother who died from SIDS. Surely that's enough self-exploration for one trip."

But it wasn't self- exploration at all. It was a telling of the family secrets. A cleaning of the closet where all the skeletal remains had been left to rot.

A small roadside church drew my attention. Since traffic had stopped for a light, I brought the car to a halt near the church's marquee. *Isaiah 41:10—Hope for the Fainthearted.* I read the message a second time and then the travelers behind me honked and I realized traffic was again moving.

The sign intrigued me, and I found myself suddenly desperate for a Bible. I looked around at the shops and finally spied a bookstore. Surely they would have a copy of God's Word, I thought sarcastically.

"May I help you?" a woman asked almost immediately upon my entry.

"I . . . well . . . do you carry any Bibles?"

She smiled indulgently. "We don't have much of a selection, but there are a few on the shelves at the back of the store, along with some other inspirational books."

I nodded and made my way through the store, to where the Bibles had been tucked away almost as an afterthought. I picked one up, not sure what the differences might be between the different copies. One seemed just as good as another. After all, wasn't the Bible . . . the Bible? Hadn't wars been fought to keep it intact? Or maybe not. I couldn't remember.

The woman at the register had made me feel rather self-conscious, and lest she think me a Bible thumper, I asked her if she gift wrapped.

"No, but we have some lovely gift bags," she said pointing to a rack just inside the door.

I chose one that looked celebratory and brought it with the Bible to the counter. She rang up the purchase and took my credit card. "A graduation gift?" she asked.

It was only then that I noticed the bag's design. I nodded and signed for the purchase. Without saying anything else, I tucked the slip and my card back into my purse and picked up the sack she handed me.

"Isaiah 41:10," I murmured, driving away from the store. I couldn't very well open the Bible and look up the verse right there without revealing that I wasn't just intending to give this as a gift.

A few blocks later I found a turnoff for a marina and followed the road to an almost full parking lot. There was some sort of activity happening—a fair or craft show it looked to be. I saw one small slot at the far end of the lot and squeezed the rental into it just as another car came whipping around from the opposite direction. I saw the driver's frustrated expression as I glanced in the rearview mirror.

"I'll only be here a second," I told him even though I knew he couldn't hear me.

I pulled the Bible out of the sack and opened the box. Inside, the leather-bound edition looked quite stately. Elegant. I took it out and smiled at the attention to detail that had been given. Books were my life, and even though I was not acquainted with this one, I could recognize the quality workmanship.

I found the book of Isaiah and then the forty-first chapter. Verse ten immediately popped out at me. *So do not fear, for I am with you; do not be dismayed, for I am your God. I will strengthen you and help you; I will uphold you with my righteous right hand.*

I sat there, rereading that verse over and over. Was God really trying to encourage me? Did He work like that? I closed the Bible and put it aside, but the words rang over and over in my mind.

Do not fear. . . . I will strengthen you. . . . I will uphold you. . . .

I looked skyward. "Will you really?"

⁓

When I finally returned home, it was as if I'd never been gone. No one said a word about my disappearance, and in fact the rest of the family was gathered once again on the deck discussing our mother. My sisters seemed much more at ease than when I'd left, and Mark was nowhere in sight. Had he gone, as I'd suggested? A part of me hoped he had stayed.

"When did Mom first show signs of being sick?"

I slipped into the deck chair beside Judith. She smiled. "I made some lemonade. Would you like a glass?"

Shaking my head, I gave her the briefest smile and waited for Dad to respond to my sister. He considered her question for a moment, but I couldn't help but wonder if his thoughts were on my sudden arrival. He looked so tired.

"I don't suppose I'll ever know for sure. I tend to think she was hearing voices by the time we married. She would sometimes seem distantly absorbed, as if listening to someone who wasn't there. She suffered from depression, which was an additional problem."

"But you didn't get her help?" Geena asked.

"Like I said earlier, she didn't want help. She didn't think it was a big deal. The mental health industry was beginning to radically change. Forced care was no longer the option it had been decades prior. But despite that, I suppose even when I asked questions or sought help on her behalf—which granted, didn't happen but a couple of times—I was told she was hormonal. One of her worst episodes of depression came after having Bailee. The doctor said it was the baby blues and not that big of a deal. He said it was normal and that most women had some kind of postpartum depression."

"Even so, they should have given her help. Why didn't her obstetrician realize the situation?" Geena asked.

"Who can tell," Dad answered. "Your mother was a very private person. Maybe because of the schizophrenia, maybe because of the depression. It could have even been because of her abusive past. Her parents lost custody of her early on and she spent most of her life under the government's control."

"Why did you never tell us this?" Piper asked.

"What good would it have done, girls?" Dad questioned in return. "When your mother was alive she didn't want me saying anything, and after she was gone . . . well . . . I didn't feel like talking about it."

Piper came to sit down beside him. She put her arm around his shoulder. "I'm sorry, Daddy. You wanted to come here for a good reason—to share your happy news. We've turned this into a bad thing." She threw me a look that seemed to dare me to say otherwise. I kept my thoughts to myself.

He shook his head. "No. This isn't bad. The years of silence were bad. We can face these things together now and deal with whatever comes."

And what might come our way? I wondered. Were there symptoms already developing in our lives that would ultimately reveal a similar diagnosis?

∽

That question was still on my mind later that night. Mark appeared not long after the others had left for dinner elsewhere. I saw him and immediately felt guilty for the way I'd acted. He knocked on the deck's sliding screen door and I waved him in.

"Your father said you were opting to stay here, so I thought I might join you. Do you mind?"

I got up from the couch and shook my head. "Not at all. I was just thinking about a walk. Wanna come?"

He smiled. "I'd like that."

"I'm sorry for the way I acted earlier." His blue-eyed gaze held me motionless for a moment. "I meant it, though . . . when I said you shouldn't care about me."

"There are a lot of things in life people told me I shouldn't do," he said quite seriously. "Going into the family publishing business was one. Trusting God with my soul was another. I think the advice was given because people were afraid of what my choice might mean to me. Afraid the work would be too great or the constraints too limiting."

I looked at him for a moment and thought again of the verse in Isaiah—the verse I'd now committed to memory. "Fear seems a powerful motivator," I murmured.

He nodded. "It seems to be the first or maybe the strongest emotion we learn."

For at least twenty minutes we simply

walked and said nothing. We had forgone the beach to walk the neighborhood streets, and I found myself enchanted with the scent of flowers and spruce. The days were staying light longer and because of that I had the strange sense that it was much earlier than the eight o'clock my watch suggested.

"You've really come at an unusual time," I told Mark.

"Because of your family?"

His question seemed odd to me. "Well, there's that, but I meant the weather. We seldom have so many beautiful days in a row here. There's almost always some rain or clouds."

"Oh, I see what you're saying."

"If you'd like," I said, trying to keep the conversation casual, "we could all plan to go to Seattle tomorrow and visit Pike Place Market. It's definitely something to see if you've never experienced it."

"Sounds like a good time. Would everyone go?"

I tucked my hands into my jacket pocket. "I don't know. We could certainly offer it as a diversion for everyone. We can take the ferry over as pedestrians. That way we won't have to worry about parking."

"I think it sounds like a very interesting time," Mark replied and added, "even if it's just you and me."

I smiled. "We haven't scared you off yet?"

He laughed. "Hardly. Remember when we got that manuscript in from the German doctor who wrote about nuclear weaponry and religion? I told you then that challenges didn't scare me. They only serve to make me more determined."

"To divide and conquer?" I looked at him and raised my brow.

His expression left me breathless and he moved closer to take hold of my elbow. "Only if it advances my plan."

"Ah, I see." I didn't dare say more. There was a trembling that ran from my head to my toes, and I was sure my voice would betray his effect on me.

Mark's voice lowered to a whisper. "Don't you want to know what my plan is?"

I swallowed hard and tried to remain unconcerned. Casual. "You forget. I've been on the edge of many of your plans."

Grinning, he tightened his hold on me. "Well, this time you can't be on the edge of the plan . . . because you are the plan."

CHAPTER 18

To my surprise no one wanted to accompany Mark and me to Seattle. Of course, I still hadn't really apologized to Dad for the anger I'd displayed, but I had a feeling he wasn't holding it against me. Maybe God really had changed the way he dealt with life. He seemed happy.

Dad and Judith headed off antique shopping, while Geena had already told us the night before that she planned to sleep in. Piper told me she wasn't feeling well and wanted to stick around the house. Mark didn't seem to mind, and I was quickly coming to realize how much I enjoyed our time together. Maybe my heart really did know what was best for me.

" 'So do not fear, for I am with you.' "

"What was that?" Mark asked.

I looked up and smiled. "Oh, I was just remembering something."

I comforted myself with the fact that Mark

knew the worst about our family and still wanted to be a part of my life. Maybe with his background and schooling he felt he could handle whatever developed. Maybe it was a sort of sick fatal attraction, although I really didn't believe that.

Pike Place Market was just as I remembered it. Momma had taken us there shortly before her death. I had been terrified then—the crowds and noise were frightening to me at the age of twelve. I also had to be mindful of my sisters and their whereabouts as our mother seemed to just glide through the masses of people. I remember holding tight to Geena and Piper and fighting desperately to keep my eyes fixed on our mother. It hadn't been easy.

"You look kind of stunned," Mark said as we passed the fish market. People were gathered to watch the men throw the daily catch as people ordered their choices. It was remarkable that they could handle the slimy creatures and not drop them. I turned to Mark and tried to hide my feelings.

"Isn't this amazing?"

He raised a brow and narrowed his eyes. "Are you truly dumbfounded by the fish?"

I smiled. "Well, of course I am. Aren't you? I mean, could you throw a fish twenty feet?"

"Throw one? Yeah, probably. Catching it would be the hard part." He relaxed and took hold of my arm. "However, I have a feeling that the look on your face just now wasn't for the fish-catching exploits alone." He led me on toward an incredible array of floral bouquets. The beautiful arrangements were a bargain at five dollars apiece.

I decided to level with Mark as a man and woman began to perform. He played a wash-tub bass and she a guitar, while together they sang an old folk song.

"This place brings back memories," I told him.

He nodded. "Did you come here often?"

"I can only remember a handful of times. My sisters and I came here a couple of times with my mom and dad, but other times we were with mom alone. Those were frightening times. I feared losing my sisters, since Mom said they were my responsibility."

"She was wrong, you know." He motioned to the attendant and pointed to a ten-dollar bouquet of lilies and hydrangeas. He paid the woman and presented the flowers to me.

"Thank you, they're lovely." The pinks and whites were a perfect complement to the splashes of purple statice they'd positioned in the arrangement.

"I mean it," Mark reiterated. "She was

wrong. You were never responsible for them. Not at twelve. Not at three."

I felt something catch inside, and for a moment I couldn't draw a breath. Not at three. He was thinking of my baby brother. I'd said nothing to make him think that I was dwelling on the infant I couldn't remember.

We walked past a booth selling a variety of seasoned olive oils and declined the opportunity to sample the wares. Next came an incredible arrangement of produce and still I said nothing.

"Don't forget to go downstairs," someone told us and stuffed a flyer in Mark's hands. The paper advertised some exotic spices from the Middle East. Apparently their shop was one level below.

Mark led the way downstairs and pointed to the store. "Would you like to go spice shopping?"

I nodded. We entered the shop, and my nose was immediately filled with the heavy scents of paprika, chipotle, cinnamon, and a hundred other things I couldn't identify. We browsed the aisles and Mark pointed out a bag of orange spice tea.

"I think I'd like to try that. Why don't we take some back to the house?"

I nodded and waited for him to make the purchase. It was almost as if we were any other husband and wife shopping for the day—making choices for our home.

We explored the various levels and ended up back outside on the street. After three hours we decided we were both hungry and tired. "Where shall we eat?" Mark asked. He shifted our bag of purchases, which included not only the tea but some produce, coffee beans, and newly made cheese.

"Seems like all we do is eat," I teased. "You'll go back to Boston and be able to write a book about eating your way across Seattle and the Olympic Peninsula."

He laughed. "Might not be a bad idea. People have to eat. So where do we go?"

"I picked the place last time," I reminded him.

He pointed to a place nearby. "How about that?"

I read the sign. *Le Pichet Café*. "French sounds fine with me. I've never been there, so I can't vouch for the service or menu."

"I'm willing to take a chance."

I looked at him for a moment, feeling his statement had a double meaning. "All right. Sounds like fun. Let's give it a try."

The place was quite busy but happened to have one spot for us in the very back. I sat down on the booth side of a table and let Mark hand me the bags to place beside me.

We first ordered a half baguette and butter and café au lait to keep us from starving. The waiter's recommendation of the *potage de tomates, pêches, et crevettes grillées* immediately had my attention.

"It is a creamy tomato and roasted peach soup with marinated corn and grilled prawns. A definite favorite," the waiter assured us.

"Sounds good," I said, nodding. Mark agreed and the order was placed. When the bread and coffee arrived, Mark offered a brief prayer of thanks.

"Praying in public doesn't bother you at all, does it?"

"Why should it?" he asked. "I'm not doing it for show—I'm doing it because I'm truly grateful. God has blessed me. Why shouldn't I thank Him?"

I couldn't argue that point. I tore a piece of bread and began to butter it. My stomach growled in a gesture of approval. I was embarrassed by the noise but pretended not to hear it. Mark was gentleman enough to say nothing, so I began to relax again.

We chatted comfortably, talking about Seattle and the differences between it and Boston. While Seattle was a large city, it lacked the frantic feeling of Boston. The people seemed less stressed. Maybe it was the often overcast weather and cooler temperatures, or perhaps the fact that this city was much younger than grand old Boston.

"The history here is just as rich," Mark said. "I was reading up on it the other night. This part of the world has a wide array of stories to tell."

I was certain he was right. Every area had something to say about its past. The past. There it was again like a lingering specter.

The main course was served and we quickly sampled the fare. The soup had such a creamy, delicate flavor that I sighed out loud in appreciation. I slowed myself out of determination to appear less hurried, but certainly not because the food lacked any appeal.

Mark was on his second cup of coffee when he broached the subject he'd brought up before. "I know I made you uncomfortable earlier; believe me, that wasn't my desire. I meant it, however. You weren't responsible for the lives of your sisters or infant brother."

I took a bite of a prawn to give myself time to think about my reply. I knew he was right. However, I also knew that it didn't change the fact that I felt to blame for all the bad that had happened.

Swallowing, I felt the prawn stick in my throat. The coffee pushed it down, but my satisfaction with the meal was beginning to wane in the light of my thoughts.

"I know that I shouldn't feel guilty," I told Mark. "But there is something in me that can't quite shake it off. My mother drilled it into me. I can remember that much."

"She was wrong to do that."

I nodded. "Yes. Yes, she was. But it doesn't take away the damage done, just to recognize the truth."

Mark leaned back. "You're right, of course. There are still the aftereffects of what she did. We tend to try and forget that our actions have consequences."

"I suppose I realize now, more than ever, what a very sick woman my mother was. At least with all of us talking, I feel that we can move forward."

"But sometimes we have to make decided efforts to let go of the past. Not so we can pretend it didn't happen, but more so to lessen its power. In the Bible, Isaiah talks about forgetting the former things and not dwelling on the past." At his mention of Isaiah I perked up, but he was already moving on. "Paul speaks of it in his letters. Even Jesus made it clear that forgiveness for past sins could be given and the captive set free."

"I guess I can't imagine what that even feels like—to be free of the past." I picked up my soup spoon. "My therapist tells me that sometimes the absence of something is often more important than the presence of something else. But she also tells me that something in the past is keeping hold of me. There is something I can't remember . . . something I need to know."

"Maybe it was that you had a brother. You obviously didn't remember that," Mark offered.

"It's true, and I have considered that possibility. Or maybe it's been the need to know the truth about my mother's death." I shrugged. "I just don't know. I thought perhaps when these things came to light, I would realize immediately that this was 'the missing piece.' But now that I know about Noah and my mother, I can't say that I feel any better."

"Bailee, you've been stronger than any woman I know." There was true admiration in Mark's tone. "The more I learn about you, the more I want to know."

I found that hard to understand. It seemed to me that the complications of my family and self would be enough to send any would-be suitor running. Maybe Mark's interest in psychology just gave him a sick sort of attraction to the mess that was my family. Looking up to find him watching me, however, I didn't really believe that.

By the time we finished eating, the skies had turned cloudy. We'd only walked a block when the first sprinkles began to fall. The market was still packed, and something about the swirling mass of bodies triggered my anxiety. I ignored it at first. I told myself I was being silly. But as the tension built and I felt my chest tighten, I knew I was headed into a full-blown panic attack.

"Mommy, wait!" I remembered crying out in a similar ocean of people. I reached for her hand, but she was gone. I looked for my sisters, and they were gone too. I was alone—if a person could be alone amidst several hundred other people.

"Bailee?"

I looked up to find Mark watching me. I couldn't breathe and darkness was threatening to steal my consciousness. I tried to say something, but the words didn't come out. Mark seemed to understand and took charge. He pulled me under an awning and held me close.

"It's all right," he whispered. "You're safe."

I wanted to believe that. I wanted to feel safe—especially with him. I forced myself to breathe deeply. My therapist had long ago taught me a technique to fight my panic-induced hyperventilation. As my breathing evened, the tightness in my chest began to wane. I looked at Mark and could read the concern in his expression.

"I'm sorry." I tried to pull away, but he wouldn't let me.

"Don't be."

"I don't know what came over me. Something from the past . . . maybe another time when I was little. I remembered being separated from my mother and sisters." I shook my head and looked him in the eye. "It's like this will never end."

"But it will," he assured me.

I succeeded in pulling free of his embrace. "You don't know that, Mark. I keep trying to warn you, but you aren't hearing me." I started out down the street, knowing he would follow. Embarrassment washed over me and I found myself wishing I could make light of all that had happened. But of course, I couldn't.

∽

We said very little on the trip home, and when we entered the house I could tell something wasn't right. Geena met me in the kitchen, where I was searching for a vase. Her expression said it all.

"What's happened?"

"I don't know. Piper has locked herself in her bedroom and won't come out. I don't know why. She wouldn't talk to me. She wouldn't talk to Dad. Judith even tried."

Mark came into the kitchen just then and I

threw Geena a look to keep quiet. I instantly checked myself, however. I shook my head and handed Geena the flowers Mark had purchased for me in the market.

"I'm sorry. Could you find a vase for these? I'll go try to talk to Piper."

Mark gave me a look that suggested it wasn't my job, but while I felt I could let go in some areas, this wasn't one of them. Maybe Piper needed me. She'd turned everyone else down, after all.

I made my way past Mark and up the stairs. I tried to think of reasons Piper would have locked herself away, but nothing made much sense. This was the first time our family had been able to put the dirty laundry to soak. If anything, I would have expected her to feel better.

"Piper?" I called, knocking on her door. "It's me, Bailee. Let me in."

"Go away."

"Please, Piper. Just talk to me."

"I don't want to talk to anyone. Leave me alone."

"No." My tone was adamant. "I won't leave. I'm going to stand out here and talk to you whether you like it or not. You'll have to open the door and discuss what's wrong in order to get me to stop."

For a few moments silence greeted my

request. Then to my surprise I heard Piper unlock the door and open it. Her face was puffy from crying, but her eyes were dry. I reached out to hug her, but she moved away. I followed her into the room, somewhat at odds as to what to say next.

Piper made it easy for me. She took a seat on her bed and looked up at me. "I think I'm crazy."

I cocked my head slightly. "Why would you say that?"

She let go a long breath. "I can't sleep. I can't think straight. I'm sad all the time. I'm tired all the time. I want nothing more than to crawl into this bed and sleep forever. I hate my life, Bailee. I wish I were dead."

I took a seat on the bed beside her, but didn't attempt to touch her. Very gently I posed the first question in my mind. "Are you considering ending your life?"

Piper was quiet for a few minutes. "No. Not really. I think of how nice it would be to just not wake up, but I don't think I can kill myself." She looked at me, and I knew she was searching my face for the truth. "Does that make me crazy?"

"I don't think so," I told her. "I've wished for it all to end on occasion. We all get tired, Piper. We get to those places where we feel like we just can't go on."

"I feel so hopeless—like it will never change. Like it will just go on like this forever."

I frowned. "What will?"

"Life. Me. My thoughts and feelings." She got up and paced the room. "I feel like I will always be this sad, this misplaced. I don't belong. I know that sounds stupid, but it's the way I feel. Almost like someone sitting in an audience watching a play. Only the play is my life, and I have no control or say over the things happening on stage."

Piper's words left me silent. All of my life I had worked to fix the problems of my family, but now that my eyes were opened to just how foolish that was . . . I felt incapable of giving her advice.

"I have a consuming emptiness inside of me." She put her hand to her stomach. "I feel like it's devouring me a little each day. I can't take any more. I think I'm just as lost as Momma was."

"No," I said, shaking my head. I got up and went to her, but still she pulled away.

"Schizophrenia is hereditary."

"Can be, Piper. It can be hereditary. It doesn't have to be."

She wrapped her arms around herself as if to ward me off. "I can't go on like this."

"Then let's get you the help you need. Let

me take you to the doctor. You can get a physical and—"

"No! I'm not going to go talk to some
shrink. They didn't help Momma. They can't
help me."

"Momma wouldn't let them help her.
Momma didn't believe there was help," I
reminded her. "Her mind wouldn't allow
her to understand, but yours still can. You
know that counseling and antidepressants
are being used quite successfully. You have
a college degree, Piper. You are an educated
woman, a sensible woman. And . . ." I paused
to soften my tone. "You are a loved woman.
Piper, we love you, and we're here to help
you in whatever way we can."

"I've tried it all, Bailee. Don't you get it?
I've tried counseling. I've tried relationships
and sex. I've tried drugs and alcohol. I've tried
it all. Nothing helps. I just feel all the worse
when I wake up the next day."

My thoughts flitted to horrific images of
my little sister degrading herself in various
fashions. I longed to hold her—to assure her
that it was going to be all right.

"I binge eat and purge. I've cut myself
where no one could see. I've done things I'm
too ashamed to even admit." She looked at me
as if to gauge whether or not she'd shocked

me. I tried to keep my expression one of concern and tenderness.

"I still love you, Piper. None of those things change the fact that you're my sister." For once I didn't feel as though I were saying these things out of obligation or responsibility, but rather out of honest feelings. "I want to help you any way I can."

She said nothing, but I could see something in her expression that suggested I'd gotten through—at least in the tiniest way.

"I don't know why you care." She sat back down on the bed in a state of defeat.

Her words encouraged me, left room for explanation. "Does it matter why I care?"

"Yes," she said, nodding. "It does. Why do you care? After everything I've said and done—after the way I've treated you—why do you love me?"

I didn't even stop to think. "Because . . . you're you." I stepped toward her, but stopped. "You don't have to perform for me or dress a certain way. You don't have to work a certain job or marry a certain man. I just love you because you're Piper Cooper."

She let out a long breath. "I wish it were enough." Her eyes filled with tears. "I didn't say that to hurt you."

"Believe me, I understand. Look, there really is help out there. There are good people who can offer you direction and help. You just haven't connected with the right ones yet, but they're there." I thought of Dad and Mark and their beliefs in God. Maybe that would help Piper. "Why don't we talk to Dad?"

"No." She shook her head, crossing to where I stood. "You have to promise not to say a word to anyone."

My skin tingled. "More secrets, Piper? Hasn't this family learned its lesson yet?"

"You can't tell them. I won't admit it if you do. I'll tell them that you're lying."

I shook my head in disbelief. "You just spent the entire day locked in your room. Who do you think they'll believe?"

"If you love me as you say, you won't say anything."

For just a moment it was my mother I heard. Piper's expression was that of Natalie Cooper, and her tone clearly matched our mother's soft-spoken voice. It was so eerie that I actually backed up a step.

Piper moved forward. "I don't want to talk to Dad or anyone else just yet. Please just do this for me. I promise I'll tell him when the time is right."

Something in me wanted to scream. Instead I turned away and went for the door. "I can't do this anymore. I just can't."

In the hall I ran smack into Geena. She took hold of me and immediately plied me with questions. "What's happened? What's wrong with her? Did she tell you why she locked herself up?"

I shook off her hold. "Why don't you talk to her yourself. I need to be alone."

Instead of heading to my room, I made my way down to the beach—to the place where I'd had the breakdown the night I encouraged Mark to come. I was void of tears this time, but my heart ached with an intensity that I couldn't begin to ease.

I was glad the rain had stopped. The skies were still overcast, making the water look a gunmetal gray. The dampness of the air seemed to intensify the scents of the water, the trees, and the earth. I rubbed my chilled arms, wishing I'd thought to grab my jacket.

Without meaning to, I found myself praying. *God, I don't know what to do. I don't know what to say—how to pray. I need answers, but I don't know where to even start looking.*

I squatted down and watched the water lap gently against the shoreline. I unexpectedly remembered a Sunday school class when I was probably no more than seven or eight. The teacher was talking about prayer.

"When you don't know what to pray, just talk to God like a friend," she had instructed

us with a tender smile. *"God knows what's on your heart. Just talk to Him."*

"Okay," I whispered to the air. "I feel that same emptiness Piper described." I had even used that exact expression with my therapist at one time. "I feel alone, God. Like I know you should be there, but you aren't. Or maybe it's that I know I should be there with you, but I'm not."

I sighed and watched the water pulsate against the sandy soil. Mark said I needed a relationship with God. God wanted to know what I would do with Him now that I knew He wasn't always going to do things my way. Geena wanted answers, and Piper just wanted to hide. I pressed my hands to my head. What did I want?

"God knows what's on your heart. Just talk to Him."

I closed my eyes. *All right, God, this is me telling you what's on my heart. I can't do this anymore. I can't. I feel so alone. Please don't let me bear this alone. I'd rather have some part of you—even if you don't always do things the way I think you should.*

A stillness seemed to settle somewhere deep inside me.

People have failed me and I still love them. My mother made me feel that I was to blame for bad things. I thought my father killed her and that it was my fault for that as well. She died and you could have stopped her. She had a mental illness and you could have stopped that too. I feel like you've failed me, and yet you ask what I'll do with you? I don't understand why things had to be as they were, but if I can still love people despite their choices, then surely I can still love you.

The peace within me seemed to grow.

Was this what it was to be surrendered? Not a giving up, but a giving over? I didn't feel defeated in this kind of prayer; rather I felt myself strengthened. How could that be?

I opened my eyes and stood up. In the stillness it seemed that the entire world was holding its breath—standing in awe of the moment. "I don't want to go on without you."

Hearing a noise behind me, I turned and found my father watching me. He looked worried and I gave him a smile.

"If you heard what I just said, then you should know that I was talking to God."

He said nothing, but just watched me for a moment longer. I felt my heart nearly break. "I'm sorry, Daddy. I'm so sorry."

He came to me and pulled me into his arms. "Oh, Bailee, you've nothing to be sorry for." He held me tight and stroked my hair, just like he'd done when I was very young. "I understand—God understands."

"I probably did it all wrong," I told him.

"I didn't know all the right words to say or the Bible verses to quote." I pulled back and met his tear-filled eyes. "But I know He understands. He knows what's in my heart, doesn't He?" I felt like a child desperate for reassurance.

"Oh, sweetheart, He surely does. Just trust Him."

"I want to, Dad. But . . ."

"But?"

I pulled back just enough to look Dad in the eye. "I'm afraid. I'm so afraid."

"That He won't be there for you? That He'll leave you . . . like I did?" Tears came to his eyes and I nodded. Dad nodded too. "He won't. He's the only one who never will, Bailee. He will never leave you. Never forsake you. People will always disappoint you, but God will always be faithful."

His words sounded familiar—perhaps something I'd heard as a child. But this time was different. This time I felt the wonder of it all, and knew them to be true for myself. God really did care, and He really was right there with me . . . holding me in His righteous hand. Dad hugged me tight again and for a moment I just rested in his arms—pretending I was resting in God's embrace.

CHAPTER 19

I had thought that setting things right with God would mean that the nightmares would cease. But I was wrong. That night I tossed and turned and went from one scary scenario to another. I found myself lost and terrified, cold and frightened, even hurting from some imagined altercation. I saw my mother and heard her sharp rebukes. I searched endlessly for baby Noah . . . never to find him.

I would wake up from one nightmare long enough to get my bearings, then fall asleep and head off on another ghoulish journey. It was exhausting. Around four I awoke, determined to just get up and start the day.

I pulled on my robe and headed downstairs. My first thought was to make coffee, but then something else came to mind. I'd left the newly purchased Bible hidden in my room upstairs. It was strange, but I felt strongly compelled to read it now.

I made my way back upstairs to my room and noticed light coming from under Piper's door. Had it been there earlier? I hadn't noticed. I pressed my ear to the door and heard noises. She was obviously awake.

"Piper? Are you okay?"

She opened the door, and I could see past her to the bed, where her open suitcase was half full of clothes. "I'm leaving."

"For where?" I asked.

She turned from me and headed back to a stack of clothes. "I'm going back to Boston. This house—these memories—it's all too much. I can't be here."

"And you think the memories will leave you alone in Boston?" I didn't mean to be sarcastic, but that was the way it sounded.

Piper's look suggested I'd overstepped my bounds. She stalked to the closet and pulled out several shirts. "I didn't expect you to understand. You have all the answers. You've always had all the answers."

"Hardly. But do you know who does?"

She tossed more clothes on the bed. "A therapist?"

I shook my head. "I wasn't thinking of a therapist. I meant God."

She rolled her eyes. "Not you too. First Dad and now you. I'll tell you what I told Dad: I just don't see that it helps to involve God. It isn't that I don't believe He exists—I just don't see Him in the details."

"Why not?"

I could tell by her expression it wasn't the question she'd anticipated. "Well, just look around at the world. There are far too many problems—too much sickness—too many ugly, angry people for God to have any real say."

"That's what I used to think. God seemed pretty distant. If He was all powerful, why didn't He make the world a better place?"

"Exactly." Piper picked up a shirt and folded it. "So please don't expect me to buy into it. My own life is proof that God just doesn't care."

I wasn't knowledgeable enough to give a convincing argument. I knew there were verses that showed how we'd sinned and needed God. I knew that we were obligated to admit our sin and need for a Savior, but otherwise it was just my own personal experience that I could go on. And that really wasn't much at all.

"Piper, I won't pretend that I have all the answers. I just know that I felt like you. I had a great big emptiness inside me that I knew would eventually consume me. I felt so alone. I felt like no one in the world could possibly care or understand."

She tipped her head my way, seeming to really hear me. I went on quickly. "I didn't know how to find my way out of that. I struggled against it with therapy and work, but I only seemed to sink deeper. And believe me, I don't have it all worked out—I don't know how it can possibly all work—but I prayed yesterday, and for the first time ever I felt that God really heard me."

"That sounds great for you, Bailee. I hope for your sake that it gives you peace of mind. But I don't think God can help me. I think I'm crazy—just like our mother. He didn't help her, and He won't help me."

I crossed the room to take hold of her. "That isn't true. God was there for Momma. She couldn't always see it or understand His love, but God was there for her. Oh, Piper, please don't go. Stay at least a couple more days and talk to Dad and Judith. Let them know what you're going through."

Piper pushed me hard. "No! I told you I don't want to talk to them or anyone else."

"Please, Piper. You've done this your way for years now. You told me yourself that you've been sad for a long, long while. It hasn't worked."

"Just go back to bed, Bailee. I don't want to talk about this. You aren't in control anymore. You aren't my mother and I don't want your advice."

Her words hurt, but I didn't want to cause her more pain. I backed away a few steps and drew a deep breath. "You're right. I'm not your mother. I'm your sister. I don't want to advise you—I just want to love you."

"Well, I'm not looking for love or advice."

I thought of Mark's comment to me—how I was looking so hard for love. Piper was looking for love too. She just didn't know it. And just like Mark with me, I couldn't show her the truth.

"I don't want to leave you like this."

She looked at me oddly. "I'm not going to jump off a building like Mom, if that's what you're worried about."

Her comment sent a shiver through me. "Piper, I just don't think it's good for you to be alone. I definitely don't think you should leave without telling anyone. Please. Just wait for daylight and I'll drive you to the ferry myself. I'll even drive you to the airport if that's what you want."

"What I want has never mattered," Piper said, raising her voice. "I wanted a mother. I wanted a real family with a mom and dad. I wanted to live in a house with my sisters—not some boarding school." She shoved a pair of pants into the suitcase.

"What I've wanted all of my life was normalcy, and no one could give it to me. I wanted a puppy and friends. I wanted birthday parties and—" Her voice broke and she shook it off. Sniffing back tears, she shook her head almost violently. "No. I'm not going to have this conversation with you. Especially not with you."

Her words stung, but I tried not to show it. "If not with me, then with Dad or Judith or even Geena. Talk to one of them if you don't want to have anything to do with me."

Her expression suggested she thought I was completely crazy. "You ought to understand if anyone does," she said. "I can't talk to anyone in this family. You're all a part of the same conspiracy. Oh sure, we're all so very adult about it now. All so proud of ourselves for speaking the horror aloud and admitting there has been a monster living under the bed all these years. But it's too little too late."

"But it doesn't have to be that way, Piper." Her declaration made me even more concerned that she was contemplating suicide. "Now that the truth has come out, we can—"

"What?" she interrupted. "Fix it? This can't be fixed, Bailee." She sounded exhausted, as if any further movement would require effort she simply didn't have. "If I promise to stay until it's light, will you please go and leave me alone?"

I nodded. If that was the only way to get her to agree, I had to do what I could. It would be easy enough to keep an eye on her. I could leave my bedroom door open and watch to be sure she didn't leave. She would have to pass by my room if she were to head out.

"I'll be in my room if you need me—if you want to talk or . . . whatever," I said and walked to the door.

Piper looked hesitant. She opened her mouth to speak, then closed it. Shaking her head, she went back to the closet for more clothes. Without turning around I heard her determined voice. "Just go."

Back in my room I set my door ajar and crawled onto the bed. I could see the hallway lit by the dim glow of the night-light. I felt sick at heart. There was nothing I could do to help Piper. She was desperate and determined.

"I just want to help her, but I can't," I whispered. "I can't change the past and I can't fix the present." But even as I said it, I knew who could. Prayer was all so new to me, but at this place and time, it seemed the most natural thing I'd done in years.

"She needs you, God. Please help her. Please let the healing begin for her—for all of us."

∽

I couldn't suppress my yawns as I stepped onto the deck. I'd fallen asleep sometime after my conversation with Piper, and when I awoke, her room was empty. Dad and Judith were busy at the barbecue grill. I'd fully intended to tell them that Piper was gone, but instead I found her sitting beside Geena, sipping orange juice.

"You look tired," Geena commented.

I nodded and sank into a seat. "I am. I didn't sleep well last night."

Judith brought a plate of grilled ham to the table. "Since the rain cleared we thought we'd enjoy breakfast out here."

I noticed a bowl of scrambled eggs and a platter of toast. "It sounds great," I admitted. I looked around. "Did Mark decide to sleep in?"

"He had a conference call. Said he'd join us as soon as he could," Dad replied, joining us at the table. He offered grace and as soon as he said amen, Piper drew everyone's attention.

"I'm the reason Bailee is so tired."

Everyone stopped mid-reach and looked at Piper. Judith smiled. "Were you girls up talking all night?"

"Not exactly," my youngest sister admitted. "Bailee caught me trying to run away."

I was surprised at her candor. I reached for a piece of toast and tried to act nonchalant about the entire matter.

"Why would you want to run away?"

Dad asked good-naturedly. "You're a grown woman. Grown-ups don't have to run away when they want to leave a place. They just leave." He grew quite serious. "You were never meant to feel like you had to stay."

I completely disagreed with Dad's analysis. Adults ran away all the time. After all, he'd spent most of our childhood and teen years on the run. If anyone knew about getting away from discomfort, it was Dad. But I said nothing. I forced my silence by stuffing toast in my mouth.

Geena reached for the ham and shrugged. "I think adults run away more often than kids, if you want my opinion. When things get uncomfortable they just up and quit. They quit jobs, marriages, families, churches, relationships of all kinds. We aren't exactly a committed people anymore."

"She makes a good point," Judith interjected.

My father considered their comments and nodded. "I suppose I know that better than most."

I felt a sense of relief. I hadn't had to make a single statement and all my thoughts had been expressed. Even so, I supposed I still hadn't learned the value of just being honest and speaking up. There was some sort of war going on inside me that suggested telling the truth equated being cruel. I would need to talk to Dinah about that when we got back to Boston.

"I'm depressed." Piper's simple statement shut everyone up once again. She shrugged. "I've been depressed most of my life. I tried to talk to a counselor in school, but she just said it was normal because I'd lost Mom at such a young age. She told me to meditate on positive thoughts and look for the good things in my life and I would be fine. But I'm not."

"How ridiculous," Geena commented. "That's a bunch of bunk."

Piper sighed. "Bailee kept me from leaving before talking to you all. I didn't want to deal with this, but she gave me a lot to think about. I guess I want to get help." Tears came to her eyes, and she struggled to speak. "I'm just so afraid that I'm crazy . . . like Mom."

To my surprise, it was Judith who acted first. She put her arm around Piper and pulled her close. "Don't be afraid. We're here for you. We won't abandon you." She stroked Piper's hair and let my sister cry.

Dad looked pale and distressed. I could almost hear the questions pouring through his thoughts. Is this the beginning of schizophrenia? Is Piper going to end up like her mother? How do we handle this without making it worse?

Judith continued to deal with the matter as if

none of us was there. "Piper, we can head back to Boston whenever you'd like. When we get there I'll help you set up a physical. That's the best place to start. You may just be run down or deficient in something. Don't give yourself over to worrying about the worst-case scenario until we've at least gone that far."

Piper lifted her face to Judith. "Will you go with me?"

I ignored the stab of pain I felt at her question. I wasn't going to feel betrayed just because Piper wanted Judith to help her in this situation instead of me. I knew that it would be petty to try to make this be about my feelings, but there was that burning question in my heart. I had tried so hard all of my life to be whatever my sisters needed. What did I do wrong?

"I will go with you if you want me to," Judith agreed. "I will even help you find the right people to see."

"Thank you," Piper said. She wiped her face with a napkin and looked back to me. "Please don't be angry."

Her expression was so full of pain. "I'm not angry," I told her. At least that much was true.

"It's not because I don't love you," she added. "It's not really about you at all. I just need someone who can be . . . well . . . I guess . . ." She stammered for the right word.

"Objective?" I asked with new understanding. I was too close—too connected to the problem. Piper needed a neutral third party, although I knew Judith was anything but neutral toward her new stepdaughter.

"Yes," Piper said. "Objective."

"I think that's very wise." I reached for the coffee and poured myself a cup. This was how the healing would start, I thought. Perhaps we would one day look back on this moment and realize that God had begun to knit us back together as a family. Not because of my abilities or my desires, but because of His.

CHAPTER 20

Mark still hadn't joined us by the time breakfast was over, so Geena and I went ahead and cleared the table. Dad and Judith took Piper for a walk on the beach so they could talk, and the time afforded Geena and I an opportunity to do likewise.

"I was surprised when Piper asked Judith to accompany her to the doctor," Geena began, "so I figure you must have been pretty hurt by it."

There was no sense in lying. I put a bowl in the dishwasher and straightened. "It did hurt, but I think I'm seeing the good of it. Judith truly can be more objective than any of us. I'm not Piper's mother, and in trying to take on so much responsibility with her and with you, it's robbed me of the rightful position I had to just be your sister and friend."

Geena looked at me with such intensity that I had a feeling I wasn't going to like her next comment. "Do you think Piper is schizophrenic?"

Hadn't I already asked myself that question a hundred times? I shrugged. "I don't know, and frankly, I'm not even going to try to guess. I've spent my entire adulthood doing that. At least she's willing to seek professional help. Now I don't have to be the one to second-guess her actions."

"But surely you have an opinion. I mean, you know more about this than I do. You remember Mom better than I can. Did Mom act like Piper?"

"I don't know, Geena. I can't remember when Mom first started getting sick. I know Mom was sad much of the time. I guess learning about Noah explains a lot. Dealing with her demons couldn't have been easy."

"And maybe Piper is having the same struggle with her demons. Maybe the truth has been staring us in the eye for years."

"The truth is supposed to set us free," I said, considering all that had happened. "Even with all that's been revealed, however, I feel like there's just more work—more to confront."

"Like searching out the details for a case," Geena agreed.

"Exactly. And I can't help but feel there is something else I'm here to do—to understand.

I don't know what it is, but I'm not ready to leave until I figure it out."

Geena looked at me for a moment. "So stay. Just because they're going back doesn't mean you can't stick around. Maybe I can even stay an extra few days."

"I suppose you're right. We could stay up at the cottage and let the rentals start up here at the house. I wouldn't want Dad to lose all of his summer income." I smiled.

"Especially now."

"What do you mean?"

Geena leaned closer, although there was really no need. "I think Dad is planning to retire early. He didn't say so, but there were just little things I heard him comment on to Judith."

"Well, I certainly hadn't considered that possibility." Dad's work had seemed to be his life for so long. "Do you really think he would quit?"

"I don't know why not. He built up the business, but I know he prides himself on having trained a good team. My guess is he'll sell out his interest in it and be done."

"Then what?" I couldn't imagine him sitting at home doing nothing.

"That's where one of those comments comes in. I think he and Judith would like to travel a bit—see the world."

"He's seen the world many times over," I said, putting detergent into the dishwasher.

"Yes, but only from a business perspective, and always alone," Geena replied. "Having someone to share it with would make for a completely new adventure."

"Anybody at home?" Mark called from the front of the house.

"We're in the kitchen." I set the cycle on the machine and turned my attention to the plate we'd kept for Mark. "We saved you breakfast," I told him as he popped around the corner.

"Wonderful. I'm starved." He was wearing jeans and a black T-shirt. I'd never seen him looking so casual.

He grinned at me with such enthusiasm I couldn't help but return the smile. "Your meeting must have gone very well."

Shaking his head, Mark took the plate Geena offered. "Not at all. In fact, I have to fly back to New York immediately."

I felt a deep sense of disappointment. "Oh. Well, it's just that you seemed so cheerful." I turned away, hoping he wouldn't see my frown. I wiped the counter and tried to think of something else to say.

"I'm going upstairs to clean the bathroom," Geena said. "It's my turn. Mark, if you want to pop that in the microwave, it's there just over the stove."

"Thanks."

I heard Mark cross behind me, but I kept my focus on several coffee rings that had stained the counter. The microwave hummed to life and I remembered that we still had coffee in the pot.

"Would you like a cup of coffee?"

"I would. Why don't you pour two and come sit with me while I eat."

My feelings were back under control, so I smiled and turned around. "Of course."

He was still grinning like he'd just won the lottery or a trip to Hawaii. I cocked my head. "For someone who had a horrible meeting, you certainly seem delighted."

Laughing, he stepped forward and pulled me into his arms. I looked up without thinking and found his mouth only a fraction of an inch away from mine. "Your dad told me about your decision."

It all became clear and I pulled back just a bit. "This is about my talk with God? You're smiling like an idiot because I made sense of the voice I'd been hearing?"

"It makes me very happy," he declared.

I looked at him oddly. "And just why would it make you so happy?"

"Because it eliminates any obstacle in my way to putting my plans in motion."

"Your plans? And exactly what plans are you talking about?"

"Let me show you phase one," he said in a low, intriguing tone. He touched his lips to mine, and I felt my body melt against him.

It was like I had no will of my own. I wrapped my arms around his neck and gave in to my emotions. I stopped worrying about my sisters and our potential risk of mental illness. I put aside my insecurities and wounded feelings about having done my best to hold the family together. I even let go of my deepest fear that something was still unresolved, and passionately returned Mark's kiss.

He trailed his mouth from my lips and showered my face with kisses so tender and enticing that I thought I might very well stop breathing. Was this what it was to be in love—to know true love?

My heart was pounding hard, and I pulled away, rather embarrassed by my own desire. "Wow," I said, trying to gather my thoughts. "Phase one certainly packs a punch."

He laughed and pulled me toward him again. "Just wait until you hear about phase two."

I put my hands between us and pushed on his chest ever so slightly. "I think we need to spend some time considering this phase before we move on."

His grin didn't fade. "I thought phase one was pretty self-explanatory, but perhaps I should reiterate my point." His blue eyes twinkled, and I couldn't help but feel his joy permeate my defenses.

I quickly broke his hold and moved to put the kitchen island between us. Just then the microwave chimed and I pointed. "Your breakfast is ready."

Mark chuckled and went to pop open the door and retrieve his plate. "I thought you said there was coffee."

Steadying myself against the island, I nodded. "I'll bring it to the table. The clouds are starting to build in the sky, but I think we're safe from rain if you want to eat on the deck."

"Sounds good." He headed across the room to the sliding door.

I let out a breath and went to the cupboard for a couple of mugs. I wasn't at all sure I had the strength to explore what phase two might involve. With a shaky hand, I poured the coffee and headed to the deck. Was it acceptable to pray that God might keep me from jumping into the arms of a man who could kiss so thoroughly that I forgot my name?

Mark sat at the table with the chair pushed out. He patted his lap. "I saved you a seat."

I handed him his coffee and moved quickly to the other side. "I'll just sit over here."

He laughed and gave me a wink. "Chicken?"

"Absolutely."

That only made him laugh harder. He put the coffee on the table and scooted up. He bowed his head. "Father, thank you for this day and this meal. Thank you for answering my prayers. Thank you for this woman and thank you for what you're going to do. Amen."

I looked at him over the rim of my coffee cup. There was no way I was going to ask him what he meant by that last part. Instead, I hurried to ask him about work.

"So what has happened at the publishing house?"

"There's conflict with two different authors over two entirely different issues. Their agents are causing all sorts of problems and Dad wants me to handle it. Push all of the pro-verbial pieces into place, so to speak. He also wants to know if I've convinced you to move to New York and join our office."

After everything that had happened that morning, I wasn't sure exactly what my answer would be. If Piper proved to have schizophrenia, I couldn't help but wonder what my responsibility might be. I chided myself silently. I just didn't seem to get it. Piper wasn't my responsibility.

"*You have to take care of your sisters or bad things will happen.*" My mother's voice echoed in my head. I frowned.

"What's wrong?" Mark asked.

I looked at him, not really even seeing him for a moment. In my mind I was in a dark room and my mother was trying to hide me. The image was fleeting and Mark's face came into focus.

"My sister Piper is having trouble. She's worried that she's going crazy—schizophrenic."

"And do you think that's the case?"

"I used to think that I'd know if my sisters were showing signs of mental illness."

"But not now?" He took a bite of food and reached for the salt.

"No. I don't think I'm at all qualified. I'm an editor. I know books."

He nodded. "Indeed you do. Which is all the more reason to say yes to our offer. We need you. We need your expertise."

I heard my dad's voice in conversation. "Sounds like Dad and Judith are coming back. They went for a walk with Piper to talk about getting her help. She's agreed to see a doctor and she wants Judith to go with her."

"Not you?"

I bit my lower lip for a moment. "No. And really, that's all right. I haven't had much time to process it, but I think once I really consider it, I'm going to be happy. Judith is a loving woman."

"She certainly seems to be. Let your sister know that I have a good friend practicing psychiatry in the Boston area. He's quite trustworthy—and a Christian."

Just then I could see Dad and Piper top the stairs below. Judith was right behind them. I saw Dad put his arm around Piper's shoulder and hug her close. She seemed calm—even happy. I noticed Judith catch sight of us. She waved and said something to Dad. He looked up and gave me a nod.

Piper saw me and smiled. I felt a sense of relief. Maybe it would be all right for me to linger here once they had gone. Maybe it would work out for me to take the job in New York City.

"Guess I'll have to wait to share phase two with you until later," Mark murmured.

Piper was the first one on the deck. She greeted Mark, then looked at me. "Thanks for what you said to me this morning."

I was surprised by her comment. "You're welcome." I didn't know what else to say.

"I know I wasn't very nice to you, and I'm sorry." She leaned down and hugged me. "I love you, and I know you just wanted to help."

"You're right," I agreed. "I do want to help. I love you."

Piper straightened and looked at Dad and Judith. "I'm going to go take a shower."

She left without another word and I looked to Dad. He and Judith took a seat at the table between Mark and me.

"We're going to fly back day after tomorrow," he explained.

"Mark has to head back to New York immediately," I said.

"Yeah, I called and have a flight out this afternoon," he told them.

I hadn't realized this, but just nodded. "Geena and I might stick around a day or two," I said, toying with my now empty coffee cup. "At least I might. I guess I shouldn't speak for Geena."

"Sounds fine," Dad said. "Just let us know when you leave and we'll start up the rentals."

"If you like, we can stay at the cottage so that you can at least rent out the house."

Dad nodded. "That would be fine. I'll let the caretakers know." He reached out to Mark and touched his shoulder. "I suppose Bailee will be taking you back to Seattle?"

"I hadn't asked her yet, but I'm hoping so. I'd like the extra time. I'm still trying to convince her to take the job in New York." He looked at me and grinned. "I also have to clarify some information regarding several phases of a project she's a part of."

I felt my face flush and quickly jumped to my feet. "Well, if I'm going to drive you to SeaTac, I'd better change my clothes." It was a poor excuse, as I was dressed perfectly for the trip. Mark chuckled and I ignored him. "I'll only be a minute."

CHAPTER 21

We had plenty of time, so I opted to drive Mark to SeaTac rather than take the ferry. The overcast skies promised rain, but that didn't bother me. What did bother me was the way Mark watched me from the passenger seat. I had expected him to be talkative and full of references to the kiss we'd shared earlier. Instead he just sat there grinning like he knew I was reliving that moment over and over. Of course . . . I was.

Finally, I couldn't take it anymore. "Okay, so let's say we have a . . . relationship . . . hypothetically."

He laughed. "There's nothing hypothetical about it. We have a relationship."

"Of course. Even friendship is a relationship. And then we also have our working relationship," I said and changed lanes to avoid a logging truck. "I just meant suppose we were to get romantically involved."

"Like kissing and being breathless in each other's arms?"

I had to slam on the brakes to avoid rear-ending the white sedan in front of me. Maybe this wasn't the best conversation to have while driving.

"Look, why is it so hard for you to admit that I have an incredibly powerful effect on you?" Mark reached out to touch my hand and I nearly jumped out the window.

"Enough." I saw the exit coming up and signaled to take it. I got off the highway and made my way to the nearest parking lot. Pulling to a stop, I threw the car into park and turned in the seat.

"The last time I opened myself up to let someone affect me the way you do was . . . well . . . it was . . ." I fell silent. "All right, so the truth is I've never opened myself up that way. I've only had two boyfriends my entire life, and neither was anything more than a surface relationship and certainly nothing as serious . . . as this."

"So you feel serious about this?"

I tried to still my racing heart. "Look, I don't feel things lightly. In fact, I don't like to allow myself to feel deeply at all. You have a way of breaking down my defenses."

"And what's wrong with that, Bailee? I'm

crazy about you. In fact, I'm going to go out on a limb here. I love you."

I swallowed hard and felt the breath catch in my throat. It should have been easy to tell Mark that I loved him as well. And I did. But for the life of me I couldn't say the words. I looked at him for several minutes.

"There are still so many questions in my mind. There are things in my past that are unresolved. I don't think I'd make a very good girlfriend . . . or wife for that matter."

His expression grew quite sober. I thought for a moment that maybe I'd offended him by mentioning the idea of marriage. "Bailee, you don't have to settle everything in a day. You've gone through a lot since coming here." His hand covered mine. "I'm not going to make things difficult for you. I want to be there with you—to help with what you need."

"I don't know what I need; that's the problem." I smiled, hoping to reassure him. "I want this to work out. I do."

He returned my smile. "Then we're in agreement on that issue, because I very much want this to work." He made it sound so simple, but I knew in my heart it wasn't.

"I need time. I need to know that Piper is okay. Even if she's schizophrenic . . . I need to know that she's getting treatment and that she has what she needs."

"Bailee, she's not your responsibility."

"I know that, but she is my sister."

"You have to let go sooner or later."

His comment made me defensive. "Look, this is my family, and I don't expect you to understand. Just because I know more now about the past and the secrets that were kept than I did a week ago doesn't mean I'm ready for a commitment. I need time. I need to talk through all of this with my therapist and . . . and with God."

"But not me?" He sounded hurt. "Is she a Christian therapist?"

I shrugged. "I never worried about asking and it's never really come up. Dinah is good at what she does."

"I understand. Just keep in mind that it might become an issue. As you draw closer to God and learn more about what the Bible says . . . well, you might find that the suggestions of a non-Christian won't line up. Just be prepared. Have some options. Like I said earlier—I have a friend in the area."

I didn't want to further offend him, but the last thing I wanted to do was change therapists. The idea of Dinah being offended by my new acceptance of Christian values had never really entered my thoughts, and I couldn't honestly say how I would respond if that turned out to be the case. "I'll keep that in mind."

He looked at me like he couldn't quite decide whether I was telling the truth or not. He let out a long breath and leaned back against the seat. "Funny, I thought I knew all the obstacles I was facing in this relationship."

I looked at him and felt a strange sense of loss. Was he going to give up on us? Was it unfair of me to beg him to hang in there with me . . . to give me time to sort through my issues? Would I lose him because I needed to do this on my own?

Mark gave me a sad sort of smile. "You'd better get me to the airport or I'll miss my flight."

I wanted to say something, but the words stuck in my throat. How could I reassure him when I didn't know where my journey might take me? I wanted to pledge him my undying love, but in all honesty I knew that wasn't realistic. I was far too practical to pretend otherwise.

⁂

I was sorry to see Mark walk into the airport. Sorrier still to board the Bremerton ferry without him. I wanted to call him the moment I drove up onto dry land again. I wanted to tell him I'd been wrong—that I would take the job in New York and that I'd commit to whatever relationship he wanted. But I didn't. I knew my fear was driving my heart.

Do not fear, for I am with you. Those words offered me the only comfort I could find.

My regrets culminated as I parked the rental car in the driveway at home and looked at the house, knowing he was gone. It was raining and I had been feeling rather punk since the ferry ride. I'd thought maybe it was a bit of seasickness since the waters were choppy, but now that I was home I felt even worse. A chill rushed through me, leaving me longing for bed.

The house was empty when I went inside. I guessed that Dad and Judith had taken Geena and Piper out for supper. My watch showed that it was a little after six thirty. My throat was scratchy and I was still nauseated. Maybe some tea would help.

I went to the cupboard to look for an herbal decaffeinated blend. I didn't want anything to keep me awake all night. It was going to be hard enough to think of Mark being gone and of my family heading back to Boston. Maybe staying on wasn't a good idea. After all, I hadn't really approached Geena about how long she could remain. She might have already decided to head back with the others.

Then too, I wanted to have some time with Dinah—some intense therapy regarding all that I'd learned. I wanted to tell her about Mark and my commitment to God, and I wanted to know how she felt about a Christian point of view.

I gave up my search for tea and popped some cold tabs instead. My head was swimming and I decided to head for bed, my exhaustion quickly catching up with me. I crawled into bed and let my body slide down the pile of pillows. It was almost like being in a warm embrace. I thought of Mark and hoped he wasn't feeling as bad as I was.

I closed my eyes and wondered when we might see each other again. Could I wait until the regular monthly editorial meeting? My eyes blurred and I closed them. A veil of mist fell over my conscious mind.

"Be very quiet, Bailee. You have to stay here and be very quiet so they don't find you or the baby. Everything will be all right." She handed me my doll.

I looked up at my mother, not quite trusting her. I was afraid. She'd placed me inside an old box, and I was sure I'd seen some bugs in the bottom. Momma pressed me down with one hand while closing the box over me with the other.

"Stop whimpering, Bailee. They'll hear you."

I was so scared. I clutched my dolly close and fought back tears. I had to be quiet or the bad men would find me.

There was the tiniest hole where someone had damaged the box. I moved to the glimmer of light and pressed my eye against it. I could see Momma move to the far side of the room. She picked up my sleeping brother and put him in some kind of sack or maybe a bag. Next she put that on the floor and piled blankets around and over him. She turned to go, but paused at the door.

"Don't make a sound," she whispered. "I'll come back for you."

It seemed like hours before she did, however. I was cold and ached from sitting cramped up in the box. I had tried to get out at one point, but something heavy had been placed on top and the cardboard refused to give way.

Momma opened the box and held out her hands for me. "We're safe now."

I looked at her. "Were there bad men, Momma?"

"Yes," she said very seriously. "They wanted to take you away, but they couldn't find you."

I held my doll tight. "And brudder?"

"Your brother is safe too. Go get him. He's over there in the blankets."

I hurried to where I'd seen her leave him earlier. I pushed back one heavy blanket after another, but I couldn't find him. "Where? Where's brudder?"

My mother was there beside me. She pointed out the black bag. The black plastic trash bag at the bottom of the pile. "He's right here." She acted so casual about the whole thing. She opened the bag and drew out the still baby.

Noah didn't move or cry. Momma cradled him in her arms and smiled. "Now we can go back in the house. And remember, Bailee. Don't say a word to your daddy. If you tell him about hiding here, the bad men might hear."

I followed her—my bare feet cold from the chilled, damp ground. The threat of being stolen from my home was never far from my mind.

We went into the house and down a long narrow hall. Momma opened a door. It was our room. Mine and the baby's. She placed Noah in the crib and fixed me with a stern expression.

"It's your job to watch him while I go fix us some lunch. This is your responsibility, Bailee. Your job. Keep your brother safe."

I nodded, nearly dancing from the need to go relieve myself. "I have to go potty."

"Hurry up. You can't watch him if you're

not here." She left then and I hurried down the hall. My half-frozen feet tingled as they hit the cold of the tiled bathroom floor. I struggled with my pants and barely climbed onto the stool in time.

By the time I finished and climbed my little stepstool to wash my hands, I could hear that my father was home.

"Daddy!" I squealed in delight as I ran down the hallway. He lifted me in the air and twirled me in a circle. It was always a treat to have him home.

"Bailee, you're supposed to be watching the baby."

"He sleepin'," I told my father.

"Let's go see." Daddy tousled my hair and carried me to our room. "Ah, there he is," Daddy whispered.

"He sleepin'," I repeated.

Daddy put me down and went to the crib. "He sure is." My father reached out a finger to touch Noah's cheek. He pulled back his hand and looked oddly at the baby. He flicked on the lamp beside the bed and gave Noah a shake.

"Natalie! Natalie! Come quickly. It's the baby—he's not breathing."

My mother rushed into the room, her face pale. "What are you saying?"

Dad had picked up Noah by this time. He

was shouting at my mother to call the police—to call for help. My mother began screaming. She tried to rip my brother out of my father's arms.

"Go call them, Natalie. Hurry."

Daddy began blowing into Noah's mouth. I backed into the corner of my room and put my thumb in my mouth. So many people came and there was so much noise. My mother cried and screamed at everyone. My brother kept sleeping, but somehow I knew this wasn't right. Still I sat in the corner and rocked back and forth.

At one point my mother caught sight of me. She came to where I sat and yanked me up from the floor. "What have you done? This is your fault. Your fault!"

"No! No! I did good. I did good. I was quiet. I didn't make noise. The bad men didn't take me." I was rambling and crying as she shook me.

A uniformed police officer came to my mother and took me out of her grasp. "Mrs. Cooper, I know this has been a terrible shock, but it's not going to help for you to shake your daughter. The baby died from SIDS."

I had no understanding of what SIDS might be; I just knew that it was very, very bad and that my mother blamed me.

"If she'd been in here watching him like I told her to, he wouldn't be dead."

The officer held me tight. "No, ma'am. She couldn't have known he was in distress. He passed on in his sleep. There was no struggle. She's just a little girl. She didn't know. You could have been sitting right beside him yourself and you wouldn't have known."

My mother slapped me so quickly that the officer didn't even have time to protect me. The pain was intense. My father came up from behind her and took hold of her as she ranted and screamed and fought. I screamed as the policeman took me out of the room.

"It was your job to keep him safe!" my mother screamed. "Your job, Bailee!"

"Bailee, wake up. Bailee!"

I opened my eyes to see my father standing over me. Judith was at the foot of the bed and my sisters were standing in the open door.

My breath came in rapid pants and my throat was so dry I could hardly recognize that the screaming and moaning I heard was coming from my own throat. I sat up but the room swam before me.

"It was just a nightmare," my father said. He touched my face. "She's burning up. Bailee, are you sick?"

Just then my stomach churned. "I'm gonna throw up."

Judith reacted quickly. She grabbed my

empty waste can and brought it to the bed just as I began to dry heave. "Piper, would you get your sister some water? Geena, do we have something for a fever?"

"I'll go look," Geena said.

My stomach finally calmed a bit and I gave a shudder and moan. "It was so horrible, Dad."

"The nightmare?"

Dad sat down on the bed beside me, and I grabbed hold of him like there was no tomorrow. "No," I said hoarsely. "It wasn't just a nightmare. It was . . . a memory. It was when Noah died."

My father frowned. Judith turned to take the glass of water Piper had just brought back. "Here, just take a sip and spit it out." I did as instructed.

Geena returned with a couple of aspirins. "These ought to help with the fever."

"Thank you," Judith said and passed me the pills. "I know your stomach is upset, so maybe wait a little bit before you take these."

I nodded and Dad took the pills from me and placed them on the nightstand. He smiled and pushed back my hair. "Now then, I'll send the girls to the store for some soda and crackers. That ought to help with the nausea."

"Oh, have them get some chicken soup too," Judith suggested.

I was frustrated that no one wanted to hear about my memory. I pulled on Dad's arm like a small child might. "Dad, listen to me. I know what happened to Noah. I remember what happened."

"That's fine, sweetheart, but you need to rest." He looked at Judith and then to my sisters. The look on their faces suggested a problem. Did they think I was crazy? Were they afraid of me—of the scene I'd just made?

The memory lingered and wouldn't let me go. "She killed him," I said. "Momma killed Noah. She said it was my fault, but it wasn't. It was hers."

My father shook his head. "No, Bailee. It was SIDS. Noah died of Sudden Infant Death Syndrome. It wasn't her fault or yours."

I pulled back. "No, you don't understand. She took us out and hid us in the garage or some sort of shed. She hid Noah in a garbage bag and put me in a box. She buried Noah at the bottom of a pile of blankets."

Dad's eyes widened and his face paled. "What are you saying?"

"She used to hide us. She said bad men were coming to take us away. She said if I told you, the men would overhear and find me. She told me they would take me away forever. She hid us that day. I don't know how long we were out there. When she came back for us . . . when she told me to get Noah, I couldn't find him." I began to sob. "Oh, Daddy . . . I couldn't find him."

My father reached out and took hold of my arm. "Bailee, it's all right."

I shook my head over and over. "She took him out of the bag and he didn't move. He didn't cry. He never woke up again. We went in the house, and she put him in the bed. I thought he was asleep, but he wasn't." I put my hands to my face and wept as I never had before. My head throbbed from the tirade.

Dad pulled me into his arms, but his embrace was one of someone in shock. It was like he'd lost his son all over again, and this time . . . this time it really was my fault.

CHAPTER 22

When Mark called later that night to let me know he'd gotten back to New York safely, Geena happened to be the one checking on me and picked up the call.

"Bailee's phone, this is Geena," she answered.

I saw Geena nod. "She's right here, Mark, but she's sick. Caught a bug of some sort."

I held up my hand to take the phone. Geena didn't hesitate. She handed me the cell, but refused to leave.

"Hello?" My voice was gravelly and dry.

"You sound awful. What happened? This afternoon you were fine."

"I'm not sure. It hit me pretty fast." I coughed to clear my throat but it did no good. "I was on the way home when I just started feeling like I was catching a cold or something. Anyway, I'm sick."

"Well, I just wanted to let you know I'd

made it back safely." The tone of his voice sounded detached—almost like he was purposefully trying not to feel too much.

"I'm glad," I said and my energy began to fade. I wanted to tell him about my memory, but I didn't have the strength. I wondered if Geena would mind filling in.

"I'll let you go then. I need to be up early."

"Oh—all right. Good night."

"That was short," Geena said, taking the phone from my hand. I nodded and closed my eyes. Had I sabotaged myself? I couldn't think clearly and struggled to make sense of it all. Maybe it was just the sickness talking, but I felt as though I'd just lost my best friend.

The night passed with me slipping in and out of sleep. At one point I woke up in a sweat, despite only having a sheet over me. I threw back the soft Egyptian cotton cover with the strength of a newborn kitten.

"Don't get chilled," Judith commanded. She got up from the overstuffed chair and came to the bed.

"How come you're sleeping in the chair?" I asked.

She drew the sheet back over me, then reached out a hand to touch my forehead. "Because you had a fever of 103. That merits some special attention. If it wasn't lower by morning, we planned to take you to the hospital. You feel cooler now, however."

"I feel much better. Not so achy."

"That's a good sign." She took up a washcloth and wiped my forehead. "We've been worried about you."

"Anybody else sick?"

She shook her head. "No. Not yet anyway."

She was so very tender with me. Her gentleness made me think of how many times I'd longed for a mother's gentle touch.

"Judith, may I ask you a question about your childhood?"

"Of course." She stopped her ministering and sat beside me. "What is it you want to know?"

"Did you have a good relationship with your mother?"

She smiled and pushed back my damp hair. "I did and still do. Why do you ask?"

"I don't know. I guess because I never did, but I saw other girls who did. I always envied them. They were proud to have their mothers around—they liked doing things together. To see some of them openly show their love. . . . I can't explain how it affected me."

"That had to be hard on you."

"It still is. When I watch television or a movie where someone has that kind of relationship, I find myself wavering between bitter anger and a longing so deep it threatens to stop my heart." I shook my head. "Well, maybe not that—but it is painful."

Judith put her hand on mine. "I can't imagine the sadness of being a child in your position. To grow up without the affection and attention you deserved must have been hideous. To instead find yourself responsible for things and people that you had no business safeguarding was not only difficult, but most unfair. No child should have had to face the things you did."

It was only then that I thought of Dad and how my revelation must have devastated him. "Is Dad okay?"

My stepmother looked at her hands. "He's very upset. Of course, he's worried about you more than anything."

I tried to sit up, but my head was still a mess. I fell back, dizzy, and closed my eyes. "Do you think he'd come and talk to me here?"

She nodded. "I know he would. He sat with you part of the night."

The thought of that touched me, and I refixed my gaze on Judith. "He did?"

"He would have stayed the entire night if I'd let him. Instead, I insisted we take shifts and that way we could be rested for the morning in case you were worse and needed to go to the hospital." She got up. "I'll get him."

I waited for his return, feeling weak and completely incapable. Whatever bug I'd managed to catch was clearly doing a number on me.

"Hey, babe, are you feeling better?" Dad asked as he came into the room. He was wearing a T-shirt and matching baggy sleeping pants. But he didn't look like he'd managed much rest.

"My head still hurts and I'm dizzy. My aching is better though, and I don't feel like I want to heave my guts onto the floor."

He smiled and sat down beside me, where Judith had been only moments before. I reached out and took hold of his hand. It wasn't something either of us expected. In fact, it was rather foreign to the both of us.

"Dad, I'm so sorry for just blurting out all that stuff about Noah and Mom."

He put a finger to my lips. "Never apologize for the truth."

I let my breath out in a whoosh. I hadn't realized I'd been holding it. "So you . . . believe me?"

"Of course. Why shouldn't I?" He shook his head. "I should have known. I should have at least guessed. People kept telling me there was something wrong with your mother—that I shouldn't leave you kids alone with her. I just figured their concerns were unfounded."

"Who was concerned?" I asked, feeling my strength give out.

"Neighbors, and later teachers, school officials. It was one of the reasons I kept us moving. If we stayed too long in one place, people started asking a lot of questions. Why is your wife so obsessed with her children? Why doesn't she see to it that the children attend school regularly? Things like that."

A thread of anger coursed through my body. Despite being sick, I looked at him hard. "And even though people were asking questions, you just let it go on?"

He nodded and looked away. "I'm sorry. I just never thought your mother was a danger. You girls always seemed pretty happy. I remember things were bad for a while after Noah died, but everyone—the doctor, your mother's pastor, my mother—everyone said it was normal for your mother to act out her feelings and focus them on the child who survived."

"So you left me to her mercy?" I could hardly make sense of what he was saying. I closed my eyes. "How could you just turn your back on me?" I drifted into a haze of questions that had no answers. It felt like a battle was going on inside of me and the winner would determine how I responded to my father.

"Bailee?" At the sound of Dad calling my name, I opened my eyes.

"What?"

"I was talking to you, but you fell asleep." He touched my forehead. "We can talk about this later."

"But you're leaving to go back to Boston," I protested.

"No. We'll wait until you feel better—we all agreed that it was best."

I gave a weak nod. "If you promise that we'll talk later."

"I promise."

∽

When I woke up again it was late in the afternoon. On the dresser opposite the bed stood a huge bouquet of flowers. Stargazer lilies and white roses dominated the cluster, and I couldn't help but remember the bouquet Mark had bought for me at the market.

I started to get up and investigate, but noticed that someone had put a dining room chair beside my bed. There was a bell and a note on it. I picked up the paper.

Ring for service, it read.

The thought made me smile, and I gave the bell an enthusiastic shake. I was still ringing when Piper and Geena popped in.

"You certainly look better," Geena declared. "Terribly pale and disheveled, but better."

"Gee, thanks," I replied.

"Man, you scared us all half to death," Piper said. "Are you hungry?"

I considered her question for a moment and shook my head. "I could stand something to drink. I was really just wondering about the flowers."

Geena laughed and retrieved a card from the arrangement. "Who do you suppose sent them?"

I took the card from her and opened it. " 'Will be praying for your speedy recovery. Mark.' "

"Just 'Mark'? No 'forever yours' or 'with deepest love'?" Piper asked. She seemed far cheerier than I'd seen her in a while.

I put the card aside. "I'm not sure what he feels."

"Oh please." Geena rolled her eyes. "He's crazy about you." She took a seat on the chair and Piper perched on the bed beside me.

"And do you love him?" Piper asked innocently enough. "Are wedding bells ringing?"

I shook my head. "I don't know. I think I . . . I do love him, but marriage is out of the question—at least for a time. I have a lot to sort through after coming here and remembering Noah. This has been such a hard time."

Piper reached out and took hold of my hand. "You saved me from dying like he did."

"I'm sure you saved me as well," Geena

said. "I'm so sorry, Bailee. I'm sorry for all you had to go through. What a nightmare it must have been."

"You must have felt so alone." Piper drew my hand to her own. "I'm so sorry."

Their declarations made me feel strange. I was relieved that they finally understood about the past, but I was confused as to where to go from here.

"Judith had a suggestion," Geena began. "She thought maybe it would be helpful if the three of us girls went to counseling together. We could have some sessions where we talked from our own perspective about . . . Mom and those times."

I looked from Geena to Piper, who was nodding. "And you'd both be willing?"

"I think it's time we put it all to rest," Geena declared. "It might even help Piper with her sadness. Most of all . . ." She paused and looked at Piper and then back to me. "Most of all I'd hope it would help you."

I felt her squeeze my hand. "I think it would."

CHAPTER 23

I was feeling much better by the second day, and when Dad came into my bedroom to talk, I felt ready to deal with the matters at hand. He pulled up a chair and sat down, looking for all the world to be bearing more weight than ever before. I wasn't surprised. As I'd been lying in bed thinking about baby Noah and my mother, I continued to come back to my father's role in it all. It still made me angry that he had his suspicions and yet did nothing.

"Since you're feeling better, Judith thought you might want to talk."

"I doubt it will be pleasant."

He nodded. "I suppose it's to be expected. I did you wrong, Bailee. I'm not just saying that so you'll forgive me and move on. I'm saying it because I mean it. When you told me what had happened with Noah, it . . . well . . . it sort of confirmed my worst fears."

I scooted up in the bed and stuffed an extra pillow behind me. "In what way?"

"The night before your brother died, your mother was restless. Around midnight she all of a sudden got up from bed. I asked her where she was going, and she told me she had something to do. I suggested she take care of it in the morning, but she said it couldn't wait and she wouldn't be long. She kissed me and told me to go back to sleep. I started to do just that, but I couldn't shake the feeling that I ought to follow her. I deliberated for several minutes, arguing with myself that I was just being paranoid.

"You see, Bailee, your mother was very good at hiding the truth. She appeared so perfectly normal most of the time. But that was in the early years of her disorder. I knew she often 'talked' to her grandmother—who had died when Natalie was six or seven. But there was a part of me that thought that was just her way of coping with the loss of her family. I had no understanding until later that she really saw her grandmother—thought she was alive and well."

"What does that have to do with that night, Dad?" I wanted desperately to keep him focused for fear he'd go off on a rabbit trail that would never return to the path I needed to follow.

"Well, I heard your mom talking to someone, and so I got up and followed after her. She was standing in the doorway to your bedroom—yours and Noah's. She seemed to be having a conversation with someone and it wasn't at all pleasant. She was upset, but her voice was hushed so that she wouldn't wake you."

"What was she saying?"

"She was talking to her grandmother. I couldn't hear it all, but your mother kept saying, 'Don't be mad at me.' Then she said, 'I promise to take care of it; I just can't do it now.' I couldn't imagine what in the world she was talking about, so I interrupted her. She stared at me like I wasn't even there. She seemed so distant—so empty. I took her back to bed and stayed awake until she fell asleep.

"The next morning I asked her about getting up in the night and what was going on. She denied it. Said I must have dreamed it or else she was just sleepwalking. She reminded me we'd both been keeping long hours—me with work, she with a newborn—and were overly tired. It made sense to me—I suppose because I wanted it to. I told myself she'd been sleepwalking and nothing more. I think a part of me even wanted to pretend I had just dreamed up the whole thing."

"But surely you knew the difference between reality and a dream," I said.

Dad folded his hands and leaned back against the chair. "I thought I did. But you have to understand—your mother was so convincing. I went to work that day and told myself that it must have been exactly as she suggested. You have to understand, it was really the first time I'd seen something like this happen. Especially something that involved you kids."

He paused and fixed me with a hard stare. "Bailee, do you remember your mother ever hiding you away before the time with Noah?"

I thought about it for a moment. There were all sorts of nightmares where Mom was hiding us girls, but I honestly couldn't remember times prior to Noah, except for bits and pieces. "I have images of Mom and me alone, but not the fear and anxiety I felt after the others were born. In fact, I didn't realize until now that some of those nightmares I've been having revolved around what happened with Noah—because I didn't remember having a brother. I always figured the baby was Geena or Piper."

"See, I saw a marked change in your mother after she found out she was pregnant with Noah. We had taken precautions because she fully intended to go back to college. Your mother had plans to go to school and do something great with her life. She was really depressed when she found out she was pregnant with Noah."

Imagining Mom so young, realizing she would have to put her dreams aside . . . I immediately felt sorry for her. It couldn't have been easy. Here she already had one unplanned child—me. Now she was going to have another.

"I hate to admit this," Dad went on, "but I suggested she get an abortion. I knew she didn't want another child, and I figured if she aborted the baby she could go ahead with her plans to return to school."

"What happened?"

"She considered it, then decided to talk to someone at her church. They were quite hard on her. They convinced her that she was being purely selfish and that it would be murder. Of course, I believe that now—but I didn't then. Abortion seemed an easy solution.

"Your mother convinced herself that if she had an abortion she would go to hell. The church folk would even call her at home and plead with her to stand strong and carry the pregnancy to term. They even suggested she give the child up for adoption, but when she mentioned that to me . . . well . . . I have to say, I wasn't exactly congenial."

I could well imagine my father's anger at the interference being caused by the church. Dad would have rebelled at even the hint that a supreme deity need run his life.

"When I found out we were having a boy, I no longer wanted her to abort. I told your mother that we needed to go through with this, and then afterward we'd decide how to keep from having additional children. I told her a boy and a girl was a perfect combination and that we could put two children in daycare as easily as one, and she could still go back to school."

"What did she say?"

Dad rubbed his hands along the front of his jeans. "She seemed to agree. I mean, the church folks had convinced her abortion was murder, and now I was glad they had. I wanted a son, and when Noah was born, I couldn't have been happier."

"And Momma?"

"Well, I think she was happy that she'd pleased me, but I think another baby just overwhelmed her. She never did seem to really adjust, and I worried about her. The doctor said it was normal—especially since she hadn't wanted another baby. The doctor said in time she would come to terms with the situation and that I just needed to give her space.

"Your mother seemed to adjust once she

was home, and in the days that followed, I
felt more confident that the doctor had been
right. Your mother appeared quite willing to
care for Noah and you, and even though I
thought she was being too liberal with the way
she allowed you to watch over him and even
carry him at times, I was relieved that things
seemed normal again."

"But they weren't," I said as if he'd forgotten.
He shook his head. "No, they weren't."

"So what happened?"

"Well, like I said, she convinced me that
everything was fine. I went to work, and when
I came home that evening . . . that was when
I found Noah . . . dead."

I put my hand to my mouth. I couldn't even
speak for a moment. I kept thinking of how
awful it must have been for him to know that
something hadn't been quite right, but having
no proof, he'd had to put aside his concerns
and do his job. Then to come home and find
his son dead . . .

"The memories you had . . . from your
nightmare . . . I have to believe were true. I
have no reason to think otherwise. I think your
mother was overwhelmed when she realized
Noah was dead—maybe her mind wouldn't
even accept it when she took him to his crib
after hiding you both. Instead she needed
someone else to blame."

"Me." I shook my head. "She put the blame on me."

He looked away. "Yes."

"I remember the policeman took me away from her because she was so angry. She was shaking me and yelling at me."

Dad met my eyes. "Yes, that happened."

"She told me it was my fault. And she slapped me hard. The police officer was angry with her. You came and took hold of her."

He nodded. "It was just like that."

I closed my eyes. "The officer took me out of the room and Mom continued to scream after me. I was so scared. I thought the officer was a bad man taking me away. I thought I would never see any of you again." I felt the fear tightening around my throat.

Dad reached out and took hold of my hand. "I'm so sorry, Bailee. I'm sorry that you remember any of that."

All of my life I had lived with a guilt that couldn't be explained. I had taken on responsibility for my sisters—motivated by a fear that I couldn't understand. There had been such desperation in our relationship. Now I understood why.

"A few nights after Noah's death, I found your mother wandering around the backyard. She was in her nightclothes and it was cold for March in northern Texas. She was murmuring to herself, and as I drew closer I realized she was talking to her grandmother again. I didn't understand then, but I do now."

"What was she saying?" I asked, almost afraid to know.

"She kept saying over and over, "See, I took care of it, Grandma. Don't be mad. I took care of it.""

I felt a chill come over me. "She killed Noah on purpose? It wasn't just an accident caused by her paranoia?"

Dad didn't need to answer. I could see the truth in his expression. Until that moment, I hadn't realized just how many pieces were missing from the Cooper family puzzle. I guessed we all had our places that were filling in little by little.

"I'm so sorry, Daddy." Thinking that Mom had just been scared and negligent in hiding a baby in a trash bag had been one thing. Knowing she had purposefully ended the life of her son was another.

Tears streamed down his cheeks and I couldn't help but want to comfort him. But still, why did he allow Mom to be alone with us girls? What if all those times of hiding us, she'd really been trying to kill us as well. Maybe she thought that if she could just get rid of her children, her sanity would return. I shook my head. Mom didn't think she had a problem, so she would never reason in that manner. So what had been her innermost purpose?

"I'm the one who's sorry, Bailee. I know I can't go back and do right by you girls. I was wrong to leave you in her care. I was wrong to have my suspicions and do nothing with them for fear of where they might lead. I wanted my family—my perfect little family."

"A family that never existed," I countered. "We were never perfect. We weren't even close." A thought came to mind. "Why did you have more children? If Mom didn't want them—"

"But she did," he interrupted. "I mean after Noah's death, she was almost desperate to have another baby. I couldn't deny her—it seemed like a healing kind of thing."

"So Geena was a consolation."

He nodded. "And Piper was our last attempt to have another son. It was after she was born that I came to realize how serious your mother's condition really was."

"But still you did nothing."

"I know." He wiped at his eyes. "I did what I thought was right. I got help for the house and figured it would be enough. I took her to doctors, hoping the medicine would restore your mother back to the woman I married." He leaned back in a dejected fashion, tears continuing to stream. "It's my fault. I can't make the past right, Bailee. There is nothing I can do to go back and be the man that I should have been. Please . . . please forgive me."

I was crying now too. I reached out and took hold of his arm. "I forgive you," I whispered, barely able to speak. "I forgive you."

∽

"Seems like I've missed out on all the excitement," Mark declared on the phone a few nights later.

"Yes, I suppose you could say that." I'd just filled him in on all the details of my illness and epiphany. "It's the kind of excitement I'd just as soon avoid."

"Geena said you were pretty sick. I was just about to resign my position and fly back out to Seattle."

"So does that mean you aren't giving up on me . . . on us?" I asked.

For a minute he said nothing and then I heard him sigh. "I wasn't sure you wanted me to keep trying."

"I wasn't exactly sure what I wanted either, until I really thought I might lose you." I gazed at the water from the deck table. The aroma of sweet honeysuckle wafted on the air. "Mark, I know our relationship has been a challenge, but I . . . well . . . I want it to work out."

"I'm glad to hear you say so."

"Me too," I had to admit. "I'd like it all to work out."

"So does that include the job? Dad's been bugging me to get a commitment from you."

I drew a deep breath. "I've never been good at commitments, but you can tell him yes on the job. With one provision."

"Name it."

I smiled. "I need some time to work from Boston."

"What are you proposing?"

"Well, I've been thinking about that very thing. I'd like to suggest that I work out of my home and come into New York City twice a week. For example Tuesday and Friday."

"Tuesday and Friday. For how long?" he asked, seeming to give the matter serious consideration.

"Just until the end of the year."

I could almost see him frown and calculate exactly how many months we were talking about. When he answered, I nearly laughed aloud.

"That's six months."

"Yes. I need that time, Mark. If it won't work," I said, sobering, "then I'll have to say no to the job. However, if you'll give it a chance, I promise that you won't be sorry. I'll do the work of two editors. I'll keep extra long hours when I'm there."

He actually chuckled. "I wasn't so concerned about the job having your attention as I was me having your attention."

"I considered that too." I smiled. "I thought maybe, if it was necessary to have face-to-face communication more than twice a week—maybe you could come to Boston for a day or two. For instance, you could come back on Fridays with me and stay at my condo in the city while I stayed at Dad's. We could have the weekend to see each other—even work together, and then focus on work Monday and take the train back to New York on Tuesday."

"I have to say, I like the way you think. But what am I supposed to do Wednesday and Thursday without you?"

I laughed. "There's always the telephone and email."

"Not the same, but I suppose it's a doable compromise."

I grew serious again. "It would just be until the first of the year. I think I can wrap up things by then. I want to use this time to go to counseling with my sisters and see what the outcome is with Piper's health. And I think we need time to adjust to our new . . . relationship."

"So you'd move to New York City full time after the first of the year?"

"That depends."

"On what?" Mark's curious tone only served to make me feel ornery.

"On the next phase of our project together."

He was quiet for a moment, and I thought perhaps I'd said the wrong thing. I was just about to backtrack when he spoke again.

"Well, phase two is quite a serious portion of the project."

His statement took me by surprise. "I see, and what might that involve?"

He chuckled. "Well, phase two will require a commitment."

"What kind of commitment?"

"Nothing too major . . . just you and me together forever and ever and ever."

"Oh. Is that all?" I glanced at my left hand and thought of how a ring might look. "Well, I suppose that's something to take under consideration." I got up and walked to the deck railing. The Seattle ferry was approaching and I couldn't help but think of that first trip I'd taken with Mark. I'd been so unnerved by his nearness, but at the same time there had been a comfort and ease I couldn't explain.

"I like the sound of permanency," I said without really thinking. "Forever is something I've never really felt I could count on."

"Well, if I have anything to say about it, you can count on it with me." Mark's voice stirred my heart. "And you know you can count on it with God. Between Him and me, you should never need to worry about being loved."

"Love?" I questioned. He had told me he loved me when I took him to the airport, but I still had a hard time believing it. I longed to hear Mark declare his love for me again. He didn't disappoint.

"Yes, love. I love you, Bailee Cooper. Haven't you figured that out by now?"

I gave a contented sigh. Finally my life was moving forward. The chains of the past had been broken. "I was hoping that was part of phase two. I think I like the way this is coming together." I thought I might start to cry from the sheer joy of it all.

Mark didn't seem to realize the importance this moment held for me. He gave a chuckle and added in his teasing manner, "If you like this phase, just wait until you hear what I have planned for phase three."

CHAPTER 24

The months passed in a most productive manner. I was happy to discover that Dinah not only approved of my new Christian values, but was in fact a Christian herself. She had done a remarkable and professional job of keeping her faith to herself, but when she learned of my life change, the first thing she did was invite me to come to her church. Our counseling also changed for the better, as she was free to help me explore more biblical ways to experience healing. It wasn't long until Dinah was actually talking about the day I would be able to stop seeing her as a therapist altogether.

I gave Dinah's nondenominational church a try and found it very much to my liking. Judith and Dad even joined me one Sunday, and by October it became a habit. Mark attended on the weekends when he could be in Boston—which were most of them. Geena and Piper still wanted little or nothing to do with religious matters, but that was all right. They were both willing to attend counseling with a new therapist we had chosen together. It wasn't Mark's friend, but rather someone the friend had recommended, and the changes brought on by our time together had been remarkable.

Overall, autumn brought with it a healing of hearts that I had never thought possible. We still had our issues and I continued to have nightmares occasionally, but now I had better ways to deal with them. I found prayer to be a remarkable help. Perhaps the best thing about my life now was the sense of freedom I possessed. My past had always held me hostage, but no more. It wasn't that the past had changed, but I had. And that made all the difference in the world.

My new routine became something I cherished rather than avoided. Mark and I had just arrived back in Boston after a grueling and chilly Friday in New York. The economy was forcing some changes in the way things were being done at the publishing house, and freelance editors were to be the norm instead of the exception. Mark and I had worked long and hard on a schedule that would fit all of our needs. Because of that, we generally spent our weekends in Boston.

The minute we stepped off the train, my cell phone rang. I checked the ID and then answered. The call was coming from the Cooper house. "Hello?"

"Hi, Bailee. Are you and Mark back in Boston?"

"Yes, just arrived in fact." I mouthed to Mark that it was my stepmother, then turned my attention back to her as we made our way to the cab stand.

"Can you two make dinner tonight? We have several things to discuss and we wanted you girls to be there."

"Just a minute. Let me ask Mark." I turned to him. "Do you have a problem with us going right over to Mom and Dad's?" I had only recently started calling Judith *Mom* and it always seemed to bring a smile to Mark's face.

"That's fine," he said. "I'll get us a taxi."

"That'll be expensive," I countered. "We could just take the T."

"Cozier this way. I've had enough of crowds."

I shrugged and uncovered the phone. "He said that would be fine. We'll grab a cab and be there as soon as possible."

"Wonderful. We'll be waiting."

Mark had us settled in a taxi in no time. The driver wove us in and out of traffic like a madman, but I didn't mind. I snuggled into

Mark's arms and let the world disappear. I loved the feel of his cashmere coat and the way he smelled. I pretty much loved everything about him, although in all these months I'd never told him so.

This made me frown. Why couldn't I say those words? I felt them. I knew they were true. I'd asked Dinah on more than one occasion why I found it so hard to just tell him how I felt.

"He has to already know how I feel about him," I told her. "My actions certainly confirm it, even if my mouth isn't able to."

Dinah had assured me that when the time was right—when I felt safe enough, sure enough—I would say them. So what was the hold up?

We arrived at the house after eight o'clock and I was starving. Geena had arrived only minutes before us and was still standing in the foyer dumping a backpack of books to one side.

She was dressed stylishly as usual in knee boots, black tights, pencil skirt, and a pumpkin-colored angora sweater. I leaned forward and kissed her, feeling rather frumpy in my black suit. "Gorgeous as always," I declared.

"It's what all the fashionable law students are wearing." She turned from me and gave Mark a hug. "How's the publishing world?"

"Wordy," he said with a cocky grin.

"Come on, you three," Piper declared from the archway. "Judith and Dad are waiting for you."

"What? We can't sit and have a nice chat before dinner?" I teased. "What's the rush? Oh yeah, I'm starved. Let's move it, folks."

Mark laughed and gave me a slight push. "You lead the way."

I gave Piper a quick hug as I passed and dragged her along with me. "Come on. I understand there is something important to be discussed. Maybe you could clue us in first?"

She shrugged. "I have no idea. But I do have my own news."

"Good news I hope?" I said, noticing her smile.

Nodding, Piper glanced over her shoulder at Geena and Mark. "I think so."

Mom had prepared a feast and I breathed in deeply. "What is that delightful smell?" I asked, straining to see what she was bringing to the table.

"Stuffed green peppers," she replied. "Oh, and Piper put together a nice Caesar salad for us."

"And homemade Parmesan biscuits," Piper added. "It's a new recipe I got from one of my friends." She started to take her seat and added, "And just wait until you see what Judith made for dessert."

I let Mark help me with my chair and waited for the others to be seated. After Dad offered a blessing for the meal, we all began to pass the food.

"This is really great," Dad said, putting a couple of biscuits on his plate. "I wasn't sure you'd get a chance to join us at this late notice."

"So what's going on that you want to share with us?" I asked.

"Well, Piper has news first," Dad said. "Go ahead, Piper."

She nodded and put down her fork. "My thyroid tests are back and the medications are balancing out my blood levels. The doctor feels confident that we've finally got the right dosages and types of medications."

"That's wonderful news," I said. Piper had learned some months earlier that her thyroid levels were desperately low. Her fatigue, depression, weight issues, and inability to concentrate at times were all symptoms of hypothyroidism and not clinical depression or schizophrenia.

"I feel like a completely different person," Piper declared. "I have energy and ambition, and I don't feel like walking off a long pier anymore."

"Thank God," I said. "It's amazing to me that something like that could cause so many problems."

"The doctor said I may have had these problems all of my life. They probably led to my struggle with my weight, which caused me to binge and purge."

"And now that is under control as well?" Geena asked.

Piper nodded. "Very much so. I'm getting counseling about it and seeing a dietitian. I've had to realize a lot of my thoughts and beliefs about food are just plain wrong. I guess a lifetime of battling to stay as thin as your sisters or friends has caused me to really look at food in all the wrong ways."

"I think that's easy enough to do for most folks," Mom interjected. "Having a healthy attitude toward food isn't something that people have been encouraged to understand until recently. Food, however, isn't the enemy. It's nothing more than fuel. It's the importance we place on it and how we allow it to control us that matters."

"Funny we should be having this conversation at the dinner table," Dad said. "Especially given that I saw your flourless chocolate cake and toffee sauce sitting on the counter awaiting our attention."

Everyone laughed at this, but Judith held

up her hand. "It's made with all the best and most health-conscious ingredients possible, and a little bit won't hurt anyone."

"But who wants just a little bit?" Dad said with a teasing wink.

I was so relieved to hear Piper's news that I'd almost forgotten that Mom and Dad had something to tell us. "So what's your big news?" I asked, looking to Dad.

Geena leaned forward. "Please don't say you're going to have a baby. I don't think I could handle another sister. These two keep me busy enough."

Mom laughed. "Bite your tongue. I have no desire to have a baby at my age. Besides, I'm much too selfish. I want your dad all to myself."

"Which is why we're going to take an extended trip," Dad told them. "We're going to leave shortly after Christmas and be gone for most of the year."

"That's some vacation," I said, looking at Mark.

"Well, not exactly a vacation," Dad replied.

This brought my attention back to him. "Then what?"

"We're going to work with a missions agency to help start business ventures in third world nations. We're starting in Burundi, Africa, and will move around the continent with the organization."

I was stunned. I had never imagined my father doing something like this. "Does this mean you're getting out of your business here in the States?"

"Not just yet. I'm arranging for new management. Judith and I are training a team of men and women to handle the company while we're gone. This missions venture is just a test run to see if we truly feel God would have us in this kind of work. We figure if it goes well, we can expand. See, the attitude of this company is to help native peoples be able to grow their own business and meet the needs of their people. It's a sister project to go alongside the spiritual missions work."

"I think it's brilliant," Piper said, smiling. "I think it's far more important to teach a man to take care of his own needs rather than encourage government handouts."

"Well, in most of the places we'll be, there isn't much in the way of government help either." Dad's expression seemed thoughtful, yet his enthusiasm and excitement were evident.

A thought came to mind, however. What about Geena and Piper? I'd be moving to New York City after the first of the year. As if reading my mind, Dad continued.

"That brings me to the next announcement. We've already discussed this with Piper and Geena, so it will come as no surprise to them, but we're selling this house."

"What?" I was stunned. "When did you decide to do this?"

"When I told them that I was going to take the job in London," Piper said matter-of-factly.

"You what?" This was really a night for surprises. "I thought you lost that opportunity last summer."

"I thought so too." Piper pushed back her hair and shrugged. "The person who ended up taking the position didn't like living abroad. They called me three weeks ago and asked me to reconsider the position."

"But you said nothing," I countered, trying to get used to the idea of my baby sister moving to England.

"I talked to Dad about it, and my therapist." She grinned. "I figured the rest of you could wait."

Mark gave a chuckle. "You know your big sister. She still thinks she should be the first to hear any news when it comes to you two."

I elbowed him. "That's not true. I'm not that bad. I'm just surprised." I looked to Geena. "What about you? Are you moving off as well?"

"No. I'm taking your condo. That way when Piper comes home, she'll have a place in either Boston or New York City to visit."

Dad got back in on the conversation at this point. "That's right. I figured to keep the condo and sell the house. There was no sense in this place just sitting empty. I have no way of knowing for sure how this project is going to work out for us, but I have a feeling it's going to be a good one. If that's the case, we might even end up getting an apartment in London."

"A flat," Piper interjected. "Not an apartment."

Dad grinned. "See there, she's already made the move in her mind."

The rest of dinner passed quickly with discussions about how soon everyone would act upon these new life decisions. Piper was to leave within the next couple of weeks, so most of the discussion focused on her. By the end of the evening, Mark was ready to head back into the city and stay at my place. I was anxious to head up to bed.

"I have plans for us in the morning," he said as we stood at the door saying good-night. "In fact, plans for the entire day."

"Where are we going?"

"It's a surprise."

I looked at him oddly. "What should I wear?"

"Hmmm, I'd recommend clothes." He grinned.

"What type? Casual? Dressy? Warm?"

"Casual and warm is fine. I'll pick you up at eight."

"That early, eh?" I checked my watch and found that it was nearly eleven. "All right. I'll be ready. Are you renting a car?"

"No. Your dad is loaning me his."

Now I was really intrigued. Mark had definitely put some thought and planning into this. "All right. I'll be ready."

෴

At seven-thirty the next morning I was dressed in jeans and a sweater and ready to head off to the great unknown. I found Judith in the kitchen making coffee.

"I see you're already up and running."

She turned around to beam me a smile. I swear the woman was always happy. She made a good mother for this family, I decided. We had been too long without cheerful people.

"Your father and I plan to take the T into the city and spend the day at the Marketplace. Should be a lot of fun."

"Do you know where Mark is taking me?"

She shook her head. "Even if I did, I wouldn't tell you. It's a surprise. I don't think your father even knows."

I nodded. I was sure Mark had kept this entire adventure to himself. He loved to plan surprises for me, and while such things used to strike me with terror, I was starting to kind of enjoy them. When he knocked on the door a few minutes later, I was more than ready and waiting for our adventure.

"So where are we going?" I asked.

"I told you it was a surprise," Mark replied.

"Yes, but now we're actually participating in the surprise."

"It doesn't work that way," he said, helping me into the car. He hurried around to the driver's side as I secured my seatbelt. Once he was in the car and ready to go, he threw me a grin. "Just be patient. I think you're going to like this."

We headed out and away from Boston. I could see that we weren't going to be driving to the coast, so that eliminated a few ideas from mind. By the time an hour had passed, I was fairly certain we were heading to Connecticut, but I had no idea as to why. When we took the ramp for Hartford, I fixed Mark with a curious look.

"This is definitely holding my interest."

"Good. I'm happy to say that we've very nearly arrived. Just enjoy the fall colors. You know tourists pay good money to come here just to see what's in your backyard."

I laughed, but he was right. The scenery was incredible, and the rich tapestry of golds, oranges, reds, and browns made autumn clearly one of the most beautiful times of year for this area of the country.

It was only a short time later that we arrived at the Harriet Beecher Stowe Center. "Surprise!" Mark exclaimed. He brought us to a stop in the parking area and turned the car off. "I figured because we're book people we should take advantage of all the book-related places in our corner of the world."

"I agree." It wasn't at all what I had thought we might do. I had envisioned a walk on the beach or picking apples or some other wonderful outdoor activity, but coming here was even more delightful. I loved the thoughtfulness of the plan. "This is perfect," I said.

"I'm glad you think so."

We toured the facilities and talked about the woman who'd written *Uncle Tom's Cabin* so long ago. I marveled at how impressive it was that one piece of literature could have such an impact on society.

The leaves crunched beneath our feet as we passed the area where Harriet had once gardened. " 'A garden is a healing place for the soul,' " I murmured, quoting Harriet's own words. Her gardens had been a passion of hers.

"I can see why," Mark said, taking hold of my hand. "There is a certain anticipation of new life, working with the soil and seeds."

"I think I'd like to have a garden someday. Of course, I'd have to learn how. I kill my houseplants, so I can only imagine what I might do to an entire yard full of flowers."

"You can always learn. I'm sure Harriet wasn't born with all her gardening knowledge."

"I don't know. She was a phenomenal woman," I said. "I'm so glad you thought of coming here."

"You're quite phenomenal yourself." Mark raised my hand to his lips.

I smiled. "Thank you. You always make me feel that I am."

"It's true, though." He tucked my arm close against him.

Walking for several moments in the autumn air, the swirl of colorful leaves beneath our feet, the temperature chilling our cheeks, I found I'd never been happier. I stopped all at once and turned to him.

"I love you," I told him. My heart beat faster. "I honestly and truly love you."

He looked at me intently for a moment, then grinned in that self-assured way of his. "I know that." He pulled me into his arms and kissed me soundly on the mouth. "But I'm glad you finally got around to saying it," he whispered against my lips. "Makes what I want to say so much better."

He let me go and reached into his pocket.

Dropping to one knee right there in the middle of the sidewalk, Mark opened the box and held it before me. "Will you marry me?"

I could hardly believe he'd just proposed in Harriet Beecher Stowe's yard. I looked at him and then to the ring sparkling inside the box. He wanted to marry me—to spend the rest of his life with me.

"Well?" he asked.

The things that had once haunted me no longer seemed a barrier to a future filled with love and companionship. "I will," I said, fighting back tears.

He got up and pulled me into his arms once again. "I'm so glad you said yes. My knee was freezing on that pavement."

I giggled. "Is that the only reason you're glad?"

Shaking his head, he took the beautiful antique ring and slipped it on my finger. "No, silly. I'm also glad because now we can move ahead to finish out phase two and go right into phase three."

"And exactly what might that entail?" I raised a brow.

His blue eyes twinkled. "A wedding will complete phase two quite nicely. I suggest a lovely Christmastime wedding. I know it's short notice, but I have friends and we can pull strings if you need some exotic designer gown and special location for the ceremony."

I shook my head. "I only need you." I could scarcely believe this was happening. Six months ago I was mired in the past. Now I felt almost as though I could fly.

He kissed me again, and I leaned into the solid strength of him. Weak in the knees, I finally pulled away. "And phase three?"

"Ah," he said in a low husky voice. "The honeymoon."

"Hmm." I imagined a warm location with long days spent in each other's company. "I think I shall very much enjoy working with you through that phase . . . and all the others."

Laughing, he put his arm around me and we headed for the car. "I think, Miss Cooper, that this will be the first of many successful projects together."

CHAPTER 25

We set the wedding for two days after Christmas. Piper had already journeyed to London but arranged to be back for the celebration. She and Geena agreed to be my dual maids of honor and dressed beautifully in black and white and red; they made a striking addition to the church decorations.

Mom had helped me to arrange the décor. She teased that since Mark and I were both in publishing we should have everything done in black and white, but that was a little too stark for me, and we added red in honor of the holidays. The church, already dressed for Christmas, needed very few additional touches. We'd decked the sides of the pews with pine garlands trimmed with red bows earlier in the month as a donation from the Cooper family for the holidays. That not only worked well with the season, but also with our plans for the wedding. Several artfully designed arrangements of red roses and calla lilies, as well as beautiful brass stands of candles, rounded off the setting. I was quite pleased with the way it had turned out. It looked tasteful and elegant without being pretentious.

I wanted a simple wedding and so did Mark. In fact, he suggested more than once that we elope and put an end to the festivities. I held my ground that a girl only married once, hopefully, and that I wanted to have this moment to remember. He understood, as I knew he would. We decided against having lengthy sermons or singing. A short exchange of vows along with the recitation of Scripture that had become very important to us would keep the focus on what was most important— our covenant with God and each other.

"You doing all right?" Dad asked before he escorted me to the altar.

I smoothed down the lines of my strapless white silk gown and nodded. He reached over to touch my cheek. "You're so very beautiful."

"Thank you, Dad. May I say that you're quite dashing in that tuxedo."

He smiled and pulled at the lapels. "So your stepmom already told me."

I laughed. "I'm sure she did."

Geena and Piper popped into the alcove and hugged me. I couldn't help but remember all the times we'd huddled together as children. Those had been dark days, but now we were sharing a moment of light.

"I'm so excited for you," Geena whispered against my ear.

Piper leaned in to do likewise. "I hope you'll always be happy."

"With God's help," I said, holding tight to them for a moment, "I pray we'll all be happy."

My sisters nodded and pulled away. Geena stepped toward Dad and straightened his bow tie, while Piper adjusted her sash and glanced at the wall clock.

"It's time," Piper said. "Do we look all right?"

Piper gave a turn in her sleek strapless black dress. A sash of white, overlaid with a smaller one of red, trimmed her waist and accented the flowers she held. Her bobbed hair only served to accent her elfish face. Geena had left her hair to cascade down her back. I thought they both looked incredible. "You look stunning. You both do."

"You too." They both smiled and Geena cocked her head to the door. "Come on."

I drew a deep breath and looked at Dad. "I guess it's time to give me away."

"Mark's a good man, and I know I can trust him to do right by you. You're going to have a good life, Bailee. I just feel God's hand is upon you and this marriage."

His encouragement brought tears to my eyes. "Don't make me cry," I said, hugging him one more time.

We followed Geena and Piper, who had already taken their spots at the back of the church. The processional began to play and Piper stepped forward and then Geena. At the front of the church I saw Mark standing beside two of his longtime friends, Chris and Thomas.

"He's waiting," Dad whispered in my ear.

I met Dad's gaze and drew a deep breath. "And so phase two concludes." He looked at me oddly, but I only giggled. "It's a long story."

Mark looked so very serious as I walked down the aisle. With each step I found my heart picking up speed and my breathing quickening. And then he smiled at me, and I felt as if the entire world had disappeared. How could it be that one man could so completely change my life?

His grin deepened as my father brought me to stand beside him. Mark leaned close.

"I thought maybe you'd changed your mind."

I smiled and touched the sleeve of his tux. "Not likely," I whispered.

∽

I can't say that I remember all the details of the ceremony. I was so nervous about doing everything just right that when the moment finally came and the pastor said we were man and wife, I wanted to take hold of Mark and drag him out of the church. I was tired of crowds and fanfare and wished only to be alone in his arms. Instead, we kissed very briefly.

"More of that later," Mark whispered.

"Phase three, eh?" I said in a very serious manner.

He winked. "You have no idea."

Geena leaned in. "Get a move on, you two. There's a reception and dinner to be completed before you can go traipsing off on your honeymoon."

I looked at her over my shoulder and shook my head. "Nobody says we have to stay for either one."

Mark chuckled and pulled me down the aisle. "You are creating a major scandal, Mrs. Delahunt."

"Mrs. Delahunt," I breathed. I liked the sound of that very much. Bailee Delahunt. Sounded like a strong and successful name. A fleeting thought passed through my head, but I pushed it aside. My twenty-eighth birthday was shortly after New Year's. Thirty wasn't that far off, and so far I had no reason to worry that schizophrenia would play a part in my future, the way it had my past. The blessing, however, was that Mark and I had thoroughly discussed the matter. He knew it was a possibility, but we both agreed it wasn't going to be a sword hanging over our heads—neither would we allow our home to be a house of secrets. I thought of a quote by Harriet Beecher Stowe and smiled. *The past, the present and the future are really one: they are today.*

I will live for today, I told myself and smiled at my new husband. With God's help and his, I felt there was nothing I couldn't accomplish—nothing I couldn't endure. I would do as God said in Isaiah and fear not—and in doing so focus on the other verses that Mark had shared with me.

Forget the former things; do not dwell on the past. See, I am doing a new thing! Now it springs up; do you not perceive it?

I could smell the sweet scent of my bouquet and took in a long, deep breath. "A new thing," I whispered as we reached the end of the church aisle.

Mark seemed to completely understand. He looked at me and smiled. "A new thing."

DISCUSSION QUESTIONS

1. According to the surgeon general, mental illness affects approximately one in five people. Given these statistics, most people will know someone who has a mental or emotional illness. Has your life been touched by someone like this?

2. In *House of Secrets*, the sisters find it necessary to hide the truth of what they believe happened to their mother. Have you ever found yourself the keeper of a potentially life-changing secret? If so, how did you deal with it and did you eventually let the secret be known?

3. Sisters can often have both rewarding and strained relationships. Discuss the positive and negative ways that Bailee, Geena, and Piper interacted.

4. *House of Secrets* focuses on the scars left from childhood trauma. If you've suffered from similar events in your past, how did you deal with the trauma? Were you able to overcome the bondage it placed you in? If so, how?

5. What does the Bible say about mental illness? How can we as Christians reach out to the mentally ill in our community?

6. Secrets tend to damage more than help, but they are almost always at the base of emotional trauma. What does that kind of bondage look like to you?

7. How does Satan use secrets to keep us in bondage? What tools do we have as Christians to overcome such bondage?

8. If you were diagnosed with a mental illness, how would you handle it? Would you actively seek help? Would you let the people around you know? Would you fear being ostracized?

TRACIE PETERSON is the bestselling, award-winning author of more than 80 novels. Tracie also teaches writing workshops at a variety of conferences on subjects such as inspirational romance and historical research. She and her family live in Belgrade, Montana.